Beyond *The Tempest*

The Tempest Series

Beyond *The Tempest*

A Sorcerous Tale of Bermuda

The Tempest Series

Barry H. Wiley

I long

To hear the story of your life, which must

Take the ear strangely.

The Tempest V. i

William Shakespeare

1611

eISBN 978-1310-43460-0

ISBN 978-0692480854

ISBN 0692480854

What seest thou else

In the dark backward and abysm of time?

Act I, ii

The Tempest

1

A memory trained for spectacular feats, as Tony DiMarco had trained his over fifteen years, always has a subtle drawback -- mixing memories from one show or demonstration with another. By using the ancient Greek loci system of memory, DiMarco was able to avoid the confusing intermingling of recalled images. Before each show, he would stroll through a local area rich with distinctive impressions: statues, tombstones, fountains and so forth. Later during the show, he would disentangle all the names, numbers and objects from the memories of previous shows by linking each local memory to its respective local loci, as a stained glass window, a grave, a cobblestone path, and even once, the individual stones on a path to his rental car, as necessary.

On a hill behind Hamilton, Bermuda, Paget Street Cemetery appeared empty as DiMarco scanned it swiftly, laying out the pattern he would follow. His walking pattern had to be logical so that it would hold together by itself, reducing the effort needed during his show to retain the pattern in place. He decided to begin inside the church ruins, ignoring the red warning signs about falling masonry, to follow a pattern using the largest tombs as markers and finally the arched gateway to the cemetery as the finish. As he walked quickly, DiMarco noticed for the first time a tourist near one of the ornate tombstones on the far side of the graveyard. Short-sleeved, heavy, his bulk was exaggerated by two cameras with elaborate lenses slung about his neck. The plastic water bottle and white straw hat balanced on the edge of the tomb must be his, DiMarco mused, but then began the process of clearing his mind for the loci exercise.

The tourist replaced the hat on his head, took a sip from the bottle, and began fumbling again with the lens of one of the cameras.

Paget Street Church had been built in the eighteenth century, rebuilt in the nineteenth, ignored in the twentieth, and forgotten in the twenty-first. Only small yellow birds were sitting in the choir stalls, the pews were rubble. DiMarco could not identify any of the multitudes of small trees, vines and countless flowers covering the exposed brick columns and cracked crenelated walls. The fragrances of hyacinth and cedar permeated the air. The effect was of a perfumed fantasy world untouched, unharmed by reality. He grinned. Wouldn't be surprised to encounter a unicorn grazing outside the church. But with the lowering sun and the growing coolness, DiMarco couldn't delay his calculated walk through the roofless church.

He started from the altar under a young sapling through the choir stalls, then moved down the narrow weed and twig strewn central path between pews, stopped for a moment at the remains of a baptismal fount, and then outside under an arched portico. Chunks of dull-red brick were sprinkled throughout the church. Those red warning signs meant what they said. DiMarco paused to fix the walk in his mind.

He glimpsed the tourist still fumbling with his cameras as DiMarco passed a large marble tomb to start down the overgrown pathway to the rear of the cemetery. It would darken there first, so had to be covered first. Images had to be clear to be useful. Random calls and whistles of restless birds were fading with the light, so DiMarco stepped a little quicker. Epitaphs, weathered shapes, a tree stump with two metallic dark green lizards nose to nose, an

3

odd wrought iron grave marker. He knelt abruptly, to examine its crude design more closely. DiMarco chuckled softly to himself when he heard the muttered curses of the tourist. Thankfully photography had never been one of his compulsions. He stood, still for a moment, breathing in the sweet honeysuckle.

***

The heavy .41 slug penetrated DiMarco's skull just above his left ear. The short muffled bark didn't disturb the birds in their daily finale of song. DiMarco's extraordinary memory instantly stored the image of the big red-faced tourist, no longer clumsily fumbling with cameras, a grim satisfied smile set on his heavy-jawed face. Red face from sunburn? Can't tell. The mushrooming slug plowed through the left brain hemisphere, dismembering and erasing DiMarco's arduously constructed logical interconnections. His motor nerve centers were severed cleanly, instantly stopping his heart and breathing.

An odd memory, DiMarco's last, noted what a unique locus the red-faced killer made, so easy to recall. The electro-chemical trace that was the physical memory raced along tangled neural trunk lines like a frantic lost thing, stopped at one juncture, it started down another, and another, weakening as it went, striving to register its message, to complete its mission. It faded and finally disappeared when its path ended in torn empty synapses. The flattened .41 slug ripped out about two square inches of bone as it exited DiMarco's skull above the brain stem to mash itself into a peach tree.

As DiMarco's disconnected body twisted away and began to slump, a small .32 bullet blew his dead heart open. The sharp loud report drove the birds from the trees and hibiscus shrubs, the wary lizards from the walls.

2

It was the dream. She knew what was going to happen, but had no power to change it.

Kaarin Larsson wrapped her black coat more tightly around her as the swirling winds picked up, moving and bending the dark-green thickets. Clouds roiled, shifted, transforming as she watched, from dingy white to dull sepia laced with glowing red, violet and satin gold. She walked slowly up the steep rise, through dried stumps of stiff grass which scraped against her bare ankles. Vaguely she knew she was looking or expecting something, but couldn't think what, only that she needed to reach the top.

Contorted gaunt pine trees marked the ridge line. As she drew near, their shapes changed as time rushed to darkness, only to meld them into the darkness too. This was where she was to be, but for what? For months she had returned again and again to this grim place.

"What am I here for?" Kaarin shouted into the emptiness about her. Her voice startled her. It wasn't *her* voice. It was strangely muffled. "Here I am," she cried again. "What is it? Why am I here?" That strange voice again.

Darkness swept unnaturally across the horizon,

cleansing the sky of matter. Kaarin knew darkness couldn't come that fast except in an eclipse, or a raging storm. But there was neither here. What was happening to her?

Darkness became blackness with brightening stars beginning to form into comfortingly familiar constellations as the last remnants of light dissolved. As Kaarin turned, eyes wide, to penetrate the dark to find where she was, the constellations began changing into shapes impossible to calculate. Her mind strained to find the equations to describe what she saw, but the shapes kept changing. She tried to cry out, but the freshening wind whipped her hair across her face and mouth. She pushed it away – then – felt the call. Deep inside her being, something stirred warmly.

She turned her head, holding her long yellow hair high and away from her ears – her coat flinging itself out from her – straining to catch the sounds, to locate their direction and source. There were only the brightening stars moving outside any physical law.

Kaarin tried to reach out. "Here I am," she cried in her strange voice. "Here, here!" Then stepped suddenly back, something was coming. Illogically she had given herself, her presence away without knowing what was there, but she could see only the empty deep black starscape. Kaarin squeezed her arms around her, pulling her coat close, as though to recover her anonymity, to hold

7

in her presence, to conceal herself until she could understand what was there, what had responded to her searching. That's why she was there – it was she who was searching for something here on this slope, returning again and again.

It whipped across her mind, jarring all of her senses simultaneously. She could even taste it, a dry sweetness. Too much! There was too much! She turned to run – to hide. It was all over her. What did it want? Her! All of her! Her feet were tangled in the grass. She couldn't move them, couldn't wrench them free. She screamed. A sharp pain in her head. She screamed again, this time it was her own voice, loud and sharp.

***

Kaarin was awake, sprawled half out of bed in a silent dark room, coarseness rubbing against her face, her bare shoulders and arms. Her short nightgown was twisted up around her face and throat, her naked body arched, thrusting up hard.

Calming, Kaarin reached out with her fingers. It wasn't dry grass, it was cheap carpeting. Her head throbbed. She slowed her breathing and listened for a moment. There was nothing, then, a low moaning, grinding sound. She looked. It was the cheap digital clock on the night stand: 3:43 with the glowing red dot next to A.M. The

8

torment of the dream defied her understanding, defeated her peace. Or was it simpler, she was just lonely and horny?

Kaarin pushed herself back up into the bed, shivering with perspiration. She breathed deeply, once, twice, pulled her nightgown back into place, and discovered she was wet between her legs. Everything looked dully familiar when she turned on the night stand lamp that only pushed the shadows away, the far corners still featureless voids. Her breathing was coming back to normal, but her head still ached. She must have hit the night stand when she fell out of bed.

It always resembled her childhood nightmares. In the orphanage the nightmares had become even more threatening. A mysterious 'thing' coming, her feet glued down, unable to run. But the starscapes were vividly alive, overpoweringly real, but utterly wrong in shape and color. It wasn't her universe, the universe she had so tenaciously and joyously studied, then taught for five years before her mind had begun to splinter beyond her control. There had been that irresistible urgency again in her searching that had driven her to expose herself without regard for her own safety.

Kaarin slumped back against the pillows. One was moist. The muffled voice she heard must have been her crying out with her face buried in the pillow.

Kaarin looked around the room, recognizing the flame-pink satin and silk dress from her performance the night before lying carelessly over the back of a chair. She had broken her rule about always leaving promptly after a show, and not mixing with her audience who, after seeing her do an hour of mentalism, mindreading, usually only wanted private readings or fortune telling – or the men, or an occasional woman, just made raw propositions. She was lonely, worn thin from seeking answers from people who couldn't, or wouldn't, understand what she was talking about. Kaarin groped to recall what had happened last night. The show went well enough. There was only a glass of Amaretto and what passed for a few minutes of relaxed intelligent conversation. But *where* was she? Everything in the room looked like a hundred other motel rooms. Panic gathered at the edge of her senses. Was the dream really over? Or was she dreaming *now* and the shifting starscapes real?

She stood beside the bed, laughing nervously. "This is crazy. I don't know where I am. Too many motels!" The telephone had a room number, but no identification or outside telephone number.

Kaarin pulled opened the curtains. Only a back alley, with some obscured neon lights at the end. Could be anywhere.

There was no marking on the Gideon Bible in the night stand drawer. No stationary on the small dresser, and nothing but her own clothes in the drawers. She could see her unzipped garment bag hanging in the open closet. Her knapsack was there beside the bed as she always liked it to be which held critical performing apparatus difficult to duplicate along with a notebook for her thoughts. There had to be a location written somewhere.

After eight rings Kaarin hung up. No response from the switchboard. They might think I was drunk or spaced out on something anyway, she thought.

The room key card was only a generic green and white striped card with nothing except the manufacturer's name on it. This was getting really crazy. Where could there be something with the motel name on it, anything that could locate her? She pushed her hair up and far back, shaking her head. She pressed her hands tightly against her temples, feeling the familiar ridges under her fingers, trying to squeeze recall from her numb memory.

Kaarin stood in the center of the room, hands on her hips, slowly rotating hoping to trigger some association. "Stupidest thing in the world!" she snapped impatiently.

Garden Suites, Springfield, Massachusetts, was written on the soap wrapper she found in the bathroom

11

wastebasket. On her knees on the cold tile, Kaarin smiled wanly. It had actually been three Amarettoes, with their dry sweet taste. The conversation had only been a couple of guys trying to get their rocks off at the expense of the 'hired act'. It was Springfield and Edsel Bingeton in the morning.

Was he her last chance for sanity?

***

Dr. Edsel Bingeton, prominent anthropologist and psychical researcher, was her last name. Those others on the list that Mentavo, her mentor in the mentalist scam, had given her, people he had assured her who could help, people that Kaarin had located who had been either dead, disappeared or deranged in a nursing home unable to understand anything. Uneasy from his initial hostility, Kaarin felt Bingeton studying her closely through his small gold-framed bifocals. The room's only light, a dim archaic floor lamp, stood next to Kaarin's chair, backlighting her.

"Are you sure you aren't a reporter, Miss Larsson?" he asked sternly. "Bingeton doesn't give interviews. I know too many secrets," he repeated a second time. "But then no reporter as young as you appear to be would know so much about that old fraud, Mentavo," he answered himself. "You have pretensions at being a mentalist, too?" he asked, her

12

publicity material lying unread on his lap. "Even now in my retirement, I'm 96 you know, the museums and universities still bother me for answers they know only I can give. Even the British Museum" – he shook his head slowly – "even there, I have to help them on the tough ones."

"Mentavo told me …," she started.

"Mentavo and his wife, what was her name? Laura," he answered as Kaarin started to speak. He nodded. "I knew them all: Zancig, Dunninger, Piddington in England, Nelson – he'd sell his soul, then write a book about it and sell that too – Al Koran, that British barber turned mindreader after the war, and that drunk Ted Annemann, who killed himself just before the war. After Dunninger's success in 1919, everybody wanted to be a 'mentalist', not just a lowly mindreader. And Anna Eva Fay, a pretty blonde like you … now she was a flawless gem" – he paused – "but a fraud like the rest of 'um. All dead now, I think. God, there's been a lot of 'um. Knee-deep in mindreaders and *you* want to be one, too?"

"No. I want something more important. You are the last on the list of names Mentavo gave me of people who might be able to help me, if anything happened to him."

"Last on the list?" he interrupted again. "Well, that's good for you anyway. And I'm not surprised.

Mentavo was always looking for angles, but was always short on answers," he said, slowly, rhythmically moving his head back and forth as he spoke, like the pendulum on a worn grandfather clock. "I know many secrets. Seventy-five years I've collected and studied man. How many file cards do you think I have over there in my office? Go ahead, guess." He paused, waiting expectantly.

"Ten thousand?" Kaarin said, his interruptions were beginning to grate, heating her temper.

"107,564 cards! Almost 108,000! Cross indexed with subtle insights that no stupid computer could ever match."

"That's impressive," she said honestly, but without interest.

"So what questions do you have? I have probably already answered them sometime before." Again the tick-tock motion of his small narrow head.

Kaarin started again, speaking quickly to get it out without interruption: "I have clairvoyant visions that overwhelm me; I have a warning sense that confuses me. And now, now more frequently, it seems I can hear odd sounds as well." She tensed, to wait for the familiar ridicule.

Bingeton sat in his stained Morris chair, his body rocked slightly, forward and back, while his head pivoted in pendulum fashion. Finally Kaarin had to look away into the darkened living room, walled by glass-fronted bookcases. It appeared he would come apart at every joint.

"So? You certainly seem to have the full catalog," he said. "Many people desire such things, or at least a belief that there are people who can read omens and signs. What do you hear? Voices? Like Plato, or like pathetic Joan of Arc, that hysterical peasant girl?" His expression, his voice did not change, nor did his body motion.

"But *I don't want them* ... these visions," she pleaded. "They come at random. I have no control. I cannot see any way to control, to understand what these hideous starscapes I see are all about. I've had to leave my life work in physics at UC Riverside because those visions were tormenting me, destroying my thinking, forcing their way into my mind.

"Mentavo seemed to understand, at least at first, but now I'm not so sure. How can I control this power that won't leave me alone? How can I get rid of *IT*?" Her voice fell to a desperate whisper. "How can ..."

"I'm not surprised Mentavo couldn't help," Bingeton interrupted. "Oh, Mentavo and his wife were good performers who believed in the reality of what they were doing, while they were on the stage as they had to, to be convincing entertainers. But they knew nothing at all

15

about what you are asking. They were <u>fake</u>," he said. "Just fakes."

"But Mentavo said Laura had visions, felt what I feel. He's the only one who actually *knew*. No one at my university knew, no one. The psychologists talked silly jargon and wanted to wire me to a box while I slept, and … oh, endless *senseless crap*. I am a scientist, by God, a physicist, a good one! I know sound experimental procedure. I know God's universe. My life has been centered on wrestling with Him for His secrets, His equations. And I have seen things in the universe through my equations that no one had ever seen before. I have never known such pure joy, but now all that is gone, because of what's eating in my mind." Her voice shook in agony, but Kaarin was growing afraid. If Mentavo really didn't know, *then was she alone*? Was there no one who understood? Bingeton's blunt indifference was draining away her hope.

"You expect too much, Miss Larsson. Mentavo and Laura were only professional fakes. They were good, even, I dare say, great, for a few years in their prime in the late sixties to the early eighties. I think. I can look it up. They're in my card system somewhere.

"Really now! Mentavo was only guessing."

Kaarin's heart sank.

Bingeton smiled without warmth. "You appear pale.

16

Would you like some tea and cake? I just baked it. I don't need any help, even at 96." He rose. "I'll get more lights on. Take a look at the books while I prepare the tea. My pornography collection is in that case." He stepped around a small table. "Here, I'll unlock it for you. Regrettably, I recently gave most of the gadgets used for ingenious sexual expression that I had collected over the years to the New York Public Library. I've only kept my first one here. And New York'll get these books as well when the time comes. Their pornography collection is second only to the British Museum in the world, you know."

He swung the glass doors open.

Rising from her chair, Kaarin saw a short length of smooth copper pipe covered with yellowish-green blotches and worn knurling on one end. It had no rational function she could imagine.

Edsel Bingeton lifted it gently. "This has several names in various languages, all of which usually translate as 'the in-law'. Such ingenuity apparently is not culturally limited." He held it delicately at his fingertips and turned it slowly. "This was the first. It started my collecting career. At one time, a hundred years ago, it was gold plated. I found it being used as a door-stop" – his thin voice shook with disgust – "the ignorant woman didn't realize the *treasure* at her feet. Gold-plated." He shook his head

17

slowly. "The original owner was a true sensitive."

Kaarin asked cautiously: "What is it?"

He looked up at her, his eyebrows raised above his bifocals. "Ah … it would be indelicate to reveal its secrets without knowing you better, Miss Larsson." Abruptly, he replaced the blotchy pipe on the shelf. "Its pain is exquisitely thin, greatly heightening the final experience, but admittedly, at some" – he smiled – "risk."

"Why was it called 'the in-law'?"

"Because once involved, you can't get away from it." He smiled uncertainly. "My books are there on the middle shelf. Have you read any? Ah, but you were in theoretical physics I believe you said on the telephone. Anyway, help yourself." His frail body disappeared into the gloom, after he had turned on two dim table lamps interconnected with a snake's nest of extension cords.

Kaarin felt weak, hollow inside. Mentavo had always acted so confidently that her answers lay just beyond. All that would be needed was a little extra insight from someone on that list. Kaarin was ready for some hard frustrating work. But she hadn't been prepared for – *for nothing*!

Her final hope a 96 year old porno expert? Kaarin had to smile. The absurdity of it. Pulling out one of the French books at random, its pages flopped open at a set of photographs. Never had she felt her face become so hot and red so fast. Kaarin quickly closed the book and pushed it back in place. The human body wasn't made that way. Could people really do that? Did they really want to? Embarrassed, she looked around. Bingeton was in his small kitchen making domestic sounds. The book was ugly and degrading.

In the middle of the bookcase there was a single row of books with 'E. Bingeton' typed on yellow paper and taped across the edge of the shelf. The titles were texts and monographs on anthropology. But one Kaarin had to look at: *Social Impact of the Chastity Belt.* She read the blurbs on the royal-blue dust jacket below a picture of a much younger Bingeton, who had been good-looking, but with an unsettling sternness. She flipped through the pages to the illustrations. Her jaw dropped as she saw the spiked iron girdles with heavy locks. It was too much. Monstrously cruel insults to feminine humanity. She quickly returned the book to its place.

"Have you read it?" Bingeton asked from the semi-darkness.

She looked over as he turned on another table lamp, placed a silver tea service on a large table, then edged past another table to turn off the other two lamps. With a practiced grace, he stepped carefully around and over the maze of extension cords.

"An English publisher tried to pirate my chastity belt study, but Bingeton knows how to stop that kind of nonsense in its tracks. They didn't reckon with my mental influence in court."

Kaarin sat in the cane chair Bingeton pointed at. "Milk in your tea, Miss Larsson?" He held the partially tarnished pot, hovering over her cup. Over most of the bottom of the floral bone china cup was a thick murky brown stain, the color of long dried tea. He poured.

"Milk, yes, please." Anything to conceal that stain.

"The cake is fresh. Help yourself. A little tea and cake will help you feel better."

As she placed a piece of pound cake on her plate, Kaarin asked: "What did you mean, mental influence in court?"

Bingeton finished pouring his cup. He frowned. "I know the secret of mental influence," he confided softly. "I can turn minds at will. Used it on the English judge. My solicitors said I didn't have a chance. But I told them Bingeton could control the judge … just get me into that courtroom. I did, too. Dumbfounded everyone …even the judge."

"Have you written anything on the subject? It sounds …"

"No!" he declared sharply. "Write on it? No! It's too dangerous to let loose to an unthinking mankind. I won't say any more on the subject! I'll deny I ever mentioned it!" His eyes flashed as he bit into his pound cake. He said something with his mouth full, a shower of crumbs dropped from his lips but Kaarin couldn't understand his words.

She looked away until he finished chewing, then looked back. "Pornography and psychical research seem foreign to each other ..."

"Only to someone too dull to think," he said flatly without waiting for her to finish. "The essence of anthropology is the study of what people do to each other and themselves, and how they believe what they believe. I have devoted myself to the extremes of that essence. It's truly a wonder, what people will do to each other, and what they can believe ... are capable of believing," his voice mumbling with a mouth full of pound cake, "... a wonder", crumbs falling from his lips. He forked another piece of cake. "Psychical researchers are like homosexuals. They are so intensely jealous of each other because there is so little real stuff around. They will destroy a decades old relationship because of some slight disagreement ... without hesitation. I know. I was cut off from the Society for Psychical Research in England just because I wouldn't

21

support their maudlin rubbish. They wanted Bingeton's name on their stationary but I told them: off with it! I told Houdini the same thing, that crusty fart. You've got to stand firm ... solid. Bunch of psychic fags is all they are." He shook his head sharply and swallowed a large mouthful of pound cake.

"People think," he said, in between rapid sips of tea, "that because a thing can be faked, it can therefore also be real. That's not so. The human imagination is, at the same time: expansive, selfish and" – he jabbed a finger at her – "afraid."

"Are you saying there is nothing psychic in nature? Nothing at all? But what about what I have felt and experienced?"

"Coincidence, Miss Larsson, delusion, and/or hysteria," he replied around another bite of pound cake. "Women are prone to it. That's why the Catholic Church has so many more female saints than male."

"No!" she protested sharply. "I am not crazy! I am not hysterical!" The name Margery suddenly flashed across her mind, a face, yellow hair. She shook her head, bewildered. The image passed.

"You probably aren't human then, Miss Larsson," he said carelessly. His eyes lifted to the shadowed heights of his bookcases. "Not in seventy-five years of psychical study have I seen anything genuine. *Seventy-five years.* And I knew them all: mediums, swamis, psychics of all colors and shapes.

"Oh, I was converted once … for two days in 1927 by Margery, that *delicious* Boston witch … also blonde like you." Kaarin shuddered. "She liked to do some of her séances in the nude, among other clever innovations. And I always thanked her later for showing me that shifting, swampy other side. She died a drunkard, in 1943 I believe … it's on a file card … claiming to the end that she was genuine.

"But no. If you are seeing real visions and telling real fortunes, you cannot be human, because I've *absolutely proven* in my work that humans cannot do these things. No one has… ever!" He closed his mouth firmly; his head cocked up to one side. "But would you like another piece of cake?"

3

Bingeton had coldly dismissed Kaarin's anticipation of the name and image of Margery: "You saw her framed signed photo next to my chair and guessed." There had been the photo, but Kaarin had been unaware of it until Bingeton pointed to it as she left. He had an answer, a might-be, that was enough, no reason to investigate further, no reason at all . . .

But Mentavo had frequently experienced what he called moonshots that he would play during a show. They were odd thoughts that had nothing to do with what was going on, that would suddenly pop into his mind, but he would always play them, as he instructed her to do. If she hit, it would be a miracle, if not then it would just add credibility to her powers. After all, he had laughed, only con-men, tricksters, and politicians claimed to be always right. The more you play the moonshots the more often you hit, he had instructed, but he didn't know why. And neither did she.

During one show his moonshot, an odd image of green grass, had hit with spectacular results. Mentavo had suddenly stopped, pointed to one side of the audience, and said simply: "There is green grass there, *now* in someone's mind, bright green grass that needs mowing." A woman screamed, deeply shaken, the thought regarding her lawn had just crossed her mind for only an instant. Later Mentavo had laughed: "I couldn't stop and tell the audience that that one was the real thing, all the other stuff was tricks. If I do it right, they can't tell the difference, so you, the performer, are the only one who experiences the thrill of genuine telepathy… or whatever."

Margery had been a successful moonshot, whatever.

Then suddenly Edsel Bingeton had become slack, non-social, degenerating into a morbid monologue of yearnings for death to end his imprisonment in an old and disintegrating body. There was no God, he kept repeating, even as they walked to the elevator.

"*Boskop* … possibly," Bingeton said curtly, his jaw set, his eyes staring straight ahead without interest, as the elevator doors closed on her final question: "If not human, then what could I be?" Instead of helping her, Bingeton had only added confusion, laced with uneasiness.

***

"But what does it mean to be *Boskop*?" Kaarin snapped in angry frustration over the wind noise in the car. Bingeton's strange off-hand dismissal crawled under her

25

skin. One of the rental car windows wouldn't close completely, surrounding her with a steady muted roar.

How can I not be human? How can anyone *not be human?* She couldn't think how to even begin to deal with that question.

Two more hours on the Massachusetts Turnpike back to Boston, then tomorrow her first television appearance on the Sarah Randolph talk show, *Boston Today*. Chuck Watson, Randolph's producer, had informed her that Sarah didn't like mentalists and psychics, thought they all were cheap cons and other gutter things, but Paul Capriotti, a senior vice president at Randolph's long time principal sponsor, Pilgrim Fidelity Bank, had applied pressure to get Kaarin on, pressure which had pissed off Sarah even more.

"Be careful … and be prepared," Watson, like Capriotti, had warned. "Sarah completely destroyed one so-called psychic on camera a couple of months back." Watson had been completely nonplused when she had explained the stunt she intended to do on camera. "That can't be done … just can't be done," he had finally said.

Kaarin had to push Bingeton and Boskop from her mind to focus on the scam ahead. Find some place along the way to stop and watch Randolph's afternoon show to get a sense of her, her style, then a quick visit later to the station located on Route 128 two exits south from her motel to obtain some necessary props for her planned routine. Her fingers tingled in anticipation. Randolph's reputation was as a tough champion of the consumer against the cons of the world. *Good for her!*

In the scam, Kaarin planned to duplicate on-camera a random drawing that Sarah Randolph would make behind closed doors and then sealed inside two envelopes which would never leave Randolph's possession until in the studio in front of the audience when the cameras were on. So far as Randolph would be concerned, Kaarin would have absolutely no chance to learn anything of the drawing without having actually read her mind, or demonstrated clairvoyance, or whatever. That was the plan, but as Kaarin had learned, in mentalism anything can happen.

Turning onto an exit ramp, Kaarin smiled. Whatever Randolph did to destroy that other mentalist, I'll beat it. Her fingers tingled.

***

Justine Carlson looked at her watch again. Only eight minutes to go, the lobby would clear, the night shift would come out, and she could go home and get out of her dull gray security uniform. She could look as good as any woman in the studio, if she ever had the chance. On the large television screen set into the wall across from her,

27

Oprah Winfrey was shaking her fist at the camera making some kind of point, but the sound was too low to know what. Justine wished she could change channels some days, but that would never be allowed at WCVB, or probably in any other station's lobby. The other walls had colorful abstract renderings of various aspects of the television industry hung in large frames on the gray fabric covered walls. The artist certainly liked lightning bolts and arrows, especially red ones. Numerous plaques and awards hung in between the pictures.

A few men came out through the double doors from the office areas behind her. One nodded to her as they slowly rounded the corner into the long windowed hall that led outside, but Justine didn't know who he was. Walking out from behind them, a young woman in washed denim jeans and a leather jacket not quite concealing a lacy white blouse, suddenly stopped as though remembering something, dodged around the men and came back toward her. She pushed her heavy glasses up onto the bridge of her nose as she approached, a floppy wide-brimmed hat covered her hair.

"Excuse me, but I need some business envelopes to get more of my resumes out tonight. Do you have any that I could sort of, well, you know, like have?" she asked. "I've run out at my place."

28

Justine nodded. "Sure … but they say WCVB on them. I don't have any plain ones here."

"That's fine. It will make me look more important … maybe get to the top of the pile." She smiled.

Justine pulled open the desk drawer. "How many?"

"A handful should do it for tonight. I'll buy more tomorrow."

"You've got it," she said as Oprah disappeared for a commercial, her own signal to finally head home. "Good luck," she offered to the back of the woman who looked around and waved as she started around the corner. As she pushed back from the desk, Justine considered for a moment that maybe it was time for her to start on a resume of her own.

***

As Kaarin Larsson approached the glassed-in production offices, her nervous edge sharpened as increased adrenaline started pumping through her. If she had eaten breakfast she would be vomiting now. She dodged around workmen cautiously pushing a large table on a dolly through the groups of people clumped along the hallway. A different receptionist was on from last night when Kaarin had started her scam, but you never can know, maybe this one was just a coffee relief.

Her black skin luminous in a pink suede suit, Sarah Randolph towered above the group surrounding her. Her eyes went cold when they connected with Kaarin's. She turned to a balding gray-haired man in a leather sport coat, said something, then turned away to write on a clipboard held up for her.

Kaarin waited as he approached, pushing and patting his sparse hair into position. Half-glasses hung at his chest tied with a long shoestring around his neck.

"Chuck Watson," he said, extending his hand. "We've talked."

Kaarin smiled as she shook his hand. She noted the back of his clipboard had PANIC! in bright red painted on it.

"C'mon, Sarah's waiting. I've explained what you're up to, the piece you described. She thinks you're crazy, knows no one can do it. She comes on a little strong at first, but actually she's great when you get to know her. I've produced her show for five years … she knows how to make money for her sponsors." He took Kaarin's arm, and pushed through the shifting crowd, pulling her behind him.

Her blonde hair brushed out and hanging half-way down her back, Kaarin had worn black silk pants with a black and white jacket without a purse. A small black leather bag hung from two brass chains from a wide black leather belt. During a scam her hands always had to be free. She had carefully positioned a sealed WCVB envelope which contained another folded empty WCVB envelope under her jacket on the left side, while two other WCVB envelopes were on the right. Her fingers were tingling, her mental edge mounting.

Up close Sarah Randolph was beautiful, her face carved of polished onyx, framed in large folds of glistening black hair. Kaarin looked up as they were introduced and smiled.

"This better be good, lady, or it will be your last," Sarah said, her voice a low rasp. "I have had a belly full of phonies with their phony powers. Without Paul Capriotti at Pilgrim pushing, you wouldn't be here now. You wouldn't even be in this building. And I have a show to do in thirty minutes. So listen … you will be on eighteen minutes into the show after a Pilgrim commercial, and you'll have seven minutes max leading out into another commercial. Problem with any of that?" She glanced sharply over at Watson who stood out of Kaarin's view behind her. "So now what?" She looked at her watch, nodded at one of her aides, a young woman who immediately moved away toward the studio. The others watched silently.

"No, Sarah, I have no problem," said Kaarin. "Please go into your office alone, and with your door closed, draw a picture of anything, anything at all. Seal the picture in a letterhead envelope, then fold and seal that envelope into a second letterhead envelope. I'll wait here where I can be watched until you return. The letterhead envelopes will ensure no funny business since they could only be yours."

"No funny card tricks? And *you* are going to tell *me* what I draw without seeing it?" Sarah shook her head as she strode rapidly away toward the production offices, the flow of hurrying people parted to open a path for her. She disappeared through the first door which shut behind her. After a pause, the men in the hall turned back to their conversations.

***

Sarah was looking at her watch when she reappeared a few minutes later. She handed a sealed envelope to Kaarin as Chuck Watson immediately left to respond to someone calling his name.

Kaarin took a quick breath. The first step: Sarah was just like everyone else, they always handed you the envelope, unless you handled things like a bomb drill. Kaarin shook her head and took Sarah by the elbow to guide her to a position under a ceiling light away from the traffic in the hall.

"No, I don't want to touch the envelope," Kaarin said, as, with her shoulder turned to Sarah who walked slightly behind her, she slid Sarah's envelope down inside the left front of her jacket at the same time withdrawing the identical letterhead envelope containing the dummy envelope. Moving smoothly without hesitation her envelope switch was invisible.

Kaarin held the switched envelope up to the light. "Can you see anything through your envelope, Sarah?" she asked giving her the envelope to hold.

"No. It's completely opaque." Sarah squeezed the envelope while she held it to the light.

"Keep the envelope with you to ensure that no one can touch it until I am on." Kaarin stepped back.

Sarah raised her eyebrows. "That's it? No funny shit with cards or boxes?"

"No. It's just you and me, Sarah. And I have not touched anything." She said firmly, to plant the thought.

"Okay, lady. Just be ready. I will kill anyone who gets near this thing." Sarah walked rapidly away toward the studio where she slipped the envelope onto the clipboard handed her by one of her production assistants.

As Sarah walked away, Kaarin paused for a moment, then went immediately into the nearby lady's room. Sitting in one of the closed stalls she withdrew

Sarah's envelope from under her jacket, tore it open and examined the drawing: a sketched football stadium with the scoreboard showing a score of 41 to 19. Two pyramidal clouds were over the field with rain coming down from one. She refolded the drawing and placed it inside one of the letterhead envelopes from the right side of her jacket. She folded it and sealed that envelope into the second WCVB envelope, then slid the sealed envelope down under the left front of her jacket. Then Kaarin tore the original envelopes into smaller pieces, threw them into the toilet and flushed.

***

"Why yes, I think I know where Sarah keeps that stuff," Judy Kim, Sarah's Korean secretary, said helpfully.

Kaarin followed her into Sarah's office. While the secretary searched for the large black marker Kaarin had requested, Kaarin quickly noted the clean top of Sarah's desk; nothing extra there to build from, but always worth looking. Then, as Judy cried out in triumph holding up a package of colored markers, Kaarin saw a sealed envelope among the wadded papers in the waste basket next to the desk.

Were there two drawings? She thought. What gives? Adrenaline pumped back to a high pitch.

The moment the secretary left to find the drawing pad Kaarin had requested, Kaarin stepped back to pick up two wadded papers on top of the waste-basket. Quickly spreading one out and angling it to the light she could just make out the dim impression of two pyramids with the sun rising behind them, the sun's rays drawn out in wavy lines. The second paper was the same except no sun was behind the pyramids. Kaarin wadded the papers up and dropped them back in the waste-basket as she walked to meet the secretary at the door. The sealed envelope was best left alone, could be a trap – not worth the risk. She had enough to work her scam anyway.

"There, okay?" said Judy, grinning, a large sketch pad in her hand. "You're all set now."

Kaarin smiled. "Yes, I certainly am." Maybe Sarah had changed her mind on the drawing for whatever reason. But why?

Kaarin waited for Judy to return to her desk, then moved away from people and potentially revealing window reflections. To screen her actions, she held the pad up as though to examine it. Kaarin quickly withdrew the envelope from under her jacket and slid it up under the pad. Her fingers pressed it tightly in place. She turned back toward the studio door with the envelope containing Sarah's drawing safely concealed under the pad. As she

35

walked tingling swept over her body. Now was the time when a mentalist earned her money – making that last switch, *no matter what happened.*

***

The elaborate stage set resembled a room with a view of Boston Harbor framed by two leather chairs, a leather sofa and a low large oak coffee table. During the commercial break, the floor director led Kaarin to the seat opposite Sarah across the table. She held the envelope containing Sarah's original drawing concealed under the drawing pad that she had carried casually into the studio with her. Now, that envelope had to be switched back for the dummy envelope Sarah had been guarding. Kaarin placed the pad with the envelope hidden under it in the center of the coffee table, and leaned back into her chair.

"Why not place your envelope in the center of the table now to allow the people and the cameras to see it more clearly," Kaarin suggested casually – and held her breath, her edge at its sharpest, ready to move depending on Sarah's response.

Sarah looked at her for a moment, then finally said : "Okay." As she removed the envelope from her clipboard and laid it on the pad, she glanced over to the floor director who was gesturing a timing signal.

With Sarah's momentary distraction, Kaarin moved instantly. "Oh no," she said. "Out in the open ... away from everything." With her thumb on the dummy envelope on top and carefully aware of Sarah's eyes, Kaarin picked up and rotated the pad, which left the envelope containing Sarah's original drawing exposed on the table. She laid the drawing pad with the dummy envelope now hidden under it beside her chair. Only a brief instant of timing; the scam was now almost completed. If Sarah had delayed or hadn't looked away, then Kaarin would have done something else – whatever, to overcome that moment of maximum risk.

When Sarah turned back, Kaarin suggested: "Perhaps you should sign your envelope to ensure everyone knows it can only be yours."

Sarah cocked her head slightly, frowned, then nodded, signed across the entire flap of the envelope, then pushed the envelope back out into the center of the table. She smiled coldly. "You pull off this caper, lady, maybe you've got something. But you don't have a prayer. I had that thing every minute."

A moment later the camera's bright red light immediately ignited another surge of adrenaline through Kaarin. Her breathing picked up. Now only a little further and the scam was done. But there was still that other sealed envelope in the wastebasket, what ...?

37

Sarah nodded to the camera, introduced Kaarin, explained why she was there, then pointed at the envelope on the table.

"That envelope has been with me from the very first moment. Absolutely no one has touched it, including our guest. And to confirm that" – she pointed – "that is my signature on it. It contains a drawing that Kaarin Larsson says she can duplicate without ever seeing it, or touching it." Sarah smiled coldly into the camera that hovered over Kaarin's shoulder. "Lady, I will believe that when I see it," she rasped sharply. "You're on."

Kaarin smiled then carefully reached down and picked up the pad, holding the dummy envelope in place under it. Folding the cover of the pad over and adjusting her grip, she relaxed, the concealed envelope was now firmly held, safely hidden from any angle.

"I will draw what I think Sarah has drawn and sealed away from all eyes inside two envelopes. Right now only Sarah knows what that drawing is. It exists *only* in her mind. And to be fair, I will show the camera and the audience my drawing before Sarah opens her envelope so I cannot make any changes."

Sarah frowned and cocked her head.

Crossing her legs, Kaarin laid the pad against her knee and began to draw, stopped, hesitated, shook her head, tossed her hair back from her face, then drew again, while she tracked the timing signals of the floor director at the corner of her eye. Finally finished, Kaarin again brushed her hair away from her face and dropped the black marker on the table.

"I am committed, Sarah ... I am finished." She twisted around to show the nearest camera her drawing of the football stadium with the score, the clouds and the rain. Nearby members of the audience stood to see it better. Chuck Watson blanked out the nearest monitors to prevent Sarah's seeing it, as he had agreed to do, when Kaarin had talked with him yesterday.

Kaarin turned back toward Sarah. "Now... open your envelope and show the audience how close I have come." She held the pad face down to conceal her drawing from Sarah.

A camera moved down close to focus, to center on Sarah's hands as she ripped open one envelope, dropped the pieces, then tore open the second. As Sarah unfolded the paper on the table revealing her drawing, Kaarin laid the pad face-up beside it. A great roar erupted from the audience when they saw the drawings were virtually identical.

Sarah's jaw dropped. "Impossible! You never touched anything!" Sarah's expression of utter shocked disbelief filled the monitor screen near Kaarin, froze, then the screen snapped to a commercial. The hostess stared wide-eyed at Kaarin.

Allowing herself a small smile in response, Kaarin relaxed. Now to ditch the dummy envelope, finish the scam and slam the work home.

4

Recovering her composure during the commercial break, Sarah, a strange worried expression on her face, asked Kaarin to wait for her after the show. Kaarin had torn off her drawing, leaving it on the coffee table, and carried the pad with the hidden envelope with her out of the studio while the audience applause was just starting to subside behind her. Production personnel behind the cameras only stared at her as she passed them, but Chuck Watson grinned and gave her a thumbs-up from the control room.

***

While standing in the production offices with Sarah's staff to watch the final minutes of the show on a wall-mounted monitor, Kaarin let the dummy envelope drop from under the pad into a trash can just being carried out. The scam was finished when she casually dropped the pad on a desk and walked away. No one had spoken to her, or, in fact, had come near her.

Her face grim, Sarah pushed rapidly through the glass door with Chuck Watson in her wake. She had her drawing clenched in her fist. She stopped and shook it in Kaarin's face.

"What is going on, lady? This is not the drawing I intended. It's not!"

"You made another drawing?" asked Kaarin quietly, her performing edge returning. A mentalist's dream in the making?

"Yes, but then I changed my mind. I thought you might be able to guess from … I … I don't know what." Sarah shook her head, her jaw tight, her eyes wide. Personnel coming from the studio filled the office, but seeing Sarah, once inside their murmuring stopped. "I was quoted in the Boston *Globe* yesterday about a football game and I thought you might have seen it, so I changed to something completely out of the blue. I must have mixed envelopes … I guess." She was confused, uneasy, still holding the crumpled paper up almost touching Kaarin's face.

Kaarin waited another moment, then asked gently: "Do you want me to tell you what your other drawing is … as well?" A loud buzz instantly swept the room. All eyes fastened on her.

Sarah froze. "What? Now? <u>Right now</u>? No bullshiting?"

At the edge of a potential second miracle, Kaarin immediately turned and walked through the crowd to a large white-board on wheels, the people stepped quickly back from her as she passed. Afraid of her aura -- or maybe of her seeing into their minds? Her smile was quick and gone. Kaarin picked up a black marker from the tray on the frame of the white-board and turned around.

"Right now, Sarah," she said, brushing her hair back from her shoulders. "Right now, if you will let your mind relax a little." She paused for emphasis. "I am not trying to hurt you."

Sarah's eyes flew wide, her mouth partially opened, then closed.

Kaarin waited for a moment, looked down at the marker in her hand, frowned slightly, then nodded and began to draw a triangle, then another. Sarah gasped. When Kaarin drew a sun between the pyramids, Sarah's mouth dropped, but then she snapped her fingers and turned, pushed anxiously through her people and ran to her office.

When she returned, Kaarin had added the wavy lines to the sun and turned to face her, one hand on her hip, the marker in the other. Sarah ripped a sealed envelope open, dropping the pieces as she walked. When she finally opened out the folded paper, her voice broke: "I can't believe it! How could you know I did this? The envelopes were still sealed … buried under the trash." Sarah went grim. "What are you, Kaarin Larsson?"

Even Chuck Watson's face was pale as he pushed his limited gray hair back into position.

Unblinking, Kaarin met Sarah's disturbed eyes, held them for a moment, then smiled gently.

Shaking her head, Sarah overcame her shock within seconds, her face colored with anger. She stood with her hands on her hips while Chuck Watson and her staff shuffled about nervously, waiting. Finally she walked to the whiteboard, stopped, and looked down, within inches of Kaarin who turned, her nervous edge softening with relief, and dropped the marker back into the tray.

"Okay, Kaarin, I can't figure you. Not yet." Sarah pointed back at Watson. "Chuck, find a time *soon* for her to come back. Do your whole routine next time, lady. You can take my whole damn show. I want to see it all. I can't figure just what you are ... but, so you clearly understand, I'm going to dig, going to ask questions, check with some friends at the magic shops. Nobody gets away with setting me up" – she paused – "but if you really *have something*, then I'll be the first to beat your drum. You understand?" she rasped sharply, her parting smile a thin wintry line.

"I leave it to you to determine what I am, Sarah," Kaarin responded. "You are the judge."

44

5

The 'birdcage' on Front Street at Heyl's Corner in Hamilton, Bermuda, an open, white roofed raised platform of blue and white painted concrete just large enough for one man standing, while ostensibly manned by a bobbie-helmeted policeman to control the traffic through the central part of the city, is actually a tourist post manned at the request of merchants when three cruise ships, the maximum allowed by harbor rules, are tied up in Hamilton Harbor. It is not duty eagerly sought by any policeman, dull, and being harassed by tourists as "cute", "quaint" and *"wie hübsch"* until one day when *Vogue* magazine used the birdcage and its duty bobbie as the setting for an extensive fashion photo shoot.

When asked by his colleagues the following day, how it had been, the young black officer, Clyde Markham, sighed, his eyes rolling heavenward: "All day, man, hour after hour… lapfuls of the greatest tits and ass a man could ever dream of … and most of it in full view and …" He shook his head slowly, philosophically. "God, there will never be anything like that again … not in this man's lifetime." Markham's eyes glazed over, not reacting even when someone waved a hand across his face. A glimpse of

45

paradise can unsettle the strongest man.

Laughing, Inspector Keith R. Haggard had listened with the others to the dazed bobbie from the birdcage slumped in his chair at the Police Club. But Haggard's was another unique Bermuda concern. On September 9, 1972, while in his home, Police Commissioner George Duckett was shot fatally, and his daughter was wounded. A few months later, on March 10, 1973, with the Duckett killing still unsolved, Governor Sir Richard Sharples and his Aide de Camp, Captain Hugh Sayers, were murdered in Government House grounds. Even the Governor's Great Dane, Horsa, had been shot. Though the two assassins had ultimately been caught and hanged, a State of Emergency was immediately declared and a ban on public ownership of guns of any kind was issued. 1,440 guns were turned in during the first period of amnesty, with more being turned in later under various other conditions. The ban was formalized into law with punishment of 10 years in prison without parole for possession of a gun of any type, or possession of any part of a gun, or any amount of ammunition, even a spent shell. Permission for possession of any type of gun was at the sole discretion of the Police Commissioner. That permission had never been granted.

Now Keith Haggard had two guns, a .41 and a .32, loose somewhere on the islands. Ten years in Westgate

46

prison had been risked by someone in just holding the guns while standing on Bermuda soil. There were occasional shootings on the islands, fortunately not near any tourists, but not one as opportunistic as this one. But why had a dead man been shot? Actually, it wasn't illegal to shoot a dead man, only to hold the gun, but which gun had killed Tony DiMarco, and why had he been so hated as to be murdered twice? This wasn't a gang shooting, a concern that in Bermuda was growing in seriousness, which were usually chance killings – this one had been clearly a planned murder.

***

"Really, I scarcely knew the man, Inspector," said Roland Sommers, his back straight against the blue velvet Louis XV chair. His finely trimmed thick gray hair just touched the high white-collar of his burgundy striped shirt. There were no wrinkles in his freshly pressed gray linen suit. A great globe stood in a black lacquered antique wooden frame next to his chair, the globe nearly three feet in diameter, its continents and seas hand painted in oils. He idly pressed his fingers against the globe, rotating it silently under his hand.

"Upon the recommendation of one of my important clients who had witnessed one of Mr. DiMarco's performances and lectures on memory, in New York I believe, I secured his services for the New Century Venture Capital Conference being held in Hamilton later this week, of which I am the honorable chairman. Investment bankers have a great interest in strengthening their memories, particularly of names." Sommers glanced out at the sun-washed sea in the distance. "To help assuage our continuing tourism problems, I, with the assistance of an American banker, Marc Kane, was able to bring the Conference to Bermuda this year with its 250 or so men and women with money to spend. The Duchess management has been most cooperative."

Sommers drew momentarily on his pipe, a slim polished Savinelli briar, then, leaning forward, he laid it aside on the leather-topped carved parquet table littered with computer printouts. Haggard had stiffened. "Still fighting off the evil nicotine, Inspector?"

"Yes," he replied. "Thank you. Tobacco smoke even from a quality piece as that causes some edginess."

"How long now? I think I recall you smoking at the Club luncheon last week."

"About six days. From two packs a day to zero. The only way. Quit. Quit hard."

"That would be quite beyond me, I am afraid."

"Yes, Mr. Sommers," said Haggard, drawing a worn leather notebook from his inside jacket pocket. He wore a navy sports coat over camel slacks, an open-necked white linen shirt. "How long could anyone have known that Tony DiMarco would definitely be in Bermuda?" He flipped the cover back, his pen hovering over the paper.

"The contract was signed about a month ago, actually on his behalf by DiMarco's agent in New York. My aide can give you the exact date and a copy of the document. We learned the exact time of his arrival on Bermuda only four or five days ago."

"He was killed in the Paget Street Cemetery. Did he mention to you, or anyone that you know, that he was planning to visit the cemetery? It is not a well-known tourist location, certainly not one of the places a short-term visitor would place high on his list."

"Perhaps he'd been in Bermuda before? I have spoken myself perhaps only a dozen words to the man." Sommers pushed back from the desk. "My apologies, Inspector, but I have a crucial financing to close within the hour to meet a German deadline. And the recent down grading of Bermuda national debt by Fitch has scrambled our numbers."

"Certainly, Mr. Sommers." Keith Haggard stood.

"Ah, well, Inspector," he said, coming around the desk, his hand extended. "I do not envy your mission … however, I have my own, admittedly selfish, concern. With the tragic death of the *Gold Mind,* as DiMarco styled himself … typical show business conceit … my program now has a great hole in its mid-section that must be expeditiously filled … in three days. I will, of course, be at your disposal at any time." He walked Haggard to the door leading downstairs.

"Thank you, Mr. Sommers. I will be back to you."

Leaving the house, crossing and stepping down from the wide verandah, Haggard walked slowly toward the wooden gates set in the arched entrance in the high plaster and brick wall. "ROSE DALE" was cast at eye level into both of the white-washed cement pillars. He paused, holding the gates open for a moment, but two people knew when DiMarco would be in Bermuda and both those people knew that he would be in that cemetery *at that time.* Did the two killers know each other? Would they now be hunting each other? He shrugged, stretching his fingers and shaking his arms, then started down Queen Street toward the St. George's police station five minutes away where his car was parked. The morning sun quickly warmed his back, as the nicotine twitches subsided. Vigorous rolling sea was sparkling between the pastel buildings and houses as he walked. Six days with every hour getting tougher than the last, and a lot of hours ahead. Sommers may have been right about the tobacco.

Now I will believe there are unicorns ...

William Shakespeare

The Tempest III.iii

1611

6

"My God, Paul, you know how I feel about psychics, and you forced that blonde on me yesterday, and I get fucked in public!" Her voice shaking with fury, her eyes wild, Sarah Randolph smashed her fists against her desk. "I looked at that rerun of her so many times last night I dreamed about that bitch. I couldn't see anything phony ... nothing! And how did she get that second drawing ... how could she know *I even did* a second drawing? No con has ever beaten me ... now I've got to expose her, or kiss her ass on camera and see my ratings drop. What is she to you that you did that to me?"

Glad it wasn't him on the receiving end, Chuck Watson watched Paul Capriotti sink back into his chair, biting his lip, absorbing her fury. Capriotti was chunky ex-Harvard rugby with thinning brown hair, a gift for finance, and a strong taste for risk. A bent nose broken in forgotten scrums crowned a thick cavalry mustache. Her fury momentarily exhausted, Capriotti slowly leaned forward, his elbows braced on his knees.

"Kaarin Larsson is nothing to me personally," he said firmly. "She and her late partner did a great show for the closing dinner at Pilgrim Fidelity's annual strategic planning meeting up in Woodstock, Vermont, a few months ago. I told them we wanted them back. When Kaarin's partner died suddenly, and she went on alone, I told her my promise still held when she got into Boston again … and your *Boston Today* is the top daytime talk show in New England.

"Sarah, Pilgrim and I have supported you from the beginning. There is no way I would ever want you to look bad." He smiled warmly. "Kaarin and her partner, ah, Mentavo, did one of the best second-sight mental acts I've ever seen. She deserved the chance."

Sarah set her jaw, then sighed and nodded. "All right, Paul. I stand corrected. I'm sorry." Her smile was fleeting. "But you understand how I feel about anyone who claims to be *psychic. I want to squash them like bugs*. After what a so-called psychic reader did to my mother's life, that particular con just turns my gut."

She suddenly pointed at Watson. "Chuck, while I

get some ideas from friends about that tape, I want you and your people to question anybody who might have seen or talked to that blonde anywhere in the station. *Might have,* remember, *anybody.* Build a file right now while memories are still fresh. Everything she did or said, *no matter what.* I don't know how Kaarin Larsson got into my mind … but, by damn, I want her out!"

***

Light from the table lamp reflected a soft halo around the gazelle on the krugerrand which Paul Capriotti had pressed so warmly into her palm weeks ago in Vermont. Gentle, gentle gold. The harsh searing visions at the university that had driven her away from her life work; Mentavo's apparent understanding, but maybe only a fraud and a few lucky guesses; Bingeton's frightening off-hand comment; Sarah Randolph's quizzical look at her as she had left the studio — did any of that mean *anything,* was there anything there, any pattern, consistency in the data that could give her the beginning of understanding of what was happening inside her mind? Or was it truly only some of Mentavo's *mind dust,* a mental illusion so real and convincing, but actually utterly unreal. The dust he said he sprinkled in the thoughts of his audiences with his patter and misdirection. Could her mind be rebelling from her constant drive to force it to see beyond the limits of the perceptions of others? Had she been pushing so hard at Riverside to elbow her way past her male academic competition that her mind was starting to deliver up nonsense, not insights? Kaarin pushed the gold coin deep into the pocket of her silken grey robe, then ran her hand through her hair, pushing it away from her eyes and off her face, her fingers lightly tracing the familiar ridges at her temples.

Kaarin leaned against the window and looked down on the darkening New York streets outside her apartment building. A passing car turned on its lights. She and Chuck Watson had agreed before she left the station that she would return to Sarah's show in about a week if Sarah's prior commitments allowed, this time at a full fee not just union scale. But then Watson's quick call this morning to warn her of Sarah's declared determination to expose her on camera had left her edgy. Watson obviously had been torn between loyalty to Sarah Randolph and the potential for an ugly public setup with a studio audience loaded against her. He didn't like what the public could think of Sarah if there was a setup, even if Kaarin was embarrassed. Some ideas for her second encounter with Sarah had started forming in her thoughts as she left eagerly for her morning appointments with agents.

"A mentalist can do anything ... anything at all,"

Mentavo had taught her. "All she needs is brass … pure brass!" And an overeager skeptic was always a special prize. Sarah would require some special thought.

***

But even with miracles on Boston television yesterday, there were no follow-up bookings in New York. Five agents were impressed with her Boston DVD and with her short demo routine, but still nothing. No encouragement. Just a long and finally depressing day. But more troubling than empty bookings was the dream; again, last night. And what waited for her as more darkness came, when her eyes closed? Dear God, what was eating her insides?

Kaarin turned away from the window to pick up the library photocopies again. The material had taken only a couple of minutes to read, but she had copied it anyway:

Some unusual skull fragments found in 1913 in the Potchefstroom district of the Transvaal, South Africa, near a village called Boskop, with more fragments found a year later on other sites. Dated to about 10,000 years ago near the threshold of the Ice Age, but the evidence was very sketchy, uncertain. Maybe the Kalahari Bushmen were direct descendants of the Boskop people, and then, maybe not.

That kind of academic straddling and hedging was

very familiar to her. References listed in the article were to obscure South African anthropological journals which weren't available on-line and which the New York Public Library didn't have, but had ordered for her. She read the sheets again, then dropped them back on the table. What Bingeton had meant could be anything in that odd tick-tock head.

A deck of cards lay on the table next to her. Kaarin picked it up, did a full pressure fan, then folded the deck shut with a smooth flair of her fingers, like stroking the wind. It was sometimes easier to think while practicing card moves and sleights, a habit she had fallen into following Mentavo's example. His fingers had grown stiff and unresponsive over the years, but he persisted, frequently spilling the cards on the floor. "Dietary," he had said, laughing, stooping to pick them up again and again. "Did you ever see a fat juggler?"

Kaarin faroed the deck and snapped a waterfall finish. Pure magician, but so what? She casually sprung the deck from hand to hand, making a sound like peeling cabbage. Smoothing the cards back into a precise stack, she dropped them back on the table.

The Boskop skull fragments had been distinctive in their length and breadth, suggesting a very large cranial capacity.

<u>Eighteen.</u> She placed her hand over the deck and cut it. She counted the cards cut off. Eighteen. Dropping the cards back on the stack and shuffling to wipe out any natural breaks, she tried again. Twenty-six. No, that's too easy. Twenty-eight. Kaarin lightly touched the deck with her fingertips and lifted off part of it. She counted, though it seemed unnecessary, shit, twenty-nine. She replaced the cards, wetting her lips with her tongue, shuffled and lifted again. Twenty-eight. A simple skill to learn, given enough hours in empty hotel lobbies and bus stations, but one which always impressed businessmen. Like memorizing a shuffled deck of cards, it was something they wished they could do; and thought it remarkable that a woman could handle cards better than they could.

The physically large brain suggested by the bone fragments found at the Boskop site did not necessarily mean anything. Strangely, the Boskop people also had small undifferentiated teeth. Sarah Randolph is afraid of what I might be. Why is she so dead set against mentalists? Check her. Yeah.

So what am I?

Kaarin dealt seconds and bottoms for a moment, then shifted to dealing from the middle of the deck; a skill at which even Mentavo had marveled. Her small hands undetectably moving a card from the center of the deck

57

while appearing to deal it from the top.

Those bones from the beginning of the Ice Age. What were they? What might they have to do with me? She threw the cards on the table, watched them slid off onto the floor, and returned to the window. She'd pick them up later.

Damn that Bingeton!

***

As she leaned against the window, an encounter with Jacob Mortmann, her mentor and later thesis advisor at UC Berkeley for her Ph.D. came back:

The papers were worn thin in spots from multiple erasures. "Wretched work" was written across the top in permanent black ink. "Think better than this!" was written, precisely printed beneath. "Wretched work" had been written in graceful script. Another note, "You must, KL" had been added in washable blue ink at the bottom of page one. Kaarin flinched. The sharp remarks and the washable blue were unexpected. Her work was solid, unshakable, *original!* She bit down on her lip.

Straightening in the hard chair, she thumbed through her pages, all five. Nothing else was marked, highlighted, or noted. KL was so formal. She was scared. He couldn't lose faith in her. . .

Dr. Jacob Mortmann smiled very narrowly. "You

58

think me unfair, Kaarin?" His leaden baritone filled the barren office. The color photograph of his daughter on his desk was the only relief to the plain green of the empty walls.

Kaarin looked up, perplexed. "It's good. It's right. I believe it shows I've seen something no one else ever has," she pleaded.

"True. But it is wretched sloppy thinking ... thinking that could have been expended on another thought. You could have seen even further. You wasted a priceless moment of insight. That moment of seeing may not reoccur *to humanity* in the same way *ever again*. You haven't time to squander, KL. You are twenty. What have you done with that great basilisk of a brain you possess?" he said coolly. He shifted his heavy shoulders, his thick hands flat on the desk, his eyes holding hers.

Kaarin nervously started to speak, but hesitated. The work was good, that's all that mattered. Deeply shaken at her very core, she felt her eyes becoming moist, and she was ashamed.

Twisting in his armless chair, Mortmann reached behind him to the credenza, lifted a ream of white, unlined paper, placing it on the desk in front of him. He pulled a side drawer open, lifting out a bottle of Scripto permanent black ink. Sliding the thin-bottomed center drawer open, he took out a massive Mont Blanc fountain pen that looked like it could hold a quart of ink.

His equations formed perfect parallel rows across the papers. He wrote evenly, steadily, precisely, quietly. The equations came, virtually full-formed from the great gold nibs. After several silent minutes, he stopped. Waiting a moment for the ink to dry, he picked up the three sheets, crisp as from a printing press.

"Here are your five pages of work and your thought, simplified, clarified, without the collateral rubbish and with time for other things," he said. "Think, Kaarin, think in pen-and-ink ...*never* in pencil and rubber." His deep blue eyes were half closed. He murmured, "Your mind is too valuable to run unrestrained, to run loose."

Kaarin had bought a massive Mont Blanc -- $650. It intimidated her own students, as it had her in Mortmann's thick hand. But her mind had begun to slip loose, even using permanent black.

***

Kaarin recognized what constellations she could make out through the New York lights and haze. Starshapes forgotten, ignored by the people rushing below, going somewhere. Give up her search and quit now? Go back to UC Riverside, or try anyway, if they would take her. Tough it out. Maybe the visions and dreams will just

60

go away like a bad headache. She leaned against the window frame, only vaguely aware of some movement on the streets below.

The ringing phone intruded into Kaarin's somber brooding. Finally she recognized the sound and dove over the low vinyl sofa to get the receiver before the caller gave up. Hanging upside down over the back of the sofa, her bare legs in the air, her robe flopped open, Kaarin answered coolly: "Yes?" She tried to let her wind out slowly to avoid sounding rushed.

"Kaarin-can-you-do-memory?" the male voice erupted.

Kaarin only heard a blast of sound. "What?" she asked, forgetting and letting her breath out all at once. "Please slow down, I don't understand. Who is this?"

"You've-been-trying-to-sell-your-mental-act-to-every-agent-in-town. Right?"

Kaarin missed everything but the word 'agent'. She frantically searched her mind to make sense from the torrent of sound. Then she knew: Machinegun Morgan, the legendary agent for the elite and wealthy. She quickly pivoted to an upright position on the sofa, pulling her robe demurely about her, her legs tight together.

"Yes, Mr. Morgan?" She hoped that was the right answer.

61

'Mister!" he laughed. "I-haven't-been-called-mister-since-I-left-the-Navy." His voice boomed as he laughed again. "Look, I'll slow down." Morgan was making an obvious effort to pace his words. "It's not really fair since we've never talked before."

Kaarin laughed lightly, her hopes soaring. "That's all right, I'm catching on."

"Right. Can you do memory?"

Kaarin hesitated, then said yes, but not as authoritatively as she had hoped it would sound.

"I don't like the sound of that yes. Do you or don't you?"

"Yes, I do memory," she said. "It's that I mix it with mentalism … not as a stand-alone act. I wasn't sure how you were asking the question."

"Okay. Okay. My fault." Morgan was silent for several seconds. "I don't know that I really have time or choice." He seemed to be speaking more to himself than to Kaarin, whose heart was still pumping with anticipation. "Look," Morgan finally said. "This is the gig. You know Tony DiMarco?"

"Of course. The memory expert. The Gold Mind."

"I booked Tony into the New Century Venture Capital Conference to do a show and teach a memory training seminar. This is in Bermuda." Kaarin's hopes leaped higher. "Tony's been killed. Had his brains blown away. Bermuda police found his body in a touristy graveyard near Hamilton, draped over a tombstone or something. Lousy thing to happen. I've handled the Gold Mind over ten years. He was a quality act and a real pro. Damn shame. Just a damn shame." Morgan's voice had noticeably softened.

Kaarin was stunned. "That's terrible. Why? Have the police found the killer?" But, she felt, DiMarco deserved whatever he got.

"They think he was mugged and robbed. But Tony never carried much money with him ... told me he'd only spend it faster. Who knows? People where I came from were killed for pennies. Anyway, I have to book a replacement for Tony. I've never stiffed a client ... I've got to have a memory expert in Bermuda within four days. If you can handle it, I won't forget it. If you blow it, I won't forget that either."

"I understand." Kaarin was cautious. The show wouldn't be the problem. The seminar ... "What about materials for the seminar?" she asked. "I don't have anything."

"Use Tony's. We'll change the title page."

Kaarin then asked the question she dreaded, like laughing at the gods: "Why me?"

"No choice really. All the people I would have liked to use aren't available. Be at my office at seven-thirty tomorrow morning and bring a DVD of your Boston TV gig. I heard about that. I want to see you and some of your stuff, before I make a final decision. You-have-any-problem-with-the-time?" he erupted.

"None. I'll be there." She wrote down his address.

Kaarin was up at five unable to sleep. She carefully sorted through her wardrobe for the right effect, finally selecting a silver-grey sweater dress for her encounter with Machinegun Morgan. Simple in style, its color matched her eyes closely, which always worked well. It concealed, but didn't hide. She started to work out a follow-up routine to the Sarah Randolph scam in case Morgan wanted more, and . . .

***

Machinegun Morgan was up at five, unable to sleep, but not because of Kaarin Larsson. The telephone calls from Bermuda were more frequent and more insistent.

"What about DiMarco's replacement, Morgan?" Roland Sommers' English accent was harsh in the dark early hour. "I've three hundred investment bankers on my doorstep in three days with a hole in my program as big as the one in DiMarco's head. What are you going to do about it?"

64

Morgan scowled at Sommers' sharpened t's which the Bermudian always used for emphasis. "I'll-have-an-answer-for-you-before-noon-today," he said.

"Blast Morgan, I can't understand you!"

"You're the only one of my clients who can't," he replied slowly.

"I may not be on that estimable list much longer unless you get me answers fast! I'll give you by ten … *my time* … or our deal's off and I make my own arrangements."

"Damn," Morgan whispered. "Tony's mugging couldn't be anticipated. For over ten years Tony never missed a commitment. How could I know some two-bit hood would splatter his brains? I'm no psychic!"

Sommers was silent for a brief moment, leaving Morgan to listen to the last echoes of his words. "Our police no longer believe it was a simple mugging," he said. "It seems while DiMarco's own wallet was empty, he had five one-thousand dollar bills stuffed in the pocket of a shirt hanging in his closet. The serial numbers were matched with cash stolen in the past few weeks from a New York diamond merchant. Your Gold Mind seems to have been a bit tarnished!

"Ring me by ten!"

***

65

Cool sharp breezes in her face tossed her long hair behind her. The day, even with a struggling sun, felt good. Morgan's opportunity had lifted her spirits. Today she felt she could easily walk on water.

Kaarin had heard Morgan's name before. The principal agent for the very wealthy and elite, he provided entertainment for the exclusive parties and meetings which were always described in breathless detail in the on-line gossip columns, tabloids, *People* magazine, and even Facebook. A long way from the dismal night clubs/comedy clubs in which Mentavo had finished his career, and in which she had started hers. It could a step into a different universe.

Machinegun Morgan, with his loud booming voice and aggressive manner, must look, Kaarin reflected as she walked, like that actor on the old TV program *All in the Family*, whatever his name was. She pictured the agent as a chunky, burly man, partially balding, with his confident voice, a tough looking Naval type. She knew it. She felt positively psychic this morning. Her brief sleep had been deep, dreamless and untroubled. But to be free of the dream for even a night, that was glorious.

***

Morgan's office was not in the theatrical district, but in a towering glass paneled Park Avenue building filled

66

with the offices of law firms, financial advisors, and physicians. He wasn't even an agent, but a 'consultancy'. Morgan, Kermit T., Consultancy, 1413, the lobby directory declared in haughty stainless steel letters.

Kaarin laughed as the elevators doors closed. Her vision of a burly, rugged Naval officer needed drastic revision. How could a Kermit be rugged? They're usually small and green. She laughed again, but her nervousness climbed as each floor passed beneath her.

***

Kermit Morgan removed his tinted glasses to study her quietly for a moment as she looked closely at the vivid bold paintings hanging in his reception room. Her glossy blonde hair half-way down her back, she was ...

"They're-real-Kaarin," he boomed suddenly behind her. Kaarin flinched, and looked quickly over her shoulder. "I may be a little color blind," Morgan said very slowly, "but I know how to spell Picasso."

Morgan towered over her as he stretched out his hand to her. Her hand was small, remarkably soft. He wore a deep blue Armani pin-stripe suit, his first-time suit, until he knew who he was meeting. It made him look like a successful gray-haired Mafia capo.

To Kaarin, his designer stubble and open-necked dress shirt made him look like a cliché from some man's

67

magazine. Though a good looking cliché.

"Come in. Coffee's just finished." He held the door to his office open.

He didn't need personally autographed photos of celebrities in his large office to lend him credibility. His remarkable clients gave him that. His colors, plants and furniture were carefully arranged by a consultant to offset his partial color-blindness and to emphasize his style: earth tones, polished mahogany and money.

After casually waving her to a molded ebony and mahogany chair, which fit as closely as a racing bucket seat, Morgan settled behind a large parquet table inlaid with interlocking hexagons. He had taken Kaarin's coat to hang up, nodding in studied appreciation of her form. She looked much younger than he had expected. He nodded again as she glided smoothly into the 'witness chair' as he liked to call his DanTong original.

"I was surprised to find you so far from the theatre district," Kaarin said.

"I'm where my clients are." He waved his hand toward the ceiling. "My clients are here, or their clients are my clients, if you understand me." He paced his words deliberately.

Kaarin nodded. "A matter of marketing."

"It's all a matter of marketing." He rose to refill his

68

blue porcelain mug. "How long did you work with Mentavo?"

"Almost six months, before his stroke."

"He's dead now, isn't he?" Morgan sat deeply back into his tooled leather swivel chair.

"Yes, he died immediately from the stroke. He collapsed on stage." Kaarin shook her head again, as Morgan offered her coffee. "There was so much he still wanted to teach me."

"I booked Mentavo and Laura a couple of times a dozen years or so back. A superb professional act." He leaned back. "That Laura, even in her sixties, was a sexy witch. Lord, could she spellbind an audience. Even scare them." Morgan put his mug down. "Don't get me wrong. Mentavo was great, in his prime, and carried his full share of the act. But Laura was unique, one of a kind. She had nerve … and something else."

"What did she have? I never met her." Kaarin leaned forward. "She died the year before I connected with Mentavo."

Morgan noted her change in interest, then shrugged. "That's a good question." He leaned on one arm of the chair, propping his chin on his fingers. "I got curious one time years ago about mindreaders and such, so I picked up a few books on mindreading and mentalism, stuff that was

69

supposed to be *the* material on the subject. Annemann, Corinda, Becker, Minch, Berglas and so on. You recognize any of those names?"

She nodded once.

"Could never do the stuff myself, but I got an insight to the techniques. Not that I wanted to embarrass anybody. Just curious, you know. Well, I booked Mentavo and Laura into a chic party at the Vernon's out on Long Island. I don't remember exactly when, but I remember that show. I don't normally watch any of my acts perform. I know them all well enough, but those two I wanted to see. They were new to me then, and with all my newfound knowledge, I thought I would see through everything."

"Did you?"

He nodded. "Yeah, I caught a lot of it. Those two were smooth as fresh-woven silk. They had me several times, but I worked out the gaff later … I think. But then, near the end of their show, one of the Vernon daughters, brats every one of them, and I'll deny I ever said that, stopped the show yelling something like: 'I'm tired of your silly magic tricks. Show me something good or get out!' It bothered Mentavo a little, but it was Laura who responded. I could see her temper was up.

"She didn't hesitate. She told the kid to call any of her friends anywhere in the world. The girl decided to call her uncle who was in Monaco at the time … must have been about four or five in the morning there. Laura smiled, and I'll tell you that smile sent a chill down my spine I'll never forget. I think a spider smiles that way as she walks her web." He drained his mug, and for a moment looked down at the amber drops remaining on the bottom.

"Laura wrote something on a piece of paper, folded it and threw it on the floor in front of the girl while the kid called her uncle. When the uncle got on the phone he was mad as hell and hung over, but went along.

"Laura told the girl to have her uncle name any card from the deck … to change his mind as often as he like, but to settle on one. Then Laura said: 'I have foretold your uncle's choice on that paper on the floor.' The girl laughed and said that Laura was nuts. Mentavo was as tense as I was. The whole place was tight as hell. Anyway, the uncle settled on the four of clubs. He had filled an inside straight with a four of clubs earlier that night. A very rich card, he called it.

"Laura pointed at the paper on the floor again, and ordered the girl to open it. The brat snarled something, but opened the paper and read it to her uncle and the rest of us, then she screamed! Laura had written: A very rich card is the four of clubs! God, you could have knocked me over with a whisper. Even Mentavo went pale as a ghost. Then

71

Laura smiled that spider smile again and said: 'Now we will continue'. The place was silent as a tomb.

"They finished the show to good applause, but Mrs. Vernon told me they never wanted to see Mentavo and Laura again. They had scared everybody … but Laura, her nerve was unshakable. I've believed ever since she could do the real thing when she really had to." He pushed his mug away. "So where's the Randolph DVD?" he asked abruptly.

Kaarin waited and watched Morgan watching her on the screen. He looked back at her after a few moments as though to compare her with the television image. Her pad switch was over before the cameras turned on, so there was nothing to see, if Sarah checked the gig to find fraud, or if Morgan …

Morgan punched the eject button, and handed the disk to her across the desk. He glanced up at the ornately carved timepiece against the opposite wall. Roland Sommers. His jaw tightened, then relaxed. Some clients were more difficult to deal with, but Sommers was simply an ass. He looked at the remarkable woman now sitting before him, obviously anxious and just as obvious in trying to conceal it. A uniquely beautiful woman who would now haunt him forever. One of the peripheral benefits of being an exclusive agent, as well as the fatal blow to his two marriages.

Laura. If Kaarin Larsson was as strong as Laura, and doing a single rather than a two-person mental act, the prospects could be unlimited. He could easily find over twenty clients worldwide where …

"That was a damn sharp piece, Kaarin. Randolph trashed the act of a friend of mine on her show a few weeks back, so to get that reaction out of her took serious nerve. I haven't a clue how you could have done that. You might be the real thing for all I know." He smiled. "I have no doubts about your ability to do the show," he said. Her smile was modest.

"The performer and agent form a partnership. It may be an 80-20 partnership financially, but it really is 50-50. Neither can benefit if the other screws up. All this is to say, if I send you to Bermuda, you've got my reputation as well as your own on the line."

"I realize that," Kaarin said quietly.

Morgan continued. "Mental acts are the toughest to do and to sell. But, at the same time, if a mental act is good, then it can be a real money-maker even without visual media or Las Vegas."

Her glassy eyes never wavered, though her anxiety was still there, but more tightly controlled.

"I'm not concerned with the show in Bermuda, even

if it's straight mentalism and no memory, as long as it's entertaining. You can do whatever routine feels right for the place." He turned to the credenza. "Take a look at this." Morgan slid a thin book bound in artificial elephant-hide covers across to her.

Tony DiMarco's name was embossed in heavy gold across the cover above the title: *Mining Your Own Gold Mind.* Morgan watched closely as she scanned the table of contents, which he knew were basic standard introductory memory subjects: a general discussion of the physiological basis of memory with McConnell's strange flat-worm experiments and other apparently bizarre efforts at understanding the mechanism of memory, along with the ancient Greek and Egyptian memory systems with developments up to the twenty-first century. A few tough puns and gags relieved the steady flow of teaching. Unfortunately, Tony DiMarco was not a comedian.

"DiMarco seems in love with his subject," Kaarin said as she flipped through multi-colored illustrations used to demonstrate the basic loci mnemonic technique of the Greeks, then the peg words, the link system . . .

"He was," Morgan replied. "Tony had a collection of about three thousand books on memory and memory systems. He loved what he was doing ... and he was damn good at it."

"I don't see anything here that is different from what I have used and studied. Mentavo always felt that a strong memory should be the hallmark of a good mentalist, and we did some memory in the act on occasion." She paused. "If I were to do a memory act and seminar combination I would want to rewrite this whole thing." She laughed and shook her head, her long hair falling across her shoulders only to be brushed back automatically. Morgan stirred. "The jokes are transparent and pretty bad. I think they interfere with the teaching. Humor is a great tool for teaching. It's fun to use and my students always responded to humor. But the humor must support the point being made, not just a one-liner for the sake of a cheap laugh."

"Your students?" Kermit Morgan frowned, realizing how little he actually knew of this woman.

"No matter," she responded. "I taught a little in college."

"What subject?" he asked.

"Physics."

He leaned forward. The lady had become more awesome yet. "How did you go from physics to mindreading? That's an amazing connection."

She smiled, but pulled back in the chair, obviously uncomfortable.

"What degree do you have? Where did you teach?"

he asked, ignoring the time, and Sommers.

"I don't want my physics background to be a part of any billing I might have. But I guess you have a right to know ... since we might be partners. I have a doctorate in quantum astrophysics from UC Berkeley. I taught at the UC Riverside campus for three years, before I couldn't take the academic world any longer ... and *real* physics isn't so far from mentalism as you might think. Only a different step in imagination."

"Impressive. Damn impressive!" The cash flow prospects could be even broader than he had first thought. If the Bermuda gig goes well, there could be no limit to her potential.

Kaarin had placed the memory book back on his table. "What now? I can study the book and use my own humor. But if I am to prepare a credible seminar I must get to work ... so must you if that cover is to be changed."

"You're quite right," he agreed. "This is the deal. It's not as good as Tony's since you don't have his stature, yet," he added with optimistic emphasis. "Four thousand for the show, a grand-and-a-half for the seminar, plus expenses and your room at the Bermuda Duchess. I'll take 35 percent this time to cover the ..."

"The risk," she completed. "That's a reasonable arrangement, this time. I'm willing to make the investment in the partnership."

"I'll have the papers sent to you this afternoon to give me power of attorney to sign contracts on your behalf. There will be $1,000 cash front money, and a plane ticket, first class, sent with the papers. Your Bermuda work permit will be waiting for you when you get there. We'll talk again before you leave. One more thing. What title do you want on the memory book?"

Kaarin reflected. "Call it: *The Invisible Art*," she said. "That is what memory truly is."

Morgan nodded, noting the title. "Good words." He reached inside his jacket for his iPhone. "One final thing. What do you do after a show."

"I pack up and leave," Kaarin replied.

"Always?"

"Every time," she stated, coloring. "I don't play those games. I never have."

"Never?"

"Never."

"Good," he said. "I don't book whores, male or female."

Kaarin flushed deeply with anger.

"Hey," Morgan half rose out of his chair. "Don't-take-it-personally." He slowed: "What you do on your time is your business. But on my time …"

"I just don't play those dumb games."

Morgan watched as Kaarin's eyes became moist in her struggle to control her temper.

Speaking slowly, she said: "You have a right to set your rules, which I will observe in our relationship. Mr. Morgan, I know very well the difference between work and play." Some of her suppressed anger colored her voice, sharpening it.

Trying to cool her growing anger, Morgan sat back in his chair. "Hey, I'm sorry. Sometimes I have the grace of a water buffalo. But," he added, leaning forward, "it's necessary for us to get the ground rules set early, to avoid later misunderstandings."

Kaarin had already risen to leave.

Morgan stood up and put out his hand. "Okay?" he asked.

Kaarin gripped his hand, and nodded silently. Her plain smile appeared forced.

Helping her with her coat, Morgan smiled slowly. "I'll be in touch," he said.

Kermit Morgan watched as Kaarin disappeared into the still empty reception room. She was someone special, who would need different handling. But she was something else he couldn't define, something in her presence. He swiped to Sommers' name, the 441 area code immediately appeared. For the first time he may have met a woman who could tame a unicorn.

7

"Morgan finally find a replacement for Mr. DiMarco?" asked Crockwell.

"Yes. A lady, no less," answered Roland Sommers.

"A woman? Who?"

"A Miss Kaarin Larsson. She calls herself 'The Indescribable Phenomenon'."

Crockwell laughed as he twisted and crushed out his cigarette. "Crazy show business people! There's no end to their conceit." He fisted one hand and shook it. "An untrustworthy bunch … an untrustworthy bunch."

"Morgan says she is a phenomenon … at least physically, I gather." Sommers drew momentarily on his Savinelli, letting the smoke caress the inside of his mouth and tongue. An electric beauty, Morgan had said.

"Physically? How pleasant. How very pleasant. Did she know DiMarco, our late *Gold_Mind*?" His question was politely phrased, softly spoken, but his eyes brightened, demanding.

"Morgan wasn't completely certain. Apparently she may have, on a somewhat casual basis. We must assume that she did, I believe, and keep our options accordingly." Each word was formed precisely, and set in place with care. Ian Sanford Crockwell, whose wealth was increasingly fragile, was likely to panic at the wrong word. His money had come from inheritance and some uneasy sources, not from making tough decisions under pressure. Sommers knew his clients, how much they could handle, psychologically and financially. Ian Sanford Crockwell was fragile in both columns.

"Yes," Crockwell agreed. He tapped another cigarette against the smooth hard leather arm of the chair. "Has the killer been located?" he asked, quickly switching off the subject of show business people.

"Not yet, but soon I'm sure. Our consultant is most thorough."

"Except all blacks look the same to him. Blast! If Mr. McGraw had kept his eyes open, and acted quickly our situation would now be safely under control." He lit the cigarette, inhaling slowly, deeply. "I don't like untidiness, Sommers."

"Mr. McGraw was not retained because of his ability to identify native Bermudians."

"Rubbish! *I am* a native Bermudian … keep your classes correct, sir!" Smoke exhaled sharply from his nostrils, his widened eyes cold with contempt.

Sommers let the stem of his pipe play lightly across his lips, the bowl warm to his fingertips. Though he had lived for most of his life on Bermuda, he had been born in a London slum. Each of his two applications for Bermuda citizenship had been denied by the government who had been consistently tightening the requirements over the years partly, obviously, to keep the home vote loyal. Even with his connections and the clear financial benefit to the islands of his work, the fools were blinded with their short term political obsessions. His latest application for a Permanent Resident Certificate, though he still couldn't vote, had finally been granted. But he still could only buy property in the top 5% of value, like any foreigner, with a minimum of about $3.5 million. Sommers grimaced, damn their ... His face immediately relaxed. Never show a client any emotion. But on the basis of current law, he could never become a Bermuda citizen. But the politicians of both parties would still have their hands out.

"My apologies, sir." Sommers' tone was mildly mocking, but the man across the Louis XV desk from him did not notice. Sommers changed the subject. "Intriguing."

"What?" Crockwell's brief flash of anger faded, his flaccid features once again serene.

"Morgan said we would find the Larsson woman quite unusual."

"Oh? Well, what does an 'Indescribable Phenomenon' do? I thought she was to be just another

82

memory expert like friend DiMarco." Impatient, he exhaled two short streams of smoke through his nose.

"She apparently is also a skilled mindreader ... of all things." He chuckled. "Do you feel threatened?"

"She *would* have a hellish time reading our minds, wouldn't she?" Crockwell nodded, starting to grin at the obvious absurdity.

They both laughed loudly, startling the delicate, dark-haired young man bringing them morning tea. Sommers let the great globe rotate silently beneath his fingertips.

Safely in harbor
Is the king's ship; in the deep nook, where once
Thou call'dst me up at midnight to fetch dew
From the still-vexed Bermoothes, where she's hid
The Tempest I:ii

8

Kaarin breathed deeply, her eyes closed, feeling the acceleration of the A320 press her more deeply into the cushions. The frantic pace since Morgan's first call had left no moments for rest or reflection. Endless details, wardrobe, seminar -- the reprinted memory books misplaced at the printer according to Morgan's quick call — and another time over the Friday night show routine with some options depending on the audience and the performance space itself. Couldn't prepare in a vacuum, she needed information on the audience, to get some personal slants in order to make miracles out of tricks. Morgan had included write-ups and brochures on the conference and on the Bermuda Duchess hotel with the thousand dollars, plane ticket, contract and a small note of apology with an invitation to dinner. An invitation she had very carefully declined. Morgan would be interesting, perhaps necessary, to know, but there was so little time. Later, she had promised, after Bermuda. But after Bermuda there was Sarah Randolph wanting to pick her bones in public, and then what? The feeling that something was always there, a growing quickness to her anger, the relentless invasion of the starscapes into her dreams, a strange uneasiness that seemed to stalk her.

Even with the material Morgan had sent, Kaarin still needed more, more personal information. She could only focus on the organizers described in the conference publicity, there wasn't time for anything else. Articles in the Sunday New York *Times*, luckily retrieved from the trash, and Monday's *Wall Street Journal* had added some scraps. She checked the on-line Bermuda news sites, *Bernews* and the *Royal Gazette,* for background on the Bermuda economy and finances as that might come up at the conference. A national debt of $3.5 billion, a recent credit rating down-grade, and a marked shortage of jobs which both political parties always promised to over come. An odd brief article in the New York *Times* on a Colorado investment banker with a picture showing him standing on the porch of his childhood home, talking about the roots of his success; she clipped it when the final paragraph mentioned his attending the Bermuda conference. Maybe useful, but she had to know something about the personalities of the most prominent organizers to have something certain, something concrete to build on. With those insights nailed down, then she could wing it with whatever information she could find once in Bermuda. But it had to be quick.

Dieter Krings of Borden & Montcrief investment counselors, Chicago, could provide some fast insights into latest deals and financial gossip. Kaarin hesitated to touch the phone buttons. His number was not in her iPhone for a reason. Dieter had always been on the make. Very bright, but so obvious, since undergrad days at Berkeley, just too obvious, too anxious to get in bed to be fun. But time was short, and it was long distance which was where she wanted to keep him. And she knew he would never reveal her source.

"Kaarin! Fantastic to hear your blonde voice again!"

Kaarin laughed. "A blonde voice? Dieter, the market must be tough today. You're not rational."

"Never can be when you're around. You wouldn't dare read my mind." He paused. "What can I do for you … long distance anyway?"

"Dieter, I have a major opportunity in Bermuda to perform at the New Century Venture Capital Conference in a few days."

"Sounds like nice work. I was going to try to go, some dynamite contacts going to be there, but a couple of my deals are too pregnant. A moment … I don't remember seeing your name in the promo literature. What are you going to do?"

"Tony DiMarco, who was booked for the conference, was killed. I'm to take his place." She added, "In two days. I'm running flat out to get ready to leave Wednesday morning."

"DiMarco killed?" He stopped. "Never mind. What do you need?"

"I'm trying to get a better understanding of some of the people who will be there. Angles on their latest deals, gossip I can use to make my routines more relevant to them … more personal."

"Umm," Dieter murmured, "and here I thought you were the real thing. Lately you seem to be working the financial turf pretty regularly from what I've heard. Pilgrim Fidelity and all that."

"There's nothing regular about anything I do anymore."

"A long way from being a sensual physicist. You almost made me change my major from general irresponsibility to physics just to try to understand what

87

turned you on so hard. I still don't know… but I intend to keep investigating the subject. Why not just go back to Einstein, instead of working that showbiz play?"

"I'm not sure I can ever go back to the university. I'm still looking for some … particular answers. And I need to get some answers now for Bermuda, or I don't eat."

"All right. But it's dinner next time you're in Chicago. Shoot! I'll betray all my confidences only for you."

"All right. Dinner. Marc Kane. Who is he, does he have a sense of humor?"

"Kane, huh? A big cocky stud. Ex-pro something. Arrogant as shit. Good promoter, especially of himself. Goes for gadgets like the really-smart smartphone, and some trekkie technologies like genetic engineering, biochips, carbon nano-tubes, Internet of Things, so on. A decent, but definitely not a sparkling track record.

"A key thing, Kaarin, is to be very cautious of a technology or gadget that is too narrowly focused. It is too easy for that concept to go under if things in the market aren't near perfect. And look at the company's claimed release dates. Inside 12-18 months, probably real, beyond that, forget it." Dieter's phone was muffled for a moment. "I see that Kane just bought a big chunk of the action in a little losing operation in Texas that thinks it wants to make computers out of protein to ease implantation in the human body. Seems they think we should use steaks for calculating rather than eating. The key to their technology is the pigment from fish eyes. It'll be the only pure play in fish eyes when Kane takes them public … in 2030 maybe. He laughs a lot. Been married a dozen times. Has a multi-millionaire TV anchor-woman living with him now. Basically unpredictable. Next?"

"Roland Sommers, a Bermuda local."

"Don't know too much about him. Met him only a coupla times. Foul smelling Italian pipe, I remember. He usually likes small pieces of syndicates, usually software or social media oriented. Close-in payoff stuff. Keeps a low profile … generally low risk. Though …," he hesitated. "Don't know how much detail you want, Kaarin, but he and some Bermuda associates just put some very heavy bucks into the Cognito Thought Systems deal. Cognito … remember Descartes … was being shopped around pretty heavily. *Fast as a Thought!* was their corporate slogan. However, it seems their new ultrafast multiplexed tablet may have some serious heart pains, maybe even terminal."

"Ohh," Kaarin groaned.

"Sorry. Slip of the tongue. They needed a large input of capital to get things moving again. I looked at that deal. But so did everyone else with any room in their portfolios, I think. I know the computer marketplace, made some good money too, but Cognito didn't set right."

"Why?"

"A feeling. Same as you once said you got in your physics research. The vibes weren't right. The people were straining to make their concept look good. Talked about getting some kind of Fed loan guarantees, even without a working prototype. Even dumped a chunk of their VC money into campaign contributions in the last national elections, which is a no-no. That was enough for me to run the other way as fast as I could. Sommers was pushing too hard. Inconsistent with his low profile approach."

She wrote and underlined Cognito. "What about Sommers personally? Anything about him?"

"I understand he's an ass. Unmarried, for whatever reason. He's smart … no, that's not right. He's cunning, not smart. His smile was too processed, too smug, the two times I met him. Careful with him. He and Kane are the chief organizers of the Conference, I guess. A real interesting combination."

"I'm doing a memory training seminar on Thursday morning. What should I emphasize? Names, I would guess."

"They'll never forget you, that's certain. Yeah, names, numbers. I didn't know you were a memory expert.

What other surprises do you have?"

"I am what I am. What key trends will the conference be focused on? What subjects would be of greatest interest." She didn't want him to drift.

"If they have any spunk, what you're doing after the show, I would imagine. Nothing worse than a horny banker in the Bermuda midday sun."

"Oh, Lord, Dieter, please, there isn't time." But she laughed. She was the horny one.

He paused. Kaarin could hear him breathing. "You're right. I've got some calls hanging I've got to get to. Ah-h, the development of water-limited fracking technology that would eliminate all the environmental issues and give America almost unlimited low-cost hydrocarbon energy resources. Medical technology: the realization of a Star Trek style body scanner, the tri-corder, I think it was called. There's a $10 million award announced for the first company to do it … from a chip company, of course. A company that could come close to that would be buried under money … I hope. I have a deal gestating in that area now." He hesitated a moment. "And something up your alley. A digital sixth-sense, as it is being called. The top line smartphones have up to 18 sensors in them to tell the phone who you are, where you are and where you are going. The next step is to anticipate what you want to do … almost like digital fortune telling. It is also called contextual computing. Big bucks are waiting for that. And the Internet of Things, where every gadget talks to every other gadget. You understand what I mean?"

"Yes, I think. I was theoretical, not experimental. I wasn't even metric."

He chuckled. "Yeah, that sounds like you, Kaarin. And another thing which you may overhear, which lurks in the back of everyone's mind. That is China. The Chinese government is going all out to buy up all the technology companies it can. Bigger the better, it seems. And close off the Chinese market to anyone who might compete. The standing joke, if you could call it that, is when will China finally own Europe.

"Anyway, that all folds back into everything else. And the software, chips and networking that make it all fly. That's what Cognito and a few others are trying to do." He hesitated. "Promotion techniques. Watch out for too much hype. Lots of paper-thin, wet dream companies being shopped now. Will kill the IPO, the new issue market, if they get backing. Like what the Facebook fumbling at its IPO did to the social media IPO market for a time. Will scare the hell out of the small investor. The principal thing to know for the conference, I think, would be anything that melds with the digital sixth sense. A gadget that responds without specific commands. Toss the jargon. Throw some of your physics at them, they'll love that. A gorgeous blonde who can speak jargon ... nirvana! Venture capital jocks love jargon and playing God. I know I do. That's it. Dinner. You name the place and time."

"Thanks, Dieter, I really appreciate it. I'll call when I hit Chicago again."

"Sure you will." He hung up.

Kaarin held her cell for a moment, then tapped it off. Dieter Krings. Brilliant, irreverent, attractive with the libido of a buck rabbit. She remembered him over lunch when they had first met, using a phony accent, saying: "Vee Austrians are ferry smart people. Vee made Hitler into a German, and Beethoven into an Austrian. Und vee know how to make other tings, too." It would take a genuine mindreader to ever understand him. Well, Chicago . . . maybe. *Cognito: why the change in Sommers' investing pattern?* She underlined it again.

***

JFK fell away under her window, becoming quickly obscured by loose gray overcast. Kaarin let the seat recline a few degrees. She grinned in recalling Morgan's stunned silence when she called him yesterday to ask for help in making special arrangements at the hotel. The Duchess brochure had shown the hotel's large irregular parking lot running along the ocean with a short, but abrupt drop-off to the rocky surf below. She had estimated about a ten to fifteen foot drop and without safety fences. A blindfold memory drive around the parking lot could put her name all over Bermuda and into the other hotels, if Sommers could set it up. She had done blindfold routines before, but never an outdoor drive. Couldn't be that much different; just use the Pearl Tangley blindfold technique for forward vision, no sweat.

"Kaarin, are you sure? You don't need to do this. It's not part of the contract." Morgan had sounded concerned and worried.

"I mean to give the conference … and the Duchess … their money's worth. My plane lands about 12:30. It could be done just before afternoon tea at four."

"Damn. DiMarco never tried it. I don't think Tony ever thought of it. Damn!"

"I'm certain. Roland Sommers can let me know when I arrive if he has gotten it all arranged. It will let everyone know I'm around."

Morgan laughed nervously. "No doubt about that. Okay … assume it's on. Damn, lady, you've got guts … but it's a hell of a good idea. Solid marketing. Good luck. I-hope-you're-feeling-psychic."

She agreed. Whatever that might feel like.

Sommers, too, was stunned when Morgan called, but agreed. It would be worth seeing. Perhaps, he had laughed, even a bit indescribable.

**

The great green fish-hook that is Bermuda formed on the edge of the arc of the horizon. Isolated six hundred miles into the Atlantic on the Gulf Stream, its green sparkling with apparent inset jewels, the hook gradually softened into a beckoning arm. Kaarin pressed against the window to watch the islands approach under the left wing. Stunning white capped blue-green sea covered the deep lethal shadows of coral reefs.

Inset jewels became pastel houses in blue, yellow, pink, orange and green as Kaarin glanced back and forth from the window to the map spread on her lap. The Great Sound leading into Hamilton Harbor where two large cruise ships were at anchor. Morgan had mentioned cruise ships as a possible future market for her mentalism. Then Harrington Sound -- the Duchess, where? She had almost missed it on the southern edge of Hamilton Harbor, its slim pink towers flanked by its irregular parking lot and tennis courts and the street in front of the hotel that ran into Front Street, the main Hamilton shopping area according to the map.

Her nervous edge was sharpening. It was so easy to

be cocksure in Morgan's office and on the phone. But this was reality now. What if she blew it today, even before the conference began? Kaarin frowned, fighting down the doubts. In twenty minutes she would be on-stage for three days, then maybe a day to enjoy Bermuda like a tourist, and back to New York on Sunday. Morgan had encouraged her to stay the extra day, then she had to leave, her work permit expired. On her last day she planned to move away from the Duchess to Shadowind, a small cottage colony in Sandys Parrish near Fort Scaur at the far western end of the islands. Sands Parrish, the stewardess had corrected her pronunciation, not Sandees. Small point, maybe useful.

Kaarin watched grim Fort St. Catherine come into view as the plane gently banked to begin its final approach. The fort's stark hard-gray military geometry contrasted with the bright colors of the umbrellas on the pink beach running almost to its walls. Some resort on one side and harsh volcanic outcroppings on the other with great rusting cannon lying like drowned swimmers in the surf.

She had found two photos of Roland Sommers in the website of the *Royal Gazette*, along with some preliminary details about the Conference and some of the early arrivals of investors from Europe. She noted the names for later. The front page had a sad story of an American who had been killed in a diving accident off of

Tucker's Town. She shook her head. The American had been a family man and only 55. SCUBA had never been her interest. There was enough on dry land to worry about. When the wheels touched the runway she felt her nervousness intensify, the adrenaline began to flow starting to reach that fine edge that was needed to "do the scam" as Mentavo had so lovingly called his profession.

***

Kaarin let the plane empty before retrieving her garment bag containing her performing wardrobe. Key irreplaceable props were in the white attaché case hanging from a narrow strap over her shoulder. The rest of the props and wardrobe were in a single checked suitcase. She wore a simple deep green boat-neck sweater over narrow-leg camel slacks. She would dress differently for the memory drive.

Kaarin squinted tightly against the brilliant sun until she had levered her sunglasses into place with a free pair of fingers. The last of the passengers were disappearing into the terminal as Kaarin emerged from the plane. Figure 15-20 minutes to clear immigration, Morgan had said. Sommers will take it from there.

Kaarin gave her passport to a smiling immigration officer. Above him a portrait of Queen Elizabeth II was shadowed behind construction scaffolding.

97

"Good afternoon, miss. Delighted to see all those good Yankee dollars arriving." He chuckled softly, while flipping through her passport. He stamped it, then turned back to her photograph. "Um," he said. "If you'll pardon my saying so, miss, you're one of the few people who could not take a bad passport picture." He laughed. "And I know how that is."

Before she could reply, he stepped away from his counter to signal someone, who in turn disappeared into an office, then quickly reappeared with Roland Sommers at his side.

When Kaarin hesitated to pass the counter, the immigration officer grinned, stuffed her passport and orange card into the side pocket of her attaché case for her. "You are in the hands of the Brass now, miss. *You may pass on*," he said with mock seriousness.

Roland Sommers' greeting was coolly polite. A sharp snap of his fingers summoned a slight dark-haired young man from the office to take her garment bag.

"Do you have any other luggage, Miss Larsson?" Sommers asked.

"Yes, a single suitcase." She started to tell him he could call her Kaarin, but stopped as she realized he wouldn't anyway.

Sommers turned. "Rennie, a single bag. Miss

Larsson, you have the claim stub, and your orange immigration card?"

She quickly handed them to Rennie who accepted the bits of cardboard as though they were Crown documents and started toward the baggage area with a choppy stepping walk.

"It's a white suitcase with K L. on it," she offered to his back. He nodded in acknowledgment without turning.

"Your suitcase will be waiting in your room at the Duchess, Miss Larsson. My car is waiting. This way, if you please." Sommers took her arm gently, then released it when she began to move in the right direction.

Immigration officers had gathered at one of the counters to enjoy a short break before the next flight arrived. When Kaarin looked back as she passed through the sliding exit door, the officer who had processed her, waved. She smiled in return, then passed under the Bermuda coat-of-arms to the outside brilliance. Kaarin glimpsed Bermuda's official motto carved on a scroll below gold encrusted clear-blue heraldry: QUO FATA FERUNT — *whither the fates lead us.*

***

Sarah Randolph was sick of watching Kaarin Larsson, so while the others were grouped at one end of the small theatre watching the Larsson video play she walked

99

around the room, reached from the magic shop by a short corridor through a usually closed door. Three of the room's walls were covered floor to ceiling with colorful old magic posters and autographed photos, with one wall of glass-enclosed shelves of rare magic apparatus.. There were two large posters of Alexander, the Man Who Knows. Wish she did. She loved to watch good magic and knew a few card tricks herself, but Josh Raymond, the shop's owner, could dazzle her with cards every time with no apparent effort. He seemed to know everyone in magic and every trick ever done. When she recognized the painfully familiar sounds of the conclusion of the Larsson experience, she took a donut from the box next to the coffee pot near the back door and returned to the table as the four men stood and stretched.

"Pop the disk, John, and give it back to Sarah," growled Raymond. The young shop assistant moved quickly. "Impressive piece of work, Sarah. Heard a little of Larsson, but haven't seen her work before." He removed his black horn-rimmed glasses, cleaned them, and laid them on the table. He closed his eyes for a moment, then grinned. "Damned impressive. Some guts there, too. She had to have taken some serious chances."

"So how'd she do it, Josh?" Sarah asked, as everyone sat down again.

"Yeah, Josh, how the hell did she pull that off?"

asked Dave Blunt, casually fanning and closing a deck, then fanning again. "I couldn't catch a thing."

"Blunt, you couldn't catch someone palming an elephant." Josh grinned, replaced his glasses, then crossed his arms and leaned back silently.

"Some very thorough pre-show work, whatever it was," offered Alan Disney, a small man with a large mustache.

Raymond nodded. "Yeah, Uri Geller did a stunt like that on Boston television years ago, but his gaffus was straight forward. This Larsson girl doesn't leave any easy footprints. She looks so damn young. And that second drawing Sarah said she did after the show demonstrates she thinks on her feet and isn't afraid to push the edge of risk." He nodded again. "A little polish and luck, Kaarin Larsson could go nationwide. Where is she now?"

"I heard she took Tony DiMarco's gig in Bermuda," said Disney.

"So what do I do, Josh?" asked Sarah impatiently. "She's coming back for the whole show in maybe a week. People trust me to expose cons … that's my reputation."

Blunt snorted. "Yeah, you sure did in George Kartin a couple of months back. What'd he ever do to deserve that? He hasn't worked since."

Sarah glared at Blunt. "Him or me, Dave. That's

101

what it was, *and he didn't have the stuff!* He didn't do his homework."

"I'm not sure I could tell you, Sarah," Raymond said, ignoring Kartin. "A good mentalist is a strong lateral thinker and may not even know herself how she's going to do it until she sees the setup and actually does it. She certainly started her scam before you ever saw her. That's a given."

Sarah shook her head. "I've had my producer check with everyone who might have had any contact with her in any way for two days before the show, but nothing suspicious."

"Wouldn't be suspicious," said Disney. "Wouldn't seem out of place at all, and people don't remember things unless you do something funny."

Sarah frowned. "There was a girl who asked security for some envelopes the night before, for sending out her resumes she said. But the guard couldn't remember her face, she was just there and gone. And, that has happened a couple of times in the past."

A chime rang. "John, grab me some more coffee, then see who's out front. I'm not in while Sarah's here," said Raymond. He leaned toward her, his heavy eyebrows knotted. "Sarah, I can't give you a method that a-b-c gives you what happened on that DVD and in your offices later.

Kaarin Larsson was obviously well trained during her time with old Mentavo … she's resourceful, and careful about her claims. She has plenty of nerve and … she doesn't really claim to be the real thing, just damn close. Which winds up meaning the same thing to an audience. You stopped Kartin because he did a canned scam with a fixed method. He was asking for trouble and you delivered. He got what he deserved." Raymond reached up for his refilled coffee cup. "Larsson, I suspect, goes with the situation, looks for an opening and then does it. Some performers call that jazz mentalism. I'll bet she had adrenaline pumping through her by the gallon, and trying like shit not to show it. I know what it's like to be out on an edge like that with everything on the table … you never forget it, Sarah … and for some performers, like me and probably Larsson, that adrenaline rush becomes addictive.

"Some world-class athletes told me once that they get the same thing like skiing down a mountain at a hundred miles an hour. You miss, you're dead. You make it … you want to do it again the next day. You get to where you just have to keep pushing that edge again and again, until you meet a faster gun." He grinned. "Like you, Sarah."

Blunt started to speak, but Sarah interrupted: "I hear what you're telling me, Josh. I won't do what she might expect, and I don't leave her alone at any time, even into the lady's room. There won't be any casual time, *this time*. I'll try to push her to try too much, force her beyond the edge."

Josh nodded. "Yeah." Then he laughed: "But don't be shocked though if Larsson still pulls it off. Remember, she thinks laterally not vertically like a magician. With her, and all good mentalists, there is no method, Sarah, only a result, a finish!"

He smashed his fist against the table.

9

Kaarin couldn't take her eyes from the kaleidoscopic beauty only hinted at from the air. Sea and harbor through the car windows, deep blue-green on one side of the causeway, astonishingly clear on the other, then into a narrow road, pulling close to hard-cut volcanic walls to allow bare inches of clearance for a bus heading for the airport. Hibiscus, glowing purple morning glories, hyacinth, more dazzling flowers whose names she didn't know, darting metallic-green lizards, someone's small banana plot, then pastel houses; all without a shadow in the fierce mid-day sun. She looked back to the copy of the *Royal Gazette* that Roland Sommers had given her.

The story with her photograph was on page three. "Woman Mindreader and Memory Expert at the Duchess," the single column headline ran. "Bankers' Brains to be Probed", the sub-head alliterated. The unnamed reporter followed up with more labored cleverness describing her planned conference performance at the Duchess, but emphasizing her outdoor memory feat under: "Tensions at Tea Time". Kaarin's photo was the close-up she had given Morgan of her looking directly at the camera through a candle flame that created soft highlights on her hair flowing over bare shoulders. The effect of sultry mystery was diminished in the two column newspaper color reproduction, but her name was spelled correctly – and it brought the people, lots of people, and three mobile crews with five television cameras marked ZBM-9, VSB-11, and ZFB-7. Only the public channel, Sommers whispered, CITV, was missing.

***

Her audience started to gather at three o'clock. From the balcony of her fourth floor room, Kaarin counted the house, watched as people in and out of bathing suits, many struggling with mopeds gathered in the areas already marked off by the Duchess management. Maroon shirted Duchess men and women were rapidly distributing vivid fluorescent red traffic cones about the parking lot along the pattern she had sketched out to Morgan, who had e-mailed it to Sommers. The intent was to raise her *apparent* risk, and thus the entertainment value of the demonstration. A crew was removing sound equipment from a blue van: microphones, amplifiers and seven, no, eight loudspeakers. Sommers had certainly been swift and thorough.

Kaarin started at the sudden high pitched screams of *keee-keee-krrt-krrt* of three white and black birds with long white central tail feathers soaring up into the cerulean sky, then suddenly swooping down, banking hard left to almost

106

sweep across her balcony. She took a breath and smiled. Another friendly greeting.

The Duchess crew was tightening her suggested layout with narrower pathways and sharper turns. Garish red cones outlined the route along the rocky drop-off with twists, switch backs and dog-legs. No straight sections to make it easy for her; just as she had requested, but now with smaller margins for error. Her layout was supposed to suggest danger, show-biz; not to become almost suicidal.

Glancing upward and along the side of the pink tower which overlooked the parking lot, she could see people with afternoon drinks gathering on their balconies. A few had binoculars or video cameras hanging from their necks. Three of the loudspeakers were being positioned to project up toward the overhanging balconies.

Three-fifteen. Kaarin went back into her room to change. Her hair was already brushed and tied back, carefully arranged so that her ears were clearly visible to negate anyone thinking that she had some electronic receiver from which she could obtain help or directions. Her dress would be short simple white highlighted with black, leaving one shoulder bare, with strong sunguard heavily applied. Again to demonstrate that there could be nothing concealed on her body that could guide her. The white would contrast sharply against the black parking lot as she walked around the route. She had asked for a dark colored convertible to use, to ensure that she would stand out in white, and that she would always be visible to everyone all the time. Kaarin wanted to be sure that her audience saw everything.

Three thirty-five. If she had eaten anything after lunch, she would be vomiting it all up now, her nervousness honed to cutting-sharp. A soft sea breeze found its way into her room, gently stirring the light window hangings, tinkling a stained glass windchime hung near the balcony entrance. Its meanderings were strangely cold, though the sun was still high over the horizon.

Kaarin placed two rectangular pieces of thick cotton batting and a long strip of black velvet about four inches wide into a white plastic case. As she waited for Sommers' knock to escort her downstairs, she reviewed her lines, locking in the first three sentences. Once she got past them, she would be on her way. Kaarin was too tight to sit. She began to pace, and to wonder if she should still include the ten thousand dollar forfeiture. Ten thousand she didn't have. An ideal opportunity to impress Morgan yes, but silly to risk so much, to push so close to the edge. C'mon lady, get real, the drive itself was enough.

Still time to pull back . . .

***

As Kaarin had outlined to Kermit Morgan, she would first walk the route to memorize it, then, to apparently add to the difficulty, she would, after being blindfolded, drive the convertible over the route but opposite to the way she had walked it. Confining the drive to the hotel parking lot meant the audience would see all of it, unlike a blindfold drive through the streets, and being on private property no last minute police authorization would be required. The blindfold would be cotton batting pressed down on her closed eyes, wrapped in layers of black velvet. There would be no chance, Morgan had protested, remembering his mentalism studies, for forward vision through the blindfold. How, he had asked, could she do it? "If you miss," he had pleaded with some emotion, "they'll have to fish you out of the harbor." Kaarin had laughed then, but with Sommers' brisk knock, her stomach tightened up the final notch.

***

At exactly four o'clock, Roland Sommers was relaxed as he stepped to the microphone to introduce Kaarin Larsson. Some spectators, staying at the Duchess, were carrying small plastic trays with tea cups, cucumber sandwiches and cookies. Others clicking their phones, some with cameras, others just staring. Many wore dark blue badges indicating attendance at the Conference. She

109

noticed a bulky heavy-jawed tourist in a flaming red shirt and white hat stood at the edge of the crowd, focusing one of his cameras on her as she stood behind Sommers, waiting for his introduction to finish. The applause was respectable, but swept away by the stiffening wind that sent large flumes of white salt spray over the rock seawall onto the edge of the asphalt parking lot.

"Thank you, Mr. Sommers." Kaarin spoke slowly, evenly, giving her words coming out of the loudspeakers the chance to register before adding more. "The greatest mystery of the human mind does not lie in the wonders of the paranormal, telepathy or clairvoyance … but in that realm of the mind common to us all … our memory. My purpose this afternoon," – she slowed again to let the echoes die away – "my purpose this afternoon is to demonstrate what a trained, disciplined memory can do under very difficult conditions … at risk of property and, perhaps, of personal injury." She explained carefully what lay ahead then paused, took a breath, and committed: "The physical danger is obvious … but, if I fail to complete the route, or knock over more than two traffic cones in completing it, I will forfeit to any Bermuda charity selected by the organizers of the New Century Venture Capital Conference, ten thousand American dollars!" The audience stopped sipping their tea and started whispering. "The demonstration will be visible to you throughout, so you will see everything." She stepped away from the microphone, took a short deep breath, and walked briskly to the beginning of the course twenty feet away.

The wind had slackened, but still tossed an occasional handful of spray over the rocks, as she started down the corridor defined by the cones, picturing in her mind driving the route, comparing it with what she had seen from her balcony looking down from above. Actually attempting to memorize the route would make her actions more realistic to the crowd spread around the perimeter of the driving course and up ten floors in the pink tower soaring above her.

This was the weakest piece of theatre in the scam and had to be kept as short as possible, since obviously to the audience little would be happening. Kaarin had to rely on their anticipation of what was to come as she moved without hesitation between the cones. Wait – back across one of the pathways – that could be tricky. She noted an isolated badly scarred yellow cone to use as a landmark in case of confusion, then on straight toward the rocks and the sea, twisting slightly left, then right, then hard, hard left to avoid going over the edge. Kaarin stopped and looked back. Then retraced her steps back to the hard left, and walked it again. Stopped. She looked around, as if momentarily confused, uncertain in her next step. She walked back again to repeat once more slowly. Stopped. Then continued through the rest of the route, and returned to a two-foot wide red plastic strip fastened to the asphalt, on which she had to stop the front wheels of the car for successful completion.

"Ready?" Sommers asked over the microphone when she returned, her hair and dress slightly moist from salt spray.

Kaarin stepped to the mike. "Yes. You may apply the blindfold now." She saw cameras raised, people no longer chewed on their cucumber sandwiches. Sommers opened the white box to get the cotton batting and black velvet bandage, as J. Outerbridge, Asst. Day Manager, the brass badge read on his maroon jacket, stepped to Kaarin's side, his black features glistening with light perspiration.

"Crazy way to make a buck, Miss," Jomo Outerbridge whispered, as he took the batting from Sommers and placed the two thick cotton pads over her closed eyes.

Kaarin heard whirring from cameras with motor advances, some clicking, and sotto-voiced requests from the television crews for people to please move out of the way. She felt the cotton pads pressed gently against her closed eyes. As with every other blindfold she had done, her nose immediately started itching! She dare not appear to interfere with the blindfolding to scratch. Her nose itched more in her helplessness. Kaarin curled her toes tightly, fighting off the raging urge to scratch. She tried to push it out of her mind, onto the drive and the first turn. The long edge of the pads pressed against her nose on both sides, effectively blocking any possibility of her seeing down the sides of her nose.

Sommers was wrapping the velvet bandage tightly around her head while Outerbridge held the batting in place, apparently sealing off any forward vision. Once, twice and on the final circle, the corner of Sommers' jacket sleeve brushed across her nose, scratching her itch. She could have kissed him! Her toes relaxed.

"Can you breathe all right, Miss Larsson?" J. Outerbridge asked her, over the mike so that the audience could follow.

Kaarin nodded.

Each taking one arm, Sommers and Outerbridge led her around to the driver's side of the dark-green Honda convertible. Outerbridge opened the door, while Sommers, with gentle pressure on her shoulder and back positioned Kaarin to slide to her left under the steering wheel. Knowing Bermuda drove on the left side, Kaarin had spent an hour at a Manhattan foreign car dealer practicing

113

shifting with her left hand; another detail on her list of preparation. Two hand-held television cameras and microphones bumped loudly against the hood of the car, then she heard them shuffle back as Sommers closed the door.

Opening her eyes, Kaarin relaxed her forehead which had been twisted in an intense frown. She smiled a small private smile as a pinhole of light opened before her right eye. She could see directly ahead, though her narrow field of vision covered barely half the car hood width. Already started, the engine was idling smoothly. Now protected behind the windshield from the occasional cool winds, the sun became hotter on her bare white skin, cooking through the sunguard lotion. Kaarin picked up the position of the first set of red cones, released the parking brake, slowly let out the clutch and started forward.

The crowd gasped as Kaarin swerved hard to avoid hitting the first cone on the right side. Then she centered the car in the narrow path laid out. Instant audible response from the audience felt good. She wanted to see if they were with her.

Down, turn right, ever so hesitantly to sustain the feeling she had been rattled by the almost disastrous beginning, turn left, then right, right again, more confidently, speed up slightly – quick, quick left! *God, that near miss wasn't faked!* Left again, she slowed down. Perspiration was starting to flow down her cheeks under the hot cotton wadding. A sweat droplet suddenly blurred her vision. *Oh, damn!* She heard a cone fall over. *Too soon!* The pinhole was out of focus like a distorted fish-eye lens. Her breathing, harder, faster; her face was itching, crawling with sweat. The sun baked into her bare shoulder.

Kaarin braked to a stop. She was only about a third of the way through and she was out of control. All the details to prepare and she hadn't considered the effects of sweating under the blindfold. *Damnit!* Forcing, pushing her mind back to withdraw it from her physical discomfort, Kaarin projected an image of where she was in the labyrinth against the hot black velvet of the blindfold. It looked like a turn away from the sea, then a hard switch back to go straight at a low point in the rocks. A misjudgment here and it's into the harbor. Then a 90-degree turn to parallel the water for about ten yards, a hard right, around and back again at the rocks.

Okay, mindreader, now, let's do the scam!

She swallowed, then slowly let out the clutch. The car started to move. First a slow right. As the car turned, a cooling light spray came around the windshield. Rapid blinking had partially cleared her pinhole vision, but the tiny hole had slipped downward slightly. The tightly bound batting and velvet had shifted a fraction of an inch downward on her sweat soaked forehead and cheeks. She could now see only just a few inches beyond the end of the hood. Even pressing her right shoulder hard against the door added little to her field of vision. Kaarin could not raise her hand to touch the blindfold without triggering suspicion. She couldn't delay. The situation would only degrade further.

Hard, hard left back toward the sea and rocks. *God, was anyone still watching?* The ocean crashing up and over the rocks together with the velvet binding her head effectively muffled any crowd noises. Now, straight at the sea. Rocks were visible on the left, but dropped out of sight below the hood line of the car. Carefully looking right, her pinhole showed the Duchess crew had made the pathway very narrow next to the rocks. Kaarin turned right. She felt the left front wheel suddenly lift into the air and stop. She swallowed then pressed gently on the accelerator and twisted the steering wheel around right, hard up against the stops. The car moved, its left front wheel rising higher, then she lurched forward as it dropped suddenly. Kaarin immediately braked, to sight along the red cones on her right to bring the car back into center. She was perspiring freely now – and needed a deathgrip on the wheel to control it with her sweaty hands.

116

Ten yards, hard right, slow curve then back again toward the rocks. She braked gently, turning right, but the car skidded on the wet asphalt jolting Kaarin against the wheel when the bumper caught a projecting boulder. She pressed in the clutch, grasped the gear lever to put the car in reverse, but her wet hand slipped off. *Damn the stupid thing!* Anger surged. Clenching her teeth, Kaarin forced her mind to refocus. She put her hand under the knob on the gear lever, gripping the shaft, using the projection on the knob to keep her hand from slipping off again. The car moved back, then, once more with the gear lever, forward.

Her pinhole slipped further downward, leaving almost no vision beyond the hood. She was becoming genuinely blindfolded!

Kaarin turned away from the seawall, to start up a gentle incline to twist through a chicane. Kaarin tried to raise the blindfold by frowning deeply, then raising her eyebrows. The pinhole moved up, but when she relaxed, it slipped back. Now she had to drive with her eyebrows arched as high as possible, which let more sweat droplets run into her smarting, watering eyes.

Back around the scarred yellow cone came into view like a welcome old friend. *Ahh.* She centered the car on the pathway. Crowd noise was increasing. They were still there! She heard their groan and the sound of a cone

117

falling at the same time. *Where was it? Where was it?* She was in the center, dear Lord, there couldn't be anything in the way.

The crossover, where the pathway had turned back across itself! She had *forgotten* and aligned herself on the wrong side of that accursed yellow cone! *Stop!* Forgotten! She breathed heavily now, ten thousand dollars she didn't have and her reputation lost only one more screwup away.

Kaarin relaxed her strained forehead. The pinhole slipped downward, lower than before, her remaining field of vision drastically reduced. Her bound head throbbed with painful exhaustion. A breath, another, then again. Her confusion ebbed away. She should be about 15-20 yards away from the finish. A final deep long inhalation, then out. She raised her aching eyebrows as high as she could manage, one final effort, then let the clutch ease out, the car beginning to creep ahead. A shout from the crowd! Kaarin twisted the wheel sharply, narrowly sideswiping a cone. Oh, God! She heard it wobble, but it stayed upright.

Sweeping her struggling memory, Kaarin visualized the remaining course, now seeing it clearly as though without the blindfold, the crowd grouping around the finish, a TV crew walking toward the car, pointing at her . . . She shuddered and started to move.

The position of the yellow cone? There! Her facial

118

muscles were going numb, losing control. Stabs of pain skewered her eyes. Then left, back around again, left again. Crowd noise was much louder, rising in volume each few seconds as she rounded a last left turn to enter the final thirty feet to the red plastic strip.

The pinhole was gone.

Sweat soaked through her dress, down her back, across her shoulders and down her arms, dripping irregularly from her elbows. Her mouth was filling with wet salt.

Her face was numb. There was a glimpse of the red plastic strip, but how could she see it? She could see only black. There was no pin-hole, nothing! Agonizingly slow. Ten feet, five, three – almost, almost – now! Stop! She fumbled clumsily for the ignition, turned off the engine, then fell back against the hot seat and headrest, utterly spent.

As Sommers opened the door for her, Kaarin closed her eyes, but she was oddly aware of a TV crew appearing quickly at the hood, their camera tight on her blindfold, but she couldn't move, her numb left hand still gripped the wheel. She was floating as in a dream.

Sommers unwrapped her fingers from the wheel. "Very well done, Miss Larsson," he said blandly. He took her arm as she pivoted slowly to peel herself away from the sweat-soaked hot leather seat, someone else took her other arm when she stumbled against the car. Her closed eyes gave some relief to her exhausted facial muscles.

Once back near the crowd, Sommers stopped her, then began unwinding the velvet. She heard a whispering TV crew nearby. Outerbridge removed the batting as the last of the velvet was drawn away.

Kaarin squinted her eyes tightly against the bright late Bermuda sun. Sommers offered her a handkerchief to wipe her eyes and blotchy face. She felt dizzy and unsteady, even after draining a small glass of cold water that Outerbridge pressed into her right hand. After wiping her eyes clear of sweat and tears, Kaarin looked down at her watch. 4:45. The whole drive had been less than half an hour. It seemed forever.

Looking around, Kaarin became aware for the first time of the loud applause of the crowd. Cameras were whirring and clicking rapidly, and all three of the TV crews had five cameras on her now. There was nervous laughter throughout the staring audience as it crowded closer.

"Crazy way to make a buck, Miss," J. Outerbridge whispered to her, smiling, taking the glass from her hand.

10

Roland Sommers had smiled absently in complimenting Kaarin while escorting her back to her room. The evening was hers, he said, the memory seminar was at ten in Salon E of the Grand Ballroom, the memory books had arrived, he would have one delivered to her room for her examination, the Conference would pick up all her expenses at the Duchess, good afternoon. He closed the door.

The telephone rang three times before Kaarin, still sweaty and tired, could reach it.

"Hello."

"Miss Larsson, this is Roger Delano. I'm the general manager of the Duchess. I just wanted to compliment you on your extraordinary blindfold drive. I have never seen anything like that."

Even with her tired face, Kaarin smiled and thanked him for the compliment. His voice was very kind, like so many of the voices she had encountered at the hotel.

"I realize you must be tired, so I will be brief," he said. "If it does not interfere with your responsibilities, I would like to attend your memory seminar tomorrow morning, and your show on Friday night. Your act may be very appropriate for possible future bookings at the Duchess. I have received several queries already regarding when you might be scheduled back. So, when you find it convenient, please come to my office, on the second floor, so that I may understand more of your repertoire and your future obligations."

When Kaarin hung up, promising to meet him Friday morning, she clapped her hands in joy. Just maybe the Duchess will be the break!

***

Refreshed from a hot bath her phone rang as a bell boy was delivering her dinner. Kaarin directed him to the balcony table, then rushed to answer.

"Hey, White Witch! A memory drive of all things! Great! And Serreta says hello, too." His voice crackled with enthusiasm.

"Sugar!"

"The first time." He laughed.

"I didn't know you and Serreta were in Bermuda. That's wonderful! Where are you?"

'Hamilton." His voice calmed. "Doing some good gigs at a club here … for the last two, three weeks. Hey, lady, you looked great on the tube. The coverage was good. Wished we could have been there to cheer you on and maybe whisper some directions when nobody was looking."

"I could have used some."

"I know. It looked like things weren't all according to what I know about blindfold drives. Though never had the whatever myself to do one." He coughed. "You free tonight? Why not stop by the club, catch Black Magic in its glory, and talk blindfolds over a few Rum-Somethin's after?"

"Which club? What time? I'll be there. Sugar." She slowed. "I need you and Serreta to talk to, someone who will really hear what I'm saying ... about this afternoon."

"Anytime, Kaarin. By the way, were you aware your dress was almost transparent from sweat when you got out of that car this afternoon?" He chuckled, a feminine voice said something sharply in the background.

"Transparent?" She tensed. "How transparent?" She remembered the way people looked at her, even Roland Sommers' bland eyes had been wide.

"Like you don't have any secrets from anyone watching television this afternoon, or on the reruns tonight."

"Oh-h, dear God," she groaned, folding her arms tightly across her breasts as if to hide, feeling her face flush red.

"Like I've always said, White Lady, you know how to close an act."

She shivered, wanting to hide somewhere.

"We're at the Pink Sands, Ragan's Alley off Burnaby Street. About a 15-20 minute taxi ride from the Duchess. Our first show is at nine. I'll have a table waiting. And hey, lady, you may not have any secrets in Bermuda but you definitely have nothing to be ashamed of." He laughed. "Looking forward to tonight."

Black Magic. Sugar and Serreta Alberts, magicians from Chicago. Smooth entertainers with Sugar's effortless long-fingered sleight of hand blending with Serreta's stunning beauty and her amazing illusions. The Zombie ball, sold in every magic shop in the world for over fifty years, became a living ominous force under Serreta's control. Even with Kaarin knowing the method, Serreta's routine was impossible.

Beautiful Black Magic.

***

Lifting her plate to refill it with broiled scallops from a chafing dish, Kaarin found two small slips of paper. She nodded slowly as she read the brief notes from Mario, the bell captain. She licked her lips. He was a good $100 investment. Getting this kind of stuff she could blow their minds away. God damn, she was going to do it! And if they liked her nipples, so what! But it still hurt to smile.

***

Bermuda night encircled Kaarin with soft calmness, a gentle sweetness in the air, as the cab traversed the traffic circle at the tip of Hamilton Harbor. Kaarin relaxed, enjoying each new sight, smell and sounds. That strange whistling sound. Tree frogs, she was told in answer to her question. Black Magic! They were good, and had been reliable friends to her at a difficult time on the road.

But Kaarin shook her head. Tell the Alberts about Bingeton and the Boskops? No, she had enough confusion about what was happening to her mind. Enough. She shook her head again. The evening was too beautiful for odd little people with big heads, even for thinking about Sarah Randolph's planned vengeance. But blindfolds were something else.

Kaarin wore a bright white blouse sprinkled with small black rectangles. Its close fit contrasted with large pleated dolman sleeves. The blouse fell slightly off her shoulders, revealing a pale sunburn from the afternoon. Her black silk skirt didn't quite make it to her knees. A black leather pouch hung from two short gold chains on a wide black leather belt. The pouch, which held what she would need, eliminated the need to carry a purse. Her white shawl was folded beside her on the seat.

125

The taxi turned right at Queen Street slowly climbed the hill, passing a park hidden in darkness on one side. Another right, then right down Burnaby Street, slowed to a crawl, then stopped.

"Ragan's Alley, Miss. I can't go any further. The Pink Sands is on the left, second floor. Can you see the sign?" He had leaned down to point out the sign. "It's pink … of course." He laughed.

It was only a short walk, well lighted up the wide alley to the outside stairway leading up to the pink sign. With the evening so warmly caressing, Kaarin carried the shawl casually over one shoulder. Someone was standing at the top of the stairs.

"Miss Larsson, I'm John Nathaniel, owner and manager of the Pink Sands. Sugar said you were coming. I have a table waiting for you." Kaarin looked up, and up, to meet his eyes as she took his hand. "Your blindfold drive this afternoon was remarkable. Truly remarkable."

Her table was one row back from the dance floor. A five piece group, without tourist steel drums, was running through something Kaarin vaguely recognized. Light was low, with each table illuminated by a large pink candle set in coral.

Nathaniel held her chair. "You're a guest of the club, Miss Larsson. Your waiter will bring whatever you wish without charge. Please enjoy the show." He disappeared into the dim candlelight before Kaarin could thank him.

When a waiter appeared, she ordered a glass of cold Riesling. He quickly returned with a filled carafe and poured, leaving the carafe on the table. The group started again, with a heavy, throbbing beat. She could visualize dancing, moving, to that one. But with whom? The tablecloth was smooth, soft to her touch. Real linen. She had never performed in a nightclub that used real linen on its tables. Kaarin glanced around the room. It was about two-thirds full. Her glance also revealed that she was the only white person there.

Its set finished, the musicians, grinning and laughing, left the small raised bandstand. Crowd murmur rose. So did Kaarin's anticipation.

John Nathaniel's amplified voice in the dark announced: "The Pink Sands presents the ultimate in mystery and entertainment. Ladies and Gentlemen … Black Magic!"

Applause rose, but no one appeared. Suddenly a blue-pink spot swept across her table. A soft tap on her shoulder. Sugar Alberts, immaculate in a stylish gray tuxedo, glided past her, centered in the spot. Strengthening background music throbbed, a biting guitar writhing and moaning across it in stark emphasis.

Golden balls appeared, vanished, melted through Sugar's long gloved fingers, synchronized to the pulsating music. Rolling effortlessly across his hands, shining spheres changed from gold to silver to crystal, congealing finally into a single large multi-faceted crystal ball that tossed spectral sparks of light throughout the room.

Kaarin was mesmerized. Flawless. She could hold her own manipulating cards, but what he did with the balls was beyond her knowledge. Sugar's sparkling eyes, confident manner, total command captivated her. Real magic. He was the incarnation of the word. She hunched forward to try to anticipate his next move, his next steal. The hand was not quicker than the eye, but the mind was, misdirecting the eyes at crucial points.

The large crystal was still balanced at the very tips of his fingers gloved in gray suede. He raised a diaphanous green silk scarf – wow, where had that come from? – sent it up into the air where it spread, hovered, then began to settle softly, slowly, gently as the air itself, down toward the crystal held still at Sugar's fingertips. The silk just touched the crystal, concealing its dazzling light only a bare instant, when Sugar pulled it away to reveal a regal jungle-green parrot almost four times the size of the vanished crystal! As Sugar raised the bird sitting on his extended fingers above his shoulder, smiling knowingly at the sharp gasp of surprise from his audience and his guest, the parrot triumphantly spread wide its great thick wings.

Kaarin laughed, then applauded enthusiastically. He had her completely stopped. She sat back to watch like the other civilians.

The applause continued to rise, then, as it began to slacken, Sugar placed the parrot on a chrome steel stand with a clear glass crossbar. As he watched the bird settle itself, Sugar's head was cocked slightly to one side, as though waiting for the parrot to make up its mind. When the bird stopped, Sugar gave a short nod and raised a large black silk scarf with metallic silver slashes across the center. God, where had that come from? Stepping back, he threw the great silk into the air where, as the green silk had before, it spread wide, settling majestically downward over the parrot and the stand. As its hems grazed the dance floor Sugar grasped it casually, with a quick wrist snap flung the foulard back into the air – revealing the parrot and stand vanished -- Serreta standing in their place!

Her shining ebony skin highlighted with brilliant silver lacework and imagination, her eyes, blazing, surrounded by argent-sequined eye shadow. Kaarin gasped with shock – as did the audience. A total surprise. An utter impossibility!

Sugar had stepped out of the spot into the darkness while the audience's attention was riveted to Serreta's sudden materialization. The floor was now her's alone. Kaarin felt a twinge of envy. The Alberts knew what they were dealing with, how it would all work every time. But in mentalism she never could be sure what was real.

Serreta's smile formed slowly as she took a step forward. She drew a gleaming silver snake from about her waist, letting it flow across her fingers as though alive, a large glittering burning emerald embedded in its head. Serreta held the snake with both hands out toward the audience as if offering it to them. Then she raised it stretched between her hands, high above her head. As she lowered her hands, she began with slow deliberation to coil the silver snake into a loose ball. When her hands reached waist level Serreta held the coiled snake in her left hand, she reached with her right hand up into the blackness beyond the sharp circle of light, plucked a piece of night, a small black silk, and dropped it across the silver coils – silk and snake instantly vanished, leaving a polished silver ball with a large emerald glowing on top. Kaarin grinned, the transformation illusion was perfect. Seretta's steal of the silk from under her breast was perfect.

Responding to her intense gaze, the ball floated from her fingers a bare fraction of an inch. The background

130

music, which had been synchronized with the amazing events, went silent as Serreta stepped back from the silver ball. It held its position, unwavering, in mid-air. Kaarin strained, but could see no supporting threads or wires, and she knew where to look!

Serreta gracefully drew her hands around the hovering ball. Impossible! *There were no threads!* Kaarin's jaw dropped a fraction in wonder. She leaned forward, then she suddenly realized what the scam might be and was even more impressed.

Again a smooth silk steal. Serreta dropped a silver-black foulard over the ball. The ball instantly moved, abruptly surging toward the audience then away as though desperately trying to free itself of the power binding it to the sorceress. Dodging, darting, its form clearly discernible under the silk, the ball went wild in its frantic effort to be free. Screta scarcely held the black-silver silk at her fingertips, apparently controlling the frenzied thing only with her dominant will, her burning eyes. The ball jerked, trembled, becoming more intense in pulsating life, then savagely turned to attack Serreta, who side-stepped its onslaught, shifting the foulard from her right to her left hand, the ball's aggressive, darting movements never faltering.

With that single move, Kaarin could no longer

follow her method. Serreta had moved with inordinate skill into the highest reaches of Zombie ball manipulation. Kaarin wanted to start applauding right there, but instead leaned back her arms crossed. What a beautiful scam.

Intensely magical, the enraptured audience was under Serreta's complete command. She moved the ball back to stage center nearer, nearer to the first row of tables. She pulled the foulard from the ball – it had doubled in size! Building on the rising audience reaction, Serreta grasped the emerald, pulled it, the silver ball separated into two halves – a great burst of bluish flame leaped between the two hemispheres – and suddenly Sugar was standing beside her, a mocking smile crossing his lips. The music had risen to a crescendo, the guitar racing madly up the scale, then *stopped*. Black Magic's finish pulled the audience to its feet, applauding, shouting as the spot widened, then widened more. Only Sugar allowed a broader smile to show, while Serreta refused to abandon her role of sorceress. They bowed once, twice, then walked from the dance floor, applause filling the nightclub with thunder. Serreta glanced toward Kaarin, gave her a small, quick smile, winked and was gone.

Kaarin continued to stand and applaud with the rest until her hands hurt. Unbelievable. Their whole act was new: the business with the parrot, and Serreta's heightened

132

skill with the Zombie, her sorceress role finally shaped perfectly. Kaarin sat back to get her breath. They had it all together, everything. Yes, she admitted, she was envious. Conversations bubbled around her, as waiters returned to their stations.

"Miss Larsson, if you'll follow me, I'll show you the entrance to backstage." It was John Nathaniel, imperturbable, as though miracles were an everyday thing.

"They were absolutely marvelous, marvelous!" She let Nathaniel take her arm.

"Yes, they are. They're a superb act. They deserve a larger audience than Bermuda can provide."

Kaarin looked up, but couldn't see Nathaniel's face in the flickering candle-lit darkness.

Nathaniel stopped. "Can you see all right? The door is here." He held back a curtain.

"Thank you for everything, Mr. Nathaniel."

"A great pleasure, Miss Larsson." He was gone.

Backstage at the Pink Sands was like every other small nightclub she had ever performed in. Black Magic's dressing room was a few feet from a storage area filled with faded flats and worn plastic scenery. No worse than some of the places she had worked – better than many – but if the conference went well, she wouldn't have to worry about …

133

Sugar saw her first. He stretched his arms out until his hands were flat against each wall. Wide red sleeves of his lounging robe hung down blocking the corridor.

"Hey, Serreta, it's our favorite honky mindreader." His long face was tired, but his eyes sparkled. His warm embrace was tight, his beard tickled her cheek when he kissed her. "C'mon in, White Lady. Welcome to Ber-Muda."

Serreta waved as she cleansed her face of the exaggerated silver makeup. "Minute," she called, smiling at Kaarin in the light-ringed mirror.

Magic apparatus filled a third of the dressing room. A crystal casket for producing Serreta apparently from thin air, a menacing cage for vanishing her back, a threateningly real head chopper and cages for doves, with a special perch for the regal green parrot haughtily regarding Kaarin with large slow blinking dark eyes. Some other strange boxes Kaarin didn't recognize, never having seen them used. Thank God a mentalist only needs a pad of paper, pencil, and a lot of gall. A small table was at the room's center laid with three glasses, an ice bucket, three bottles, Gosling Black Seal rum, Bermuda Gold loquat liqueur, and a black bottle without a label.

"Three Rum-Somethin's ready in a minute."

Kaarin settled in one of the chairs scattered around

134

the room. "Unbelievable show," she said. "I was absolutely, totally stunned. Sugar, I couldn't catch when you went South with any of your loads. Where that parrot came from, Serreta's appearance, the Zombie ball … your sleights. It was great, just incredible. When did you get it all together?"

"Glad you liked it." Sugar grinned, placing ice in the glasses. Black Seal splashed liberally in one, two, he paused, raised an eyebrow at Kaarin. She showed a narrow space between finger and thumb. He nodded, and poured accordingly. "Finally fixed it up about six-seven weeks ago running through Cleveland and Buffalo. Picked up some critical help on the parrot from Josh Raymond, a solid trick man, in Watertown near Boston. Polishing now for better things."

Serreta placed the wash cloth back on the dressing table, then shifted around, extending her hands to Kaarin, who gripped and squeezed them.

"So good to see you, Kaarin. You look so beautiful."

Kaarin returned the greeting and compliment, accepted a glass from Sugar.

"Now," he said, still standing, "a toast to what we all love: mystery. May audiences always want to pay to be baffled."

135

Raising her glass in acknowledgment, Kaarin grinned. The first swallow was memorable. Her eyes widened slightly as she held her breath waiting for the fire in her throat to die out. "There's a bit more than rum in that," she managed.

Sugar grinned, twisted a chair around to straddle, and relaxed his long arms across the back. "Yeah, a bit." He sipped again, still smiling. "Lay it on us, White Lady. How'd you get to Bermuda? What's been happening to you since we saw you in St. Louis? What's going down at the Duchess?"

Kaarin slowly, cautiously sipped a little more amber liquid. "I've had some good shows, some bad shows, and some no shows at all. But a little progress. The Duchess could be the difference." She described Roger Delano's call.

Sugar sat back, nodded. "Good. That's real good. That's a solid spot. You crack the Duchess and you start traveling first class. How're you setting up Friday night?"

"I tipped two of the bell captains to keep me posted regarding any interesting conversations or activities they overhear or see with conference people. A hundred each. It's already paying off."

Sugar grinned, nodded toward Serreta. "Our honky mindreader learns quick and good. Old Mentavo didn't waste anything on you, Lady. Good, Kaarin," He set his jaw, nodded again. "Good."

"We heard you were on Boston television, Kaarin. Is that right?" asked Serreta. "I know Sarah Randolph. She's very professional, but a very tough woman." Serreta's high voice was clear, richly resonant. "And she doesn't like mentalists. Something in her family or something."

"Yes. So I learned." Kaarin quickly explained her scheduled return to Sarah's show.

"Can she find anything?" Sugar asked with concern.

"No. There's nothing on the record and all the key evidence probably went out in the trash before she thought to look. But she will be looking more carefully next time, probably try to trap me, keep someone on me all the time. She said she was going to get help from a magic shop in Boston. But I'll be ready, too." Kaarin sipped, cautiously.

Sugar frowned. "Have to be Josh Raymond, but he's not going to blow your scam. Anyway," he smiled, "you need to get a copy of your blindfold drive. Finishing with a transparent dress will open any agent's eyes."

"Sugar!" Serreta frowned.

"Hey, Doll, wait a minute before you get after me. I mean that tape would show original thinking, showmanship … and real guts". He turned back to Kaarin, raised his glass. "Damn fine scam, Kaarin. You're a natural for this business, and even a damn rocket scientist to boot."

Kaarin held her glass in both hands. "A natural what?" she asked quietly, twisting the glass around in her hands. "Something happened this afternoon, Sugar, something I need to understand."

"Go ahead, White Lady. What went down?"

"The blindfold drive ... the last half anyway ... was genuine."

Sugar arched his eyebrows. "Genuine? God, what a memory that would be!"

Kaarin shook her head. "No. Not memory. Clairvoyance, or something. I saw . . . I think I saw *through* the blindfold ... *like it was not even there*." It felt good to finally say it out loud, like exorcising a demon. She looked first at Sugar, then Serreta, but neither moved. Doves fluttered around their cages, causing the sleeping parrot to raise one eyelid slowly, then let it slide back down.

"Let me ask in straight words. You saw *through* the blindfold?"

"That's what she said, Sugar," Serreta murmured, not taking her eyes from Kaarin's face. "That's what she said," she repeated, not aware of speaking again. "Was it a vision ... like the others?" Serreta finally asked.

Kaarin slowly shook her head. "There was no

warning or anticipation. I was desperate. I had blown it. In all my preparation I didn't anticipate that the sweat on my face would make the blindfold slip downward, blocking all vision. I'd lost my peephole. That's why I was messing up, making mistakes. I strained all I could to raise it, to get the pinhole up, to get *any* field of sight. You know the drill. You know I couldn't touch the blindfold, so I tried to project a visual image of the drive route against the blackness of the blindfold ... to dredge my memory clean. To see it maybe the way I saw it from my room, from up above." She took a small sip. Their eyes fastened on her, kind gentle eyes, but Serreta's were worried. "But it wasn't memory that came. I know that. I know it. *My God, it was the real thing.* Pressure was so great I couldn't stop to examine the feeling ... I just drove on." She smiled weakly. "But it was real. Really ... real." Kaarin took a larger sip and immediately regretted it as cold fire burned through her chest.

Sugar stood up. "Funny," he said, half-smiling. "It's spirit mediums who get most scared when they see a ghost, because they know it can't be. And us" – he spread his arms, the wide red sleeves hanging down – "we make magic and you read minds, but when we experience the real thing, it shakes the shit out of us, 'cause *we know it can't be.*"

139

The parrot squawked in its sleep, its eyes closed. The short harsh sound caused them all to jump.

"Damn bird," Serreta whispered.

Sugar twisted his chair around, bringing it closer to the women as though to conceal a conspiracy. He placed his empty glass on the table.

Kaarin squeezed her glass again. "I don't know what to do. A vision has never come before when I needed it. I was desperate, so desperate … and it came. I … " She stopped. She had hoped they would, could say something that would help explain the feeling of change, of separation, permeating throughout her being. But Sugar and Serreta only looked at her, saying nothing. Only fluttering dove wings broke the stillness.

"Well," Sugar finally said, "it looks like some heavy thinking is needed. Real heavy." His lips were drawn tight, his earlier cockiness vanished.

"Sugar's right, Kaarin," Serreta said quietly, her face troubled. "This isn't the time or the place. We all need some breathing room. Why can't we meet tomorrow afternoon. You have the seminar in the morning according to the papers. It will give us some time to think, too."

It made sense, even disappointing sense, Kaarin agreed. She sipped the last of her Rum-Somethin' and stood slowly to allow for her slight dizziness from the

140

drink. "I don't know what's coming ... but something is. The sense of threat, the warning sense, was there too. I know that. But warning me of what? What good is a warning if you can't understand it?"

Sugar frowned, a growing fear moved behind his somber dark eyes. "Your warning sense too? During the drive? When?"

Seeing Sugar's dark expression, Kaarin hesitated as she placed her empty glass on the table. "I'm not sure. Almost from the beginning it seems. But I can't be certain. I was so tied in knots under that blindfold. I don't know. You know I've done blindfolds before, but this was my first drive. I pushed the edge, maybe too much, I know. I couldn't be sure I wasn't just scared shitless."

Sugar nodded slowly as he pulled his chair away. He glanced at the small clock on Serreta's dressing table. "Almost time, Baby." He looked at Kaarin. "Three a night," he said softly. "They can't get enough of Black Magic." He grinned, his eyes sparkling again.

"Tomorrow," Serreta promised.

Kaarin gathered her shawl. "Tomorrow," she agreed. "Call me at the hotel. Maybe in this paradise we can find a quiet place, what my mother would call a wild strawberry place, a special place of peace. And thanks for an incredible show ... and for caring, really caring."

She reached out to take Serreta's hands, but Serreta embraced her instead. Kaarin felt her trembling slightly. Nervousness before the next show? Serreta had once told her, laughing in a St. Louis motel lobby, that she was the only witch who tossed her cookies getting ready to cast a spell.

Kaarin caught a quick hard glance between them but she knew she might be interfering in their pre-show time. She thanked them again, refusing Sugar's offer of guidance back to the club's floor and left. Tomorrow would be soon enough. Serreta was right.

***

McGraw waited, silently, calmly as he had so many other places, so many other times, in the shadows away from the glow of the pink sign. Only, he allowed a small grimace of disgust on his large face, not alone this time. The client had insisted on a backup and had provided one without asking his approval. If he hadn't really needed the cash, he would have canceled the engagement on the spot and walked away from it. Can't do a solid professional job with client interference in operations. Can thoroughly screw a reputation. The client had even specified a head shot on the mark in the cemetery; shit, he should have walked away then. Lethal position had always been his professional choice, of effectiveness and risk, but it had to

142

be a damn head shot with no explanation.

He arched his back, rolling his shoulders.

That noise was *that black smartass* shuffling back and forth a few feet away in an adjacent dark storefront. Not a professional who could wait quietly, long hours if necessary, to do the job right the first time.

He carried a watch, but never looked at it when waiting for the mark. Counting minutes created useless artificial pressure. Time was time enough. Things were quieting down, store lights going out. *Damn his shuffling, damn it.* Never get close to the mark, leave maximum maneuvering room, maximum options. So what do they force on him as a backup? A damn cut man from Jamaica constantly eye-fucking his stupid blade. He looked up at the scintillating stars. Tourists paid a bundle for a night like this.

***

"Good night, Miss Larsson," John Nathaniel said, as she passed the maître d' podium. "A pleasure having you at the Pink Sands."

Kaarin smiled in response to Nathaniel's kindness. "A wonderful, magical evening, Mr. Nathaniel. Your customers must thoroughly enjoy Black Magic."

"Yes," he said, opening the door to the night for her. "Business is very strong around each of their shows …

9, 10:30 and midnight. Each show is a little different. A superb act, deserving of a much wider audience." He bowed. "There will be a taxi waiting at the Alley's end to return you to the Duchess. Best of good fortune during your stay on our islands." He bowed again as he closed the door.

Kaarin stood on the landing and wrapped the shawl around her bare shoulders against the growing evening coolness. Without shop lights the black sky came down into Ragan's Alley. She felt as if, like Serreta, she could simply reach up and pluck a piece of the night. Black Magic. If her Friday night show could produce the same audience reactions. She started down the stairs lost in thought and hopes for tomorrow. A taxi was waiting at the end of the Alley on Burnaby Street.

Kaarin drew the shawl tighter, the night chill clung closer with each downward step. Her hesitation with each was lengthening until, three steps from the bottom, she stopped completely. Only the Pink Sands sign cast light into the darkened Alley. Moving down the stairs with her steps the only sound in the Alley, had progressively cut off Hamilton's other night lights. Kaarin saw the taxi driver open his door, waiting for her in silence. It was remarkably thoughtful of someone, Sugar or John Nathaniel, to have the taxi for her.

Oh, God! It was like ice water pouring down her

spine into her legs, down to her toes! Kaarin had moved down the last three steps and started for the taxi, which now seemed further away. Violently shivering, grasping the shawl tighter around her, she walked more rapidly. Never had the warning sense been so intense; so cold, cold! She tried to run but her legs wouldn't respond. She stopped in the middle of the Alley, dark storefronts rising on both sides, indistinct forms in their windows. Her widened eyes searched the darkness. There were shadows only near the steps to the Pink Sands. *Which direction? Someone, something was there, somewhere, to hurt her. It was certain. Where? What?* The taxi and the steps up to the nightclub were about the same distance. Back or forward? She started backing toward the taxi, out of the Alley, searching, her eyes wide, trying to see into the darkness. She tripped, nearly falling. The shawl fell from one shoulder as she thrust out an arm for balance. She forced her panic back down. Run, run, run the warning sense demanded.

But where?

When the face floated before her eyes, it was vaguely familiar, but Kaarin didn't know why or where she had seen it before. He was behind her, she knew now, standing in a darkened shop doorway, waiting for her to pass, the pink light reflecting from her white shawl and blouse. An easy target.

But suddenly – oh, God! – a second face, black with a hook nose, grim mouth, now swam before her eyes. He was somewhere near the first one.

***

McGraw was surprised! It was obvious she knew they were there though they had made no sound once she had appeared at the top of the stairs. Even the Jamaican had stopped shuffling when the Pink Sands door opened. How? She was like a skittish fawn, searching around, stumbling, her fear growing. He glanced down at the taxi driver, who leaned idly against his cab, the passenger door opened for her. Move now! Before she got closer to the street, before anyone else left the Sands. McGraw had to make certain his only escape option stayed open.

***

Kaarin pivoted to run. On her second step she tripped. Two short muffled barks sounded near her as she sprawled across the cobblestones of the Alley, scraping her face and hands. Something warm had brushed the skin of her left arm. She rolled, pulled her legs under her to rise to get moving again. Someone was coming toward her, pink luminescence flickering from the knife in his hand.

"Hey! What's going on there?" a man shouted. "Hey!"

146

Kaarin heard but dared not look away from the shadowed form closing on her. She grasped her shawl and whipped it hard across the dark face with his pink lighted eyes, then she twisted up, lurching frantically away, stumbling up against a store window. A breeze brushed her face, her hair, her head suddenly jerked back. She fell to her knees. Kaarin groped wildly, found a few small stones, steadied herself for an instant, then threw the stones into the black face, his mouth parted, grinning.

"Hey! Hey!"

She heard running feet from the opposite direction. He hesitated, swung his knife at her, then turned and ran. Kaarin pushed to her feet, dodged and tripped over a low curbing. Her head struck heavily against an iron railing across a show window. Sharp pain, then emptiness. Her terror had transmuted to anger, angry that she didn't have another weapon.

***

"How badly is she hurt?" Sgt. Mathews asked.

"Looks all right to me, sir. Cab driver's coming probably saved her. Close though. Look at the locks of blonde hair on the stones. Knife just missed her face or throat."

He knelt down beside Kaarin. They had wrapped her in a police blanket, her feet raised on another rolled

147

blanket.

"Can you hear me, Miss? I'm Sergeant Mathews …
this is Constable Jordan." Her eyes had opened, but weren't
focusing in the lights of the large police hand-lanterns.
"Miss?" She moved, rolling to one side. "Careful, Miss.
You've had a night of it." He smiled when her eyes focused
on his face. "You're all right."

"How long?" she managed.

"You've been out only a few minutes."

"Where did you come from?"

"Cab driver called his dispatcher, who called the
station. We were down on Reid Street. Took us only a
minute to get here."

Kaarin pushed herself up with one hand, then
folded the blanket back to stand.

"Steady," Mathews said, "not too fast."

She nodded, paused. Kaarin looked up at Mathews.
"Now?"

"Now." He and Jordan lifted her, one on each arm.
They held her until she nodded.

"The world's stopped moving," she said. "I can
make it now. Thank you."

"We have an ambulance coming . . ."

"No. No need for one. Just banged my head falling.
Thanks."

Mathews watched her carefully. Nodded. "Can you answer some questions? I don't want to press you, but the sooner we can act, the better." Another policeman held a flashlight for Mathews' notebook. "Any dizziness, Miss Larsson?"

"No, only a headache. I'll answer what I can. You know my name?"

"Recognized you from the television report on your blindfold drive. How many assailants were there?"

"Two. One white, one black."

"Had you seen either of them before?"

"The white man … I think I've seen him before but I don't know where or when. Just a face that triggered something. I have never seen the black before. He had a hook-like nose, a thin face. Pink eyes, but that must have been a reflection from the nightclub sign."

Mathews wrote at length in his notebook. Jordan was folding up the blankets.

"Did they carry weapons?"

"Yes. The white man had a big gun, with something large on the end."

Mathews looked up, surprised. "A large gun? A suppresser?" He made a note. "A silencer. holy shit," he whispered.

"Yes. I saw a flash, kind of greenish, I think, but

there was only a dull muffled sound. Maybe two, I'm not sure."

Mathews wrote longer.

Kaarin pulled the shawl around her, first noticing that it had been badly slashed. Mathews saw her reaction. He let her speak.

"The black man came at me with a knife. I whipped my shawl in his face then tried to run, but he kept coming. I heard someone yell, and then I fell and cracked my head against a window railing. I tried to run ... not very brave I guess."

"Bravery has nothing to do with it," Mathews said firmly. "That's for movies and television. The idea is not to get hurt. Let the police take the risks."

"I would be delighted to," Kaarin smiled. She held up the shawl letting the pink light shine through, and shook her head. "My best one. He did a job on it."

Mathews glanced at the shawl, then at her raised arms. "That's not all, Miss Larsson. May I examine your left sleeve?"

Kaarin held out her left arm, the white dolman sleeve hanging down, shifting in a feeble breeze.

Mathews sorted through the pleated material to find what he had seen. He held out a portion of the sleeve, a ragged hole in it. "That's the entrance hole. Now for the

150

exit." When he matched the two holes, he frowned deeply.

Jordan held a flashlight close to the sheer material. He passed a pen through the holes and whistled softly. He looked at Mathews. "Inspector Haggard'll want to know about this, fast," he said.

Mathews nodded.

"What is going on?" she asked, mystified.

Mathews answered with another question. "Your purse? Did they take it? We could not find one."

"I wasn't carrying a purse. I wore this" – she held out the black leather pouch chained to her belt – "to carry what I need, so I don't have to bother with a purse. It's often more convenient."

He nodded. "Jordan, escort Miss Larsson to the Duchess. The rest of you ... I want those slugs ... tonight! Now!" he ordered. "Good night, Miss Larsson." He took the flashlight from Jordan.

Kaarin walked with Jordan to a white police car, a cone of blue light flashing on its roof. As they neared Burnaby Street she stopped. "Where's the cab driver who called you? I want to thank him."

"We have his name. You'll have a chance. We told him we would return you to the hotel, so he left for another fare. He said to wish you well." Constable Jordan opened the passenger side for her. "None of us want our visitors harmed, or even think they might be threatened. We like a peaceful Bermuda."

***

As the police car pulled away from the curb, Kaarin could see the lights of the searching police crisscrossing the walls, dodging through the plants. Their movements suddenly stopped, the lights coalesced, but Jordan had already started down Burnaby toward the cruise ships.

Kaarin leaned back, still light-headed. What had been an exotic magical evening had become instantly filled with terror and confusion. She lightly touched the hole in her sleeve: well, the blouse like the shawl was ruined. But the feeling of threat had been overwhelming; like a frigid ice bath. Sugar was right on; only a mentalist could feel the real terror of the real thing.

***

Sergeant Mathews frowned deeper still as he walked toward the wall in response to his name being called. It wasn't an opportunistic robbery, that was obvious. Someone apparently wanted to kill her bad enough to send two men to do it. Why? The size of the bullet holes, and a knife to finish! Good God, who or what is Kaarin Larsson to draw that much killing power?

152

11

Kaarin was awake. Her head still throbbed. *Good God! Two men had tried to kill her! Why?* She rolled out of bed, pulled her robe close and walked to the balcony doors. She caught her breath at the sudden in-rush of dawn coolness. A huge sun was just breaking above the horizon, backlighting long rolls of grayish-white cloud. The police would call in the morning, according to Constable Jordan, who had been very concerned. But she couldn't just sit and wait. Kaarin pulled on white jeans and a black sweatshirt and shoved a little street map into one hip pocket.

***

An exhilarating fresh wind whipped across her face. Oh, get over! She lunged the moped to the left side of empty East Broadway. The night bell captain had unlocked a few doors to get her a moped and helmet with a warning about the left side of the road.

Someone could get killed out here, for Pete's sake.

***

Kaarin retraced the taxi's route to Ragan's Alley, stopped the moped at the curb and walked the bike into the silent Alley. She put it up on its kickstand at the base of the stairs to the Pink Sands. All the shops were closed, no person was in sight. Long shadows cast by the new morning sun striped the Alley, leaving the shops on the Pink Sands side in relative darkness.

Well, scientist, what now?

Kaarin hung her helmet on the handlebars, and stood with her hands on her hips. Ragan's Alley narrowed down to an elaborate arched stone and brick moon gate at the end opposite to where she had arrived last night and this morning.

Halfway up the Pink Sands stairs, she turned and started slowly back down. Each of the shops opposite had decorated wooden awnings projecting out two or three feet from the smooth plaster finish of the building simulating a Mediterranean courtyard. At the third step she stopped, looked back at the moon gate, then slowly up the shop fronts: a yardage shop with its windows filled with a jumble of beautiful colors glittering in the small portion of sun reaching it, then a rum and booze shop with various arrangements of bottles visible, an art gallery . . .

Oh, Lord. She stepped back up one stair. The gallery window was mostly blocked from view. One step, two steps down, a large white bust of Winston Churchill was fully visible, almost touching the gallery window glass. The heavy jawed face that had floated before her eyes? She quickly stepped down the last step and across to the gallery.

Seven or eight steps, the Alley wasn't that wide. It was $6,000 (Bermuda dollars were the same as American dollars a small sign declared at the base of the bust) in glowing white Carrara marble. Churchill in open-necked shirt, his familiar defiant bulldog face set, muscles bulging along his jaws, looking slightly to his left. She looked up. Yes, the light from the Pink Sands sign would have shown on Churchill, the pink light giving a human cast to the bust, making her think she had seen a floating face? The ice cold sweep of feeling flooding her body had set off every emotional alarm she had. She had *expected* to see something, but was this the image that she had seen? What about the floating cruel black face, malevolent pink-lighted eyes and twisted nose?

She groaned.

In the adjacent window on the other side of the gallery entrance was a large bronze bust of nearly such a face with a prominent toothbrush mustache, and, yes, that was the feature she had neglected to tell the police. That little scrub of a mustache. Had she actually *seen anything* from the third step? The bronze was positioned to be more completely illuminated by the pink light of the nightclub sign. But two men *had* tried to kill her.

Very well, as her former boss at UC Riverside, Dr. Carl Grant, would say: therefore what? Kaarin stood in the

155

center of Ragan's Alley slowly rotating with her hands on her hips, the freshening breezes tossing her yellow hair across her face and eyes as she turned. The window railing she had hit. She thought she had seen the white man start running to the right, the black turning to follow as she knocked herself out on the railing.

The Bermuda police had probably already searched the Alley thoroughly, but she decided to look for herself. She brushed her hair away from her eyes. What was she, what was she becoming? What was this spooky crap floating through her mind?

There was nothing in any of the setback shop entrances. Only a small torn bit of black electrical tape on the art gallery doorsill. She put it into her pocket then walked slowly toward the moon gate, glancing over her shoulder to check on the moped. She glimpsed a man and woman walking hurriedly down Burnaby Street on the side opposite the Alley. They were talking and gesticulating wildly as they vanished from sight. No other sounds penetrated into the Alley.

On the other side of the moon gate Parliament Street was empty of people. Perhaps a car had been waiting for them. A car waiting? What for? Who could have known she was going to be there? It had to be just a typical Bermuda mugging. In which case. They probably just ran,

156

where? She turned to see the whole Alley. If there had been a car, there would be nothing to find. A walkway that ran along the inside of the wall from the moon gate led to the back side of the shops. With nothing in the street to see, she started down the walkway, noting there were no windows in the yardage shop wall.

Just Dumpsters in back, a narrow service way that opened out through slatted-wood gates at each end of the row of shops. Except for the yardage shop nearest her, all the Dumpster lids were closed. Two orange cats exploded from under the Dumpster at the sound of her approach. Kaarin jumped back, her heart pounding. A third cat charged after them. They all disappeared between the loosely hung slatted gate and the wall. As Kaarin turned, a coal black cat leaped past her from the open Dumpster, racing after the others. She took a breath to slow her heart and looked in. There were scraps of cloth, cardboard boxes, a pizza box licked and clawed clean, a green plastic Sprite bottle. Nothing much even for alley cats to eat. But the bottle, it didn't look right. She reached in. At her touch it slipped further down among the cardboard trash. Kaarin stood on her tiptoes on the Dumpster wheel, stretched down and finally got the bottle neck firmly between her thumb and forefinger.

The bottom was almost completely blown out and a

157

strip of black tape was around the neck. Its lingering acrid smell overpowered the stale pizza odor. The edges of the plastic along the ragged bottom were charred black and melted in spots, but the plastic had been ripped violently apart with cracks running up the sides. She had thought she had seen a greenish flash with the muffled barks, but after seeing the busts in the art gallery no memories of the night seemed trustworthy. But maybe, as she held the bottle up to the brightening sky, reality wasn't so far off.

There were bits of burnt green plastic in the cracks between the cobblestones about four feet from the art gallery door. Crawling on her hands and knees, repeatedly brushing back her hair as it fell forward across her shoulders, she probed for more, marking the outline of her findings with pennies.

Standing back at the gallery door and raising an imaginary pistol, Kaarin aimed for a woman at the foot of the stairs and fired. She found her extended finger pointing at the center of the crude circle of pennies glistening in the expanding sunlight. An awkward ellipse about two feet wide and almost four feet long. A hell of a blast! He must have used an elephant gun. Why so much artillery? Certainly a well placed .22 slug would have done the job. The policeman, Mathews, had looked at the holes in her blouse sleeve, but the sheer material had been badly torn, so a measurement wouldn't be worth anything. She shuddered. But why me for God's sake? She carried the shattered bottle gingerly in her fingertips and dropped it into the moped basket.

Kaarin stood at the curb and looked back into Ragan's Alley for a moment then she kicked the little moped engine to life. The oblate circle of pennies sparkled in the new sun. She set the safety helmet firmly on her head, buckling it under her chin.

Now left, damnit, left!

12

Keith Haggard reached automatically inside his jacket pocket for cigarettes that were not there. The same .41 magnum that may have killed Tony DiMarco was used to try to kill the Larsson woman. The second point in the data, but why someone with a knife? Mathews' report was clear. He slapped his hand on the desk, got up and began to pace. Four in the morning, one murder, another attempted murder, and no cigarettes. Day seven. What time does a mindreader get up? He paced faster. Day seven.

***

He pressed Send. "Miss Larsson, my name is Keith Haggard. I'm an Inspector with the Bermuda Police Service. I'm sorry if I awakened you."

"No, I've been awake for some time. I'm just finishing breakfast."

"Good. Seven can be a very early hour."

"Not for me, Inspector. Not today."

Haggard paused. "I would like to speak with you, if it would be convenient for me to come up now. It is urgent."

"Certainly. You obviously know my room number."

Her black sweatshirt said:

Psychics Do It With More Senses

in shining silver script letters with bluish highlights, to give it 'that paranormal feel', the catalog had said.

She thought of the pennies.

The data from the pennies was loose and her calculation only an awkward estimate. But then she had always been theoretical, not experimental, and it felt good to play with even simple equations again, without setting off the explosives that seemed embedded in her brain.

Four more little notes from Mario and Will, her bell captain spies, came with the breakfast tray. Amazing what they saw and heard, but wives' liaisons had to be off limits for the Friday show. Unless, maybe with the card stab stunt, a little extra tension, if she could handle it without being obvious.

When Kaarin opened the door he held out an opened dark-green leather folder. 'Keith R. Haggard, Inspector" the plastic encased card said, with a color photo and his blood type O recorded under it.

"No badge?" She stepped back to let him enter.

"No, Miss Larsson. Bermuda police don't carry badges like Americans. Our warrant card grants us all the authority we need."

"Come in, Inspector, please. I still have some hot coffee on the balcony."

His frameless glasses outlined intense blue eyes. His hair dark brown, narrow muscular shoulders. Tanned features. About six-one, she judged. She wished she had spent a little more time brushing her hair.

"Thank you," he said with a quick smile. "That would be excellent. It has already been a long morning." He followed her across the room to the balcony table.

As she poured coffee Kaarin saw him trying to read her sweatshirt. She cleared a chair of a memory book and a folder of notes, then pushed her breakfast tray across the table to make room for his filled cup.

He nodded thanks, took a slim blue notebook from his inside jacket pocket and sat down. "I hope you were able to get some rest last night. Any after-effects from that rap on the head?"

"No," she smiled, settling into a chair opposite him against the balcony railing. "None. Durability is one of my few virtues. Were your men able to find the bullets that were fired at me?"

"If you don't mind, I'd first like to review Sergeant Mathews' notes with you, to see if anything can be added. Then I have a question or two myself. And, yes, the slugs were found."

He began, quickly ticking off points, nodding as she added a detail. His technique was good, making statements that were in fact questions; like a skilled mentalist. She liked his quick smile, even if it was part of his interrogation technique.

Haggard stopped and closed his notebook. "There are some basic points which I would like to review again, but . . . those slugs that were fired at you. They were large, .41 magnums, as best our laboratory can determine since they were mushroomed badly in the wall."

"Forty-one magnum," she said. Maybe her numbers were close.

"Gun law in Bermuda is very clear and very strict. Whoever shot at you was risking ten years in prison with no parole by just holding the gun even if it was unloaded. Legal possession of a gun, or any part of a gun, or ammunition on the island can only be authorized by the Police Commissioner which has never been done. So we have someone chancing a very long prison term, what Americans call hard time, even if he never even uses the weapon. But the key point," he added quietly, "is that the bullets fired at you last night were apparently fired from the same gun that may have killed Tony DiMarco."

Kaarin stiffened. "What do you mean, may have killed DiMarco? He was shot, wasn't he?"

163

"Yes, he was. But not everything was given to the newspapers or discussed outside my office. DiMarco was shot with two bullets. A .41 magnum blew his head apart, but a second one, a .32, went through his heart. Either of the bullets would certainly have killed him. We don't know which one actually did. They came from different directions, as well, so at least two killers were involved. But why a dead man was shot, I cannot conceive ... at least not yet. When I learned the bullets fired at you apparently matched a gun from the DiMarco case, I had guards placed on your floor. One of them probably served your breakfast this morning."

The bell boy had been clumsy in handling the dishes and the cart, and left without a tip. She had simply thought he was new to the hotel. Kaarin looked out at the brilliant harbor beyond the parking lot, coming rapidly to life, a gentle promise of warmth flowing with the sea-breezes.

"I was scared shitless last night," she said. "I travel to the closest thing to paradise that I've ever seen, and on my first night two men try to kill me ... kill me two different ways no less! One would seem enough. Why two? And why *me*, for God's sake?"

"That's what I am trying to discover, Miss Larsson. Have you ever been in Bermuda before?"

"No. Never."

"Did you know Tony DiMarco?"

"Not really. I met him only once … in St. Louis. He was drunk and had decided he wanted a blonde for the night and I was to be it." She looked away, took a breath, then looked back. "An ugly situation. A friend kept him from trying tear my blouse off. Until then, I had always respected his professional accomplishments."

In response to Haggard's question, Kaarin related how she had come to be DiMarco's replacement. "No, until yesterday at the airport, I had never met or spoken with Roland Sommers."

Haggard nodded. "My men found something odd this morning in Ragan's Alley. A circle of pennies near where you were attacked."

"Not a circle actually", said Kaarin, "more just a fat ellipse. I used the pennies to outline where the pieces and bits of a Sprite bottle ended up after a bullet and muzzle blast went through its bottom. That bottle there, on the floor by the closet."

Haggard stopped, his cup hovering, his eyebrows raised. A badly damaged green plastic soda bottle was lying on the carpeting near a nightstand. He replaced his cup, rose, and walked over to it. He picked it up with his pencil in the neck and held it close. Withdrawing a small magnifying lens from a jacket pocket, he examined its torn edges, changing the angle of the bottle to get different light. He replaced it and returned to the table.

"I would like to take that bottle with me. An ellipse, you were saying?"

"Yes. I was restless, couldn't sleep, and I wanted to *do* something, not just wait to see if they make another try at me."

"When?"

"At sunup." Kaarin smiled. "Beautiful quiet mornings you have here." She explained her excursion.

"Miss Larsson, that was a solid piece of police work, but, why the ellipse of pennies?"

"Well, based on a very crude estimate of the plastic's tensile strength, and assuming the position of the gun to be at the corner of the art gallery window, and taking the approximate distribution of the plastic particles, I ... ah, did a calculation of the probable muzzle velocity of the bullet to see if that would suggest the kind of gun used. Some of my assumptions may be nonsense, but I can't just sit and do nothing. It gave me something to focus on. I estimated about 1,117.4 feet per second. That has a nice ring of accuracy it surely does not deserve. You have the bullet size, how close am I?"

Haggard laughed. "Extraordinary, Miss Larsson.

Ten-fifty is the manufacturer's number for a low-grain .41 caliber magnum cartridge."

"Um, just under ten percent high." She nodded. "I overestimated the plastic." A good morning exercise. It felt good to have something safely logical come out of her head.

Haggard looked over at the green bottle again. "Using a plastic soda bottle to suppress the sound of a shot has been done before. The bullet would suggest a revolver, not an automatic. Also we didn't find any shell casings. Did you?"

"No, Inspector. Actually, that's what I started looking for, though I assumed your people would have already done that. I thought I would be another set of eyes. I found the plastic particles instead."

"But your description of the sounds of the shots you gave Mathews suggests an automatic. A revolver cannot be suppressed only on the muzzle because sound is projected from the interface of the cylinder and isn't confined like in the chamber of an automatic. The bottle is makeshift . . ."

"So perhaps the rest is also. Maybe some foam material was taped around the cylinder? He certainly appeared to have had enough tape along."

"Yes, that could do it." He nodded slowly, his eyes drifting away in deep thought. "Yes, that could do it," he

167

repeated.

Kaarin continued: "The bottle and the tape-up would suggest the shooter knew what he was doing, and particularly that he would have to extemporize for the evening. Doesn't sound much like a casual mugger ... not with ten years at stake, for a purse of maybe cash and credit cards which I wasn't even carrying. But I'm not certain he could see that my hands were empty."

"Had DiMarco planned to do the memory drive?" Haggard suddenly asked.

"No. That was my idea. Part of the publicity for the Conference."

"But, if the Conference is not open to the public, why the publicity?"

Kaarin looked down past Haggard's shoulder at the tourists struggling with their rental mopeds, riding practice circles in the parking lot. "Actually, it really was primarily for me. The big Bermuda hotels pay well and, on occasion, hire mentalists. I wanted to be sure they all knew I'm around. It would also add authority to my seminar this morning, since my name doesn't mean anything here. I figured it was worth the risk."

He nodded. "It was quite spectacular, Miss Larsson. I watched reruns of it last night. It appeared to be quite a strain."

She felt herself blush. "It was. A few things didn't go the way they should have." She hesitated. "My name is Kaarin."

"Thank you." Haggard poked at his notebook with his pencil. "Ragan's Alley was dark, only the Pink Sands sign was illuminated. Kaarin, how could you see your attackers so clearly? Was the white man you seemed to recognize associated with DiMarco that you know?"

"I don't know where I've seen him before. I can't make any mental association that triggers anything. I have no idea what relationship he might have with DiMarco. I just saw them, that's all. I wouldn't say it, if I hadn't." He'd surely think her crazy if she described the warning sense and the faces floating before her eyes, if they really were. She wasn't sure herself anymore, but she *did see* some faces.

Haggard placed his notebook and pencil on the table. "May I have more coffee?"

Kaarin placed her palm against the silver pot. She nodded. "Still hot."

Haggard nodded as she poured. "Kaarin, you are obviously aware that something is going on that, of which, for some reason, you have become a part. I'm going to keep guards on your floor until we can be sure you're out of danger. We don't know what threat you may be to

169

DiMarco's .32 killer, as you apparently are to the one with the .41. That's a clumsy way to express it, but if two people wanted DiMarco dead, the same two may want to harm you as well."

Kaarin shook her head slowly. "Why me? I don't know where any treasure is buried."

"Perhaps someone is afraid of you."

"Of me?" Kaarin was puzzled with his suggestion. As a result of her early morning reflections, she had now decided to try to produce an element of fear in her Friday night audience, but ...

"Afraid of what you are, or appear to be. They may see you as a threat, as DiMarco's super-memory may have threatened someone, though how ..." He stopped and shrugged. "I would like to have you visit my office as soon as you can, perhaps this afternoon after your seminar, to examine some photographs of possible suspects. There may be an additional question or two, if you don't mind." He smiled.

"Certainly. I'm meeting some friends this afternoon, but we haven't set a time yet. They're going to call me after the seminar is over, around 11:30."

"Perhaps we could have lunch at my office. That would free your afternoon for your friends. The food sent over from the Police Club, however, will definitely not match the Duchess."

"No problem. I'll help any way I can, of course."

"Excellent." Haggard rose. "I'll get out of your way." He replaced the chair against the balcony railing. "Thank you for the coffee." With the Sprite bottle skewered on his pencil, he walked to the door, then stopped, his hand on the doorknob. "Do you have friends on Bermuda?"

"No. I know no one here except for the Conference officials. But I've found everyone to be very friendly. The friends I'm meeting today are from the United States."

"Perhaps you would allow me to show you a few of Bermuda's special sights? Tonight, if your plans would allow it. I believe your show is tomorrow night."

Kaarin grinned. "You know my schedule as well as I do. I would enjoy seeing more of Bermuda ... particularly with a knowledgeable native."

"Excellent. I'll pick you up for lunch and we can arrange a time for later that won't interfere with your friends ... the Alberts?"

She shook her head. "You're too quick for me. I'm afraid I don't have any secrets." It recalled Sugar's comment. She blushed, no more transparent dresses.

"My car is unmarked so the Conference and the hotel won't think you're being arrested. Nothing," he quickly added, "is in the papers or on-line about last night. Our public relations officer worked, fast, but the media can't be held off forever."

"Good. I'll see you then at about twelve."

***

As Haggard started down the hallway, he nodded to a cleaning woman near the elevator who was rearranging towels on her overloaded cart. "Anything?" he asked.

"Nothing," she replied. She pushed a pile of small soap cakes aside with her forefinger, then back. The cell phone was immediately available.

Kaarin Larsson was the most beautiful woman he had ever seen. She appeared so much younger than he had expected that it had jarred him. The problem, he entered the elevator and waited for the doors to slide shut. The problem was he couldn't get the image of her crawling across the cobblestones out of his mind. He wished he had been there, and that they had been alone. Psychics do it with more senses. He'd like to find out.

172

13

"He failed?" Ian Sanford Crockwell's eyes were alarmed. He drew deeply on his cigarette, then immediately exhaled the smoke through his mouth.

"Yes," Sommers confirmed. He suppressed his anger with McGraw's ruined mission behind a taut expression of professional detachment.

"What about the backup, the man who would *guarantee success?*"

"A taxi driver who was waiting for her at the end of Ragan's Alley chased the backup away before he could administer the finish. My understanding is that both the bullets and the knife came very, very close."

"So what! This isn't a game, Sommers. There are no points awarded. Oh, the group will not be pleased, not pleased at all with your continuing direction of this endeavor. Police?" he snapped sharply.

Roland Sommers ignored his client's impatience, letting it spend itself in the empty air. "Inspector Haggard has already contacted and interviewed Miss Larsson, so that we can assume she will be watched by the police in some way until closure of our deal.

"And recall, sir, that the Bermuda police have not

put together a sterling record of solving murders over the past several months. Killings with guns and other weapons are double what they were only 3-4 years ago. It is primarily gang violence that has not yet touched any tourists. And tourists are being warned not to go walking at night … but even then, no one has been convicted for them. It would appear that time is on our side."

Crockwell frowned. "A bitter mess, Sommers. A dangerous spreading mess." He clenched his cigarette between his teeth, a sudden warble of fear in his voice. "Haggard is the best the police have, and ..." his voice trailed away.

Sommers blew lightly through the stem of his pipe, then scooped its bowl full from a gold and green porcelain humidor on his desk. He tamped the dark fragrant tobacco shreds down into the bowl with his forefinger. He enjoyed the texture of fine moist tobacco between his fingers. "Mr. McGraw has found the killer, who used the .32," he said, as he lit and drew on the pipe. Smooth, fluid.

"He has? Who is it? What action has been taken?" Crockwell's panic hadn't subsided, only held in tenuous check. "Sommers, this business must be dispatched quickly. Every additional day damages the odds against us. We were in for a quick agile sure thing, *remember*." His attempt at sternness was unconvincing, but very correct.

174

"Mr. McGraw is watching him, to pick a time and a place. His identity is no concern to the group. Discussion in the group must be minimized. You agree?"

"Yes, yes. Certainly," he said too quickly. His panic was still simmering.

Sommers smiled, the pipe burning evenly as always. He didn't need six panic-stricken investors speculating on who and why about the man who fired the .32. It was enough that it increased his own uneasiness and necessitated killing Kaarin Larsson as promptly and quietly as possible. Her blindfolded face in his memory recalled McGraw's strange comment of late last night. She had seen him, McGraw had said, seen him in the dark. She had known he was there, though there was no warning, no light, and no sound. McGraw was certain of it. Never in McGraw's dozen years in the profession had a mark acted that way. McGraw had wanted to know what else Sommers might know about Kaarin Larsson; if there was anything else, any facts, insights he could use for preparation. Only a paid trickster, a mere conjurer, Sommers had assured him. McGraw's response, his voice, was what had caused Sommers increasing uneasiness. "Don't bet on it", McGraw had said bluntly as he hung up.

Neither of the two silent men were smiling when Rennie brought their morning tea. He circled quietly

175

around the polished leather chairs to place the silver tea service on Sommers' desk. He bowed slightly, then retreated, his choppy steps moved him around the chairs and past the large antique globe with remarkable speed. The two men, smoking rather than speaking, were indifferent to his presence and to his silent departure.

***

"All set?" asked Marc Kane.

Kaarin looked up from assembling her memory props on a small narrow table. A tripod holding a blank white flip-chart stood next to the table. Most of the memory seminar would be legitimate, but she had planned some stunts that had more showmanship than memory to emphasize specific points.

"Just about. It looks like everyone wants an early start." She was wearing trim white pants and a bright pink v-neck sweater with the sleeves pulled up to her elbows. Like her mother, Kaarin never wore jewelry except for a watch. The brochure had said the dress for the seminar would be casual, so she was casual. She smiled. Salon E was rapidly filling with men and women carrying large blue loose-leaf notebooks covered with golden money signs: $, £, ¥, €, ₩, R$, and others she didn't recognize. White memory books were already on each chair.

"Okay," he grinned. "Looks like everyone is

176

anxious to see you do your stuff again."

"That's good. I hope so. A lively audience is more fun to work with."

"How long you been in this mental business? Can't be long, I would have heard of you."

He was very big, over six feet by several inches with enormous tanned arms. His neck was the same diameter as his head. It must have been pro-football that Dieter had meant. His thick sandy hair lay over the collar of his sports shirt.

"I understand you played pro-football?" Kaarin said, side-stepping his question. She couldn't imply this might be her first big break. She didn't know yet what Sarah Randolph might bring.

Kane smiled broadly. "Yeah. About five years NFL. Colts, Patriots, once in the Pro Bowl. You follow pro ball?" His excitement was almost boyish, and Kaarin realized, very appealing.

"I would rather play football than watch it," she said and immediately regretted saying it. She didn't mean to start a conversation or get involved. Salon E was nearly full.

"Play it! You? A good wind could blow you away." He laughed. "After this is over, I want to hear about your football career. Lunch?" He had placed a large hand gently

177

against her shoulder, then withdrew it.

Kaarin smiled carefully. "I'm already committed, for the rest of the day actually. Perhaps later. It is time to start, everyone seems to be in place." His disappointment seemed genuine, which gave her sudden unexpected pleasure. She hadn't realized he had become so interesting so quickly. Again Dieter was right.

"Okay. I'll call you tomorrow." He changed tack. "You need an intro for this or just take'm on alone?"

Kaarin smiled. "No intro. I'll do what needs to be done. Thanks anyway."

Kane nodded, then moved away his stride long and determined, like he owned the place, his heavy shoulders swaying with each step to join a group of men several rows back. Her interest faded. Too much swagger, too much, too much confidence.

Her audience was dressed for the warm bright Bermuda weather, a colorful sunburnt active crowd. Kaarin was surprised that she hadn't seen Roland Sommers here, but, being local, he probably had other business. She turned to begin, feeling her nervous edge rising. She saw a dark-haired man slip in to sit in the back row at the last minute. Delano? He didn't wear a blue badge. She waited a moment longer to take a breath and to set her opening sentence in her mind.

McGraw waited. This morning he wasn't setting up to score, just to observe the mark's pattern, then with follow-up, and with some careful reconnaissance, pick the spot. He glanced at his watch: ten o'clock. Shook his head. The mark slept late. So would he when this was finished. He shifted. His thoughts moved back to last night again. But damn, the little blonde saw me in the dark! I'd swear on anything to that. Damn all hell, what kind of a spook was she?

***

"Fill your ears with castor oil," said Kaarin, "and rub the dome of your head with fresh butter! If you follow this sixteenth century memory improvement technique you will get clean ears and greasy hair, but your memory … well, you'll never forget the treatment." She smiled. "Man has tried everything to strengthen his memory: hanging dead birds around his neck as a totem, carrying mystic talismans, wearing special hats. Even Mark Twain patented a memory improvement device. But none of it worked because the five keys to a strong memory all come from *inside you … and from no where else.*"

She moved to the large flip chart. "The five keys to a strong memory." Kaarin lifted, then folded over the first sheet to reveal the five points she had written earlier in red.

179

No PowerPoint crap that these people probably saw every day. The flip chart made it more personal:

1) Motivation

2) Attention or accurate observation

3) Association of ideas

4) Repetition of experience or thought

5) Judgment

Kaarin whirled away from the chart, her yellow hair flying over her shoulder, as she moved to the center aisle. She took several steps to place herself in the center of the audience. Holding the cordless microphone in her left hand, she reached into her pocket with her right for a deck of cards.

Kaarin took another step, raised her right hand holding the cards in emphasis. "Your memory can be as strong at eighty as at eighteen. Your memory will be stronger before you leave this morning, and what will be more important, you will know how to continue to strengthen your memories even further."

Smiling, she stopped. "I need three people who are familiar with cards to join me, so that I can show you an immediate application of a strong memory ... that is if you are intrigued with games of chance, like black-jack, poker, or Texas hold'm."

She started back toward the front of the audience

with two men following her up the aisle, and a grinning third already waiting for her.

Kaarin introduced the men to the audience. All middle-aged and reddened by the treacherous Bermuda sun. They apparently were well known judging from the audience reaction. There were some laughing challenges about their already being card sharks and didn't need any more help.

A brief moment for the audience to have fun, then she took a single step forward away from the three men to gain emphasis and softly spoke a single word into the microphone: "Now." The audience quieted immediately. To free her hands, Kaarin slid the mike into its chrome stand.

Her assistants watched intently as she smoothly shuffled the deck between her hands, then cut a group of cards from the top which she handed it to Chet, his conference badge said.

"Hold these cards face down for a moment, Chet, please," she said. "Don't peek." Chet grinned widely, took the cards tightly between his hands and pressed them up against his chest.

Jimmy and Len the other badges said. More like Stan and Oliver she couldn't help thinking. Kaarin spoke first to Jimmy: "Please cut about half of the pack and give the other half to Len. Thank you" – as Jimmy complied.

"Jimmy, would you … then Len … deal the cards face up onto my hand. I will memorize them as you deal. I will then search the deck in my mind to determine what cards Chet is holding in his hands over there, which at this moment he doesn't know himself. All of you," she said, looking at each of the three men helping her, "are familiar with cards. Can you do what I am about to do?"

They each shook their heads. "If you can do it," grinned Chet, "I know a couple of casinos I'd like to escort you to *real quick*."

Kaarin laughed with the audience, then turned to Jimmy: "Please begin dealing." She stood near the mike, her left hand extended to receive the cards.

Jimmy began to deal face up, one at a time, slowly, deliberately onto her hand.

"A little faster," Kaarin said softly into the mike.

Jimmy looked up in surprise, glanced at Len, then at the audience. "As you wish," he said, increasing his speed.

"A little faster yet, please," she whispered into the mike.

Jimmy's jaw dropped. He dealt faster, as quickly as he could place one card down, he dealt another, until his hands were empty.

"Now Len. As fast as Jimmy, please," Kaarin

requested. Jimmy's reactions had been ideal.

Len began dealing.

"Faster, Len, please."

He dealt rapidly, cards flowing smoothly through his thick stubby fingers. For all his Oliver Hardy appearance, Len certainly knew how to handle cards. His portion completed Len stepped back.

"You may return to your seats now, gentlemen, and thank you." Kaarin placed the cards into her pocket without looking at them. Jimmy and Len returned to their seats, responding to whispered questions from friends as they edged down the rows. "Now Chet, it's just you and me."

"You aren't going to do it, Baby Doll. Nobody could memorize that fast," Chet declared.

"You are holding sixteen cards. That's easy, anyone could get that." Kaarin carried the mike forward so that Chet was a step or two behind her. Clearly she could not see the cards in his hands. "Now look at the cards you hold, Chet. As I call them … *only when I call them correctly*, drop each one to the floor."

Chet fanned the cards: "Sixteen. You're right."

"Five hearts: the ace, two . . . four, six and jack." Cards fluttered to the floor from Chet's hand as each was called.

The six, seven and ten, queen and king of clubs

183

joined the scattered hearts, then the seven of spades.

"You have a poker hand remaining … five cards. You play poker Chet, don't you?"

"Yes, Ma'am," he responded emphatically. The audience on her right started to titter and giggle. Chet must be doing something. He was to her right about three steps behind her.

"You're holding a good poker hand. A straight." More giggling.

"Damn," she heard Chet's surprised whisper.

"Five of spades, six of spades … seven of diamonds, eight of diamonds" But the eight didn't drop. "And the nine of hearts." It didn't drop either. She whirled about. Grinning widely, Chet held up his empty hands, fingers wide. He rotated around holding his hands higher. Now the entire audience started to laugh. Blindfold drive or not, this was the turning point of her showtime in Bermuda. She could lose everything right now if Chet could upset her. Every mentalist faced this moment in every performance – and there was never any warning. Mentavo had called it the daggerpoint. She had glimpsed Marc Kane, his hands behind his head, laughing, a smirk waiting on his face. In this crowd Chet wouldn't hide the cards just in his pocket, his shirt on the right side was … "Really, Chet, do you usually play poker with two cards tucked into your shorts? There on your right hand side … what games *do you play*?"

Chet's arms dropped as his grin faded while the audience laughed louder.

"Everyone is waiting to see if I am right, Chet … about the cards."

He hesitated, then shoved his hand down inside his pants and withdrew the eight of diamonds.

"And the nine of hearts, Chet, please, we are running late."

The audience roared as Chet turned red frantically feeling inside his pants trying to find the lost card. He finally shook his right pant-leg, the card dropped out. He meekly held up the nine of hearts.

"Not much to get in the way?" Kaarin whispered into the mike as a subdued Chet passed by to his seat. The audience exploded. Marc Kane laughed and applauded with the rest of the men. Two laughing women stood up to applaud.

After a short pause to let them have fun at Chet's expense, then: "Now it's your turn. Let's get to work. Please turn to page twelve." As they each opened their white memory books, Kaarin waited.

***

McGraw waited. His bladder couldn't handle any

more coffee. Still no movement, hell, the mark may already be dead. He chuckled to himself at the thought. But even he had limits.

"Men's room?" he asked. He moved to the rear of the small diner as rapidly as his large girth would allow. Foolish and stupid to miss the mark just to piss.

He returned to his table by the window. Couldn't have been more than two minutes. Sidewalks clear in all directions, didn't miss anything. He picked up his cameras to go back to browsing at the outside newsstand. Move. Don't get glued to one place. With people moving around you, a stationary person stands out. Swim with the marks, hit, and keep moving. He looked at his watch. If it were for the final count time wouldn't matter. Just get on the mark, get off, and go.

That S&W Model 657 .41 magnum. Jesus! Of all the cannons to have handed you. A damn Hollywood gun, all shiny stainless with an 8.37 inch barrel. They shoot bull elephants on Bermuda? He had had to wrap the whole weapon with dull electrician's tape to keep from looking like King Arthur when he pulled it out. The client said he had wanted no chances with him bringing in his own tools at the airport. A suitable pistol would be provided, then throw it into the ocean when he was finished. Fine, but it was the first time he went into an engagement without his

186

own inventory. If he hadn't needed the money to catch up his alimony payments, he would have walked on the whole deal. His ex was worse than having the FBI on him.

10:40. No movement. He began to get a little uneasy. The client had insisted on a head shot for DiMarco, but didn't care where about the blonde or this mark. A little luck last night and he would be on a plane for somewhere right now. Sommers was growing impatient, especially about that little blonde. Nervous clients could be dangerous to consultants. But that little blonde, she made his skin prickle just thinking about her. Whatever she was.

He picked up a copy of *Scientific American* off the bottom shelf of the newsstand, then replaced it. The mark was standing there on the corner adjusting his shades. Looked both ways before crossing the street. His mama trained him well. Let him go ahead, no rush. This could be the mark's last day on earth.

***

"The last key is judgment," said Kaarin. "Remember what you need, forget what you don't. Your memory is almost limitless in power and capacity, but don't waste it. Keep your memories alive … as Pythagoras taught two thousand years ago: 'Only a living memory can change lives'. The Pythagoreans felt a strong memory so important that their symbol for memory was their symbol

187

for perfection … the number ten."

Kaarin flipped the last chart over to show a large red 10.

"A strong memory isn't a system of mnemonics, though as I have shown you, mnemonics can be an aide to, but not the foundation for, a strong memory." She held the mike in her hand and walked a few steps down the center aisle to gain emphasis.

"How strong is your memory? Let me close with a bit of history. In the eighteenth and nineteenth centuries there was a small group of men called the Shass Pollak. Shass was an abbreviation of the Hebrew terms for Talmud, Pollak for Polish. The Shass Pollak continued the Jewish tradition of oral preservation of the Talmud by committing the entire twelve volumes of the Babylonian Talmud to memory. This ensured that though books and scrolls could be, and were, destroyed, the culture, the faith would live. So powerful was their memorization … if you were to open any of the twelve volumes to any page and press a hat-pin down through any word on that page, the Shass Pollak could tell you precisely each and every word on every page, both sides, that the pin passed through, on through the *entire volume*. An absolutely prodigious feat! But, incredibly, one that each of us could duplicate, if we shared the intense cultural motivation of the Shass Pollak."

The sunburned bankers were quiet and still, fastened to her words.

"George Leonard," she continued, "in his essay 'In God's Image', observed: 'Studying nature, we find that the systems are created to be used to the full. What is the purpose of the unused human capability? What is its destination?'" Kaarin took a breath. She didn't want to finish too heavy. It was Bermuda and it was beach time.

"What is its destination?" she repeated softly. "That's for each of us to determine, to achieve. But to tap, to use *all* that is within us ... that's when life is fun, really fun. Questions?"

***

"You know where he'll be?"

"Yes. I know his plans," answered McGraw. "An afternoon at Fort Hamilton. His pattern is predictable. Doesn't know he's being tracked."

"Put him away. Then her. Finish this. Then get out, *immediately*."

"I understand." McGraw hung up.

_***

Roger Delano's compliments after the seminar had made her day, and maybe opened her career. He hadn't planned to stay the entire seminar, but had found her presentation fascinating. If Friday night went well, then

Delano wanted to talk about a return engagement at the Duchess within 2-3 weeks! There was something special coming up that she fit very well. Kaarin could have flown back to her room without an elevator.

She picked up the phone.

"Kaarin, how'd the memory gig go?"

"Sugar! It went well …really well. Even Delano said he enjoyed it."

"Delano? Dynamite, White Lady! How about the three of us at Fort Hamilton this afternoon … about two-thirty? Serreta wants to bring some wine and cheese and a loaf, whatever that guy said."

"Omar Khayyam."

"Right Omar."

"That's great. I'm having lunch with the police … about last night."

Sugar quieted. "Yeah, we heard. Wasn't in the papers or on TV, but right on our doorstep. Serreta wouldn't do anything until she knew you were all right. A cop, Mathews, talked to us."

"I know. I'm to look at pictures to see if I can put a name with the two faces I saw."

"Saw? It's pitch dark in the Alley that hour."

"Saw. I saw them, Sugar. Clear as daylight. A white man and a black. Sugar, the warning sense hit me

190

like an ice truck. It terrified me, but it saved my life. There's a lot to talk about this afternoon. I need some direction ... help ... something. I don't understand what is happening to me. Why they tried to kill me? Why ... Why everything?"

"See you at the fort, Kaarin. I have some thoughts. Maybe some help, maybe not. Two-thirty. Together we'll get some answers." He paused, then added: "By the way, what did the white man look like?"

"Big heavy jaws, sort of red-faced."

She heard him whisper: "Oh, shit", then loudly: "See you at the fort, Kaarin."

Kaarin was puzzled with his reaction, but felt good about being with Sugar and Serreta. If she couldn't talk with them openly, she didn't know where to turn. Everyone else would think she was totally crazy including Keith Haggard. But the need to talk to *someone*, she couldn't keep it all inside much longer.

Too much was growing like an evanescent cancer.

14

Haggard pointed as they walked away from his car. "Criminal Records Office of the Bermuda Police Service used to share the building with Socko, the Scenes of Crime Office, but they have moved into their own building now. Socko is responsible for taking fingerprints and criminal photos at the site of any serious incident."

The CRO building itself was centered between the Criminal Investigation Department and the Administration buildings. All buildings were pastel-yellow and white, and all had a remarkable view of Hamilton Harbor. Formerly an army facility, the police complex spread over the crest of Headquarters Hill.

Kaarin listened with interest to Keith Haggard as he explained, pointing back down at the Harbor. He touched her elbow to guide her toward the low one story building in the center.

"We follow the British legal system, Kaarin, so we do not have big books of criminal photographs for you to go through. Nor do we have suspect lineups. Our procedure requires that groups of similar photos, a minimum of twelve, be used," Haggard explained, as he led her into CRO.

"Another one just coming in, Inspector," said Detective Constable Collin Hopswood. "Over two hundred in from Interpol this year. That's . . .." Rounding the corner of the communications office, he stopped when he saw Kaarin. "The world's going to no good." He stammered a modest greeting when introduced to Kaarin, his round face split in a tight-lipped smile that rose to his eyes.

"Critical?" asked Haggard.

"Interpol thinks two Turkish contract killers could be coming our way."

"Anyone we know?" Haggard said.

"Not that I can say yet, sir. We'll know quickly enough when it's run through the new database. A new set of killers, apparently a new Mexican cartel, a spinoff of FARC in Columbia; and some kind of a group from the Iranian Quds Force have been increasingly active. Different sources of financing certainly, maybe even competitors. We're consistently getting more red and green notices from Interpol about their movements now." Hopswood motioned toward a table. "Butterfield has put together some picture collections for Miss Larsson. Looking at those fellows is not my idea of a proper luncheon for a lady," He carefully pulled the printout. "I will get this distributed immediately."

***

Detective Constable Paul Butterfield had placed two piles of photographs inserted in clear plastic pages, six to a page, on an otherwise bare metal table for Kaarin to examine. As she approached she saw him look away quickly after staring at her breasts. Must have seen the reruns of her blindfold drive.

"The rules, Miss Larsson, require that the faces you are looking at be reasonably similar to ensure any identification is from your memory, and not from any police prompting," Butterfield explained nervously, forcing his attention on the pictures. "One group is of blacks and the other whites since you reportedly saw one of each. I will not comment on the people whose faces are here, other than they are all male as you had suggested." He stepped back and smiled. "If you need to look at more, we have 31, 000 photos in color and 22, 000 in black and white. But fortunately for us, they are not all necessarily relevant to this inquiry." He avoided her eyes as he stepped back to give her more room.

Kaarin nodded as she pulled her chair closer to the table. She began with the whites, hoping the haunting familiarity of the face would pry something lose. Six at a time. His strong jaw line was his most prominent facial feature. She thought of Sugar's odd reaction . . .

Six more.

Faces of sullen hatred and vacuous indifference.

Six more.

***

When Haggard returned from the Police Club with plastic wrapped sandwiches and two cans of soda, Butterfield was assembling a new pile of whites while Kaarin was finishing the blacks. Butterfield shook his head to Haggard's questioning glance.

"Some provisions to sustain your strength, Kaarin. No luck?"

She looked up, rubbing her eyes. "No. Nothing. How many so far?" she asked Butterfield.

"118 whites and 90 blacks."

"Why not take lunch now," Haggard suggested. "All the photos will start to blur into the same without a break."

Kaarin agreed, stood up, stretched and looked around. The room was scrubbed government: metal desks, wooden tables, rows of beige filing cabinets, a row of LCD screens on a table. Except for the brilliant sunlight through the windows – and the yellow and black kiskadee looking quizzically in from his perch on a hibiscus branch – it probably looked like police offices anywhere in the world.

They ate silently for a few moments. Kaarin chewed slowly. Haggard had kept glancing over at her as they had driven from the Duchess through the north roundabout to

195

Middle Road, then up Montpelier Road to Gymnasium, finally up the sweeping curve of Headquarters Hill. Well, good.

"Last night ... how do you feel?" Haggard asked gently. He had already asked once in the car.

Her small smile was quick, then gone. "I'm all right, thanks. I spoke with the taxi driver this morning, but he refused to accept any money from me."

"I'm not surprised," he said. "Ellington has a strong sense of honor toward women. Almost Victorian."

He moved his sandwich and soda can to allow room for Hopswood to put down a stack of new Interpol printouts, each with a square of color in the upper right hand corner. A red on top, some greens and blacks showing.

"You know him?" Kaarin asked.

"We know all the taxi drivers, Miss Larsson," said Hopswood. He looked over from pointing out the red tagged bulletin on top. "Very well, indeed."

She nodded. "Naturally you would. Are all those photos wanted Bermudians? It seems a very large number."

"No, fortunately," responded Hopswood. "We have about 70,000 permanent residents. It would not be a pleasant place if half of them were in our files. The photos include Bermudians, but also come through Interpol,

Scotland Yard, your FBI, the Mounties in Canada. Generally from countries with ties to the Commonwealth, former colonies … which would include the U.S., actually," he added with a soft grin. "In actual fact, Miss Larsson, I do not believe anything can be gained with looking beyond what Butterfield has piled over there now."

Haggard looked up from examining the red Interpol notice. "What is Interpol's response to our preliminary descriptions, Hopswood?"

"We included their recommendations in the material Miss Larsson has already seen, sir, with no result."

"We don't know them at all?" asked Haggard.

"Apparently not, sir, so far," Hopswood said. "I won't disturb your lunch further, Miss. When you are ready, Butterfield has prepared our final salvo for the day."

No pronounced jaw line on a wide white face, no thin black face with a scrub of mustache, broken nose and malevolent eyes.

Nothing.

***

Haggard was silent as they walked over the lawn toward C.I.D., except to explain Interpol's color coding. He was developing some questions of his own. Had she actually seen anything?

"Red is urgently wanted persons, blue is an inquiry

197

for information, green a notice to alert police that an individual should be watched, black is for unidentified dead bodies, usually with gruesome pictures attached, and colorless for stolen property transported across national borders, usually art objects, and formerly mostly Italian but now frequently Central Asian. We get about 50-60 notices a week.

"Hopswood is revising our software for our picture files, among other things, since we need faster correlation for efficient identification. Thousands pass through Bermuda daily. He has an upgraded computer system in his budget again for next year, but the Commissioner has a limited budget himself. With the growing Bermuda debt, we're over three billion dollars now, all the departmental budgets are tight or are being reduced. The Cabinet ministers have all taken a voluntary pay cut, but that's just pennies when the cuts need to be dollars. So we keep trying." He pointed. "I'm on the first floor, up there. The window at the corner."

***

His office was bland government, but personal, carefully ordered. No photographs of a wife or girlfriend, Kaarin noted quickly, while Haggard had stepped momentarily out of his office. On the wall, where direct sunlight could not reach it, was a framed old envelope. She

198

looked at it more closely. A crudely cut stamp, 'one penny' written in a flowing hand over the date 1854, was affixed to one corner. A signature, W.B. Perot, was below the date. It looked home-made. Must have some sentimental value, she thought.

On another wall hung a plaque carved from heavily aged dark wood:

WE FOUND IT TO BE THE DANGEROUS AND DREADED ISLAND, OR RATHER ISLANDS, OF THE BERMUDA. BECAUSE THEY BE SO TERRIBLE TO ALL THAT HAVE EVER TOUCHED ON THEM, AND SUCH TEMPESTS, THUNDERS, AND OTHER FEARFUL OBJECTS ARE SEEN AND HEARD ABOUT THEM, THAT THEY BE CALLED COMMONLY THE DEVIL'S ISLANDS.

WILLIAM STRACHEY 1609

Kaarin nodded. Of course, the *Sea Venture* shipwreck in 1609 on Bermuda. That had been the source for Shakespeare's last play, *The Tempest,* her favorite piece of Shakespeare, other than a couple of the Sonnets. Strachey had been one of the survivors on the *Sea Venture.* A police commentary on the islands, as well?

She turned back to the desk, smiling when she saw the upside-down glass ashtray near one corner. Must be taking the tough way out.

Hanging next to the door was a framed £1 Bermuda stamp, pinkish with the portrait of an English king in black and plum. A thin newsletter with a sketch map of Bermuda on the cover, *Bermuda High* printed at the top, was lying on a shelf of the bookcase behind his desk. She was curious about what it meant but decided it wasn't any of her business. The date was June, 1987.

"What is the significance of the envelope with Perot's signature? It looks home made," she asked, and was surprised at the light that appeared immediately in Haggard's thoughtful face. She had clearly struck a nerve dead center. Just naturally psychic … or maybe Boskop, whatever that might be.

"William Perot was the first postmaster in Hamilton. He made the stamps so he could spend more time in his garden instead of in the post office. It's from my father's collection … his special pride. He gave it to me just before he died. He wanted to hand it to me himself, not have an unknowing barrister do it."

"It must be worth a great deal with its age."

"It's not age, Kaarin, but scarcity and condition. There are stamps older than that envelope that aren't worth

200

a tenth of its value. The piece has some slight damage, but when my father purchased it in 1928 it was all he could afford on policeman's pay. I couldn't afford to buy it now. Few people could, if they could find one, that is. There are only twelve of those envelopes in the world."

"Isn't it taking some risk having it hanging out in the open like that?"

"This is a police station don't forget," Haggard observed, smiling. "In any case, I like to have it where I can see it. Some good, good memories associated with it."

"Is the one pound stamp over there also valuable?"

Haggard started to grin. "I should warn you, Kaarin, you're treading on my second greatest interest. I may inflict you with hours of information on Bermuda stamps that you never in your life would want to know."

She smiled. A stamp collector; it seemed *just right*. "What is your first interest? Then tell me about your second," she laughed.

"Police work," he said. "I located the George VI one-pound stamp in New York at a small dealer auction. The dealer didn't realize what he had ... you know, the ultimate collector's dream. Very fine, unhinged, a 'blank scroll' variety ... are you sure ... ?"

She nodded. It was an almost joyous relief from faces of desperate, angry men, and her own troubled mind.

201

A gentle unthreatening place in this strange mess.

"Do you collect only Bermuda stamps?" she asked, enjoying his eyes.

"Yes. My father started me. When my mother died when I was about twelve, it was just the two of us, so we spent a lot of time together. He taught me to appreciate truly fine things ... to collect, but not to acquire."

"It sounds almost like the same thing," she said.

"One collects beauty, but one acquires things he used to say."

Nicely put. Kaarin liked the senior Haggard.

"He always followed a single rule: Collect the absolute best you can afford at the time. Beauty, not things. That's how he got that Perot provisional. He saved for four years so that he would be ready, when he found it."

"I'm glad he found it," Kaarin said. "It must have given him great pleasure when he did."

"It did."

"What next?" Kaarin asked, sitting down under the Perot.

Haggard grimaced. "We have several disturbing problems. A .41 magnum is a large gun, not easily smuggled, not normally a professional's weapon, and not a gang weapon, though gang shootings have been growing in the past several months. The .41 is a major risk to carry through any entry port, and a ten-year no-parole sentence if convicted before the Supreme Court.

"The Bermuda Police Service, Kaarin, has been, up to recently, an unarmed force, like the English, though now more officers patrolling high crime zones are carrying pistols. An unexpected gun in an incident could be disastrous ... though escape from the islands would be very difficult." He glanced over at the upturned ashtray. "That .41 could be a hidden gun, loaned for a job, then returned to hiding. The killer then could leave the islands clean, so long as no one could identify him, or them. If that's the case, then someone on Bermuda arranged for DiMarco's killing and the attack on you."

Kaarin sat silently. "Why?" she finally asked. "I know no one here. I have never been here before. I myself didn't even know I was coming until a few days ago. How could I be a threat to anyone?"

"I don't know," he said. "But the fact that so few people could have known you were coming here might give us a starting point. Unless you accidently saw something that someone didn't want you to see. Or," he said slowly, "maybe someone is afraid of what they think you might actually be."

Haggard looked up at the framed Perot for a moment. "How clearly did you see them last night, Kaarin?

203

Could they be in CRO but maybe not the way you saw them, then? It was a dark place, you were under considerable stress … could you have only imagined seeing their faces?"

"I saw them as clearly as I see you now." Her voice dropped as she pronounced each word with emphasis as though to convince herself as well.

"How?" Haggard asked quietly.

Kaarin felt drained. She could see it coming, wanting so much to avoid it, wishing she hadn't reacted so strongly. She stood up, her hands thrust down into her pockets. Seconds passed, she didn't know what to do.

"A defense attorney will ask you the same question, Kaarin, when we catch them," he said gently. "The judge will insist on an answer. I'm not insisting … I just want to understand."

"The Alberts will be waiting for me." Her voice was flat. "Is there a phone I can use to call a taxi?" She wanted to run, that's all she could think of, no logic, just run for cover, for a chance to let her mind operate in peace. "Thank you for lunch." Kaarin forced a small smile.

"Dinner tonight?" he asked, standing.

Kaarin hesitated. "Yes … if we don't talk about your first interest."

"Agreed," he said. "I'll have one of my men drive

you. To Fort Hamilton?"

"Yes, if it's not too much trouble."

Haggard smiled, then shrugged. "I'd do it myself, but ... I have a staff meeting."

***

The brief ride to Fort Hamilton was silent. Kaarin did not respond to the constable's small talk, her mind searching for a way to turn. The police had nowhere to look, it seemed. With no identification from her where could they look? Two killers could still be there, still looking for her. Whose path have I crossed? What do they think I am? The clairvoyance, if that is what it was. Sugar might have some insight, at least something that could give her a toehold, a direction.

Nothing made sense.

***

"Kermit Morgan is clean. So apparently are the Alberts." Sgt. Oliver Bain put the FBI faxes on Haggard's desk. "And Immigration confirms that Miss Larsson has not been in Bermuda before." Haggard nodded. Bain said, "She looked a little upset when she left. Trouble?"

Haggard nodded again. "Miss Larsson could not identify any of CRO's photos ... and backed off completely when I raised the question again of her seeing the men clearly enough in the dark to identify. That's when she

205

decided she was late meeting the Alberts at Fort Hamilton."

"What next, sir?" Bain asked.

"DiMarco," he replied. "Dig deeper into DiMarco's recent career. What shows, seminars, involvements and where. He might have crossed Miss Larsson's path at some point if the same killer is after her. Morgan should be able to give us a detailed itinerary since he was getting a cut of DiMarco's income, and ..." Haggard paused. What other common thread was in the mix? "See what you can run down on the Alberts' movements. Where do they and DiMarco intersect? Morgan might be help there, too. Have someone go back to Nathaniel at the Pink Sands ... wait, I'll do that. I owe John a visit."

"Miss Larsson?"

"Get someone in plainclothes she couldn't have seen here. Crowley or Fox would fit. Get one of them to Fort Hamilton ... on a moped. He's to keep his distance, not get her upset. There's something about her, she might be able to sense being watched."

Oliver Bain raised an eyebrow. "A special sense? You think she might be the real thing? Fox is an amateur magician, told me how she might have done that blindfold drive ... though I'm not sure his method would work."

"Until we have more to go on, for her sake, I hope she has something extra. The FBI report on her arrive yet?"

"It was just coming in when I got back from the Club."

"Let's see." Haggard moved quickly away from his desk. What did she see – *and how* – last night? Then crawling about placing pennies at sunup. What might she do next? Kaarin was all question-marks, but she seemed to like stamps. Damn!

15

They waited for a moment on Happy Valley Road until some confused tourists could restart their stalled mopeds, then drove up into the Fort Hamilton parking lot. Their car was a regulation unmarked Mitsubishi police car.

"Got to give tourists the benefit of the doubt. Never know what direction they're going to go. Have a good afternoon, Miss Larsson." Constable Reilly smiled.

Kaarin started toward the entrance to the solid brooding redoubt, resolved to enjoy a few minutes free of thinking about killers with big guns. A wooden drawbridge spanned the wide moat. *Shampoo!* She paused a few steps onto the bridge. The thought was clear but had no meaning, no relation to anything. An odd moonshot, perhaps? Shampoo?

Shaking her head, Kaarin stopped again to lean over the railing on the bridge to look down into the lush exotic garden filling the emptied great moat. It took little imagination to feel the gentle susurrant breezes through palm fronds and large-leafed polished green shrubbery she couldn't identify. Kaarin could almost hear them touching.

***

"You do shampoo commercials, miz? You look

familiar, and with that mop of hair you must advertise something."

Kaarin had scarcely walked onto the fort's parade grounds when a chunky sunburned woman in a carelessly fitted sundress abruptly appeared beside her, a soda can in her hand.

"No," Kaarin replied, stunned by the moonshot. Why shampoo? This was crazy. She edged away, and walked a little faster. "I don't do commercials."

The dark haired woman, wearing owlish sunglasses, shrugged her sunburnt shoulders. "Hey. You look show biz, that's all. A body could make a fortune with shampoo commercials with your hair and looks. You ever try? You should try. That would be super exciting!"

"Shampoo commercials?" Kaarin wanted to end the encounter. This is silly, but the woman moved along with her.

"Oh! Exciting? I mean that's where it's at, really at." Kaarin edged away still faster. "You're cool, really cool. Could make a fortune in commercials," she insisted.

Kaarin shook her head. "I'm not interested in commercials. Please excuse me, I'm trying to find some friends." She abruptly turned away and walked quickly into the crowds, leaving the woman to join two others beneath the umbrella at a snack bar.

Fort Hamilton's parade grounds and parapets swarmed with every variety of tourist. An obvious newly wed couple were taking a silly selfie draped over a cannon. Privacy Sugar had promised. She dismissed shampoo from her mind as just an errant moonshot, but if bookings got scarce, maybe. She wanted to get completely free of people for a while, until the Alberts arrived, fifteen minutes or so.

***

Kaarin cautiously descended the uneven brick steps without hand railings into the fort's dark bowels, sun and noise fading behind her. Her hand against the coarse brick wall, she paused a few steps from the bottom to let her eyes adjust to the gloom. The brick-lined corridors underground were gloomy even with struggling lightbulbs about every twenty feet.

Winds, eyes and warmth were gone.

Some tourists had turned away from the wide stairway leading to the underside of the fort. "No way I'm going down in there. I'd get claustrophobia for sure." Kaarin turned and saw an attractive woman vigorously shake her head. When her bearded husband quickly agreed, they strolled away. They exhibited none of the touching of newly-weds.

Kaarin's first steps created muffled echoes. She was alone in a wide central bricked hall with corridors leading off at varying intervals. Turning right, she walked slowly, her fingertips glided across the century-old brick wall.

Some of the corridors weren't corridors but dark entrances to small windowless rooms of bricked floor, walls and ceiling. Some were dimly lighted, a sharp shadow across their interior, some just black gaps in the wall.

Kaarin turned left down the first gallery leading away from the central hall. No reason, just a change in direction. A slight moist chill began to hang around her under the sloping ceiling. Soundless brick was everywhere. She pulled her sweater sleeves down, plunged her hands deep into her pockets and walked slowly on, the floor sloped downward. Some small rooms obviously for storage, but one was a room intended, at one time, to be occupied. By whom? To be fifty feet underground in unrelieved somberness, lighted back then with only candles or kerosene lanterns. A dismal abyss a long way from the sun and camaraderie of the parade ground. What duty would require someone to be placed this far into the earth?

The passageway appeared closed off at the end. She hesitated, thinking to turn back, to the hall, the stairs, the parade ground, finally the sun. But, it looked like a window on the wall at the corridor's end. A window to what? She had to know. Maybe it would explain why someone would

211

be required to live down here. Check quickly, then back to find the Alberts.

The window was blocked with peeling rusty iron bars in the dim light. Kaarin went back a few steps, turned left out of the light into a narrow darkness with a still lower ceiling, her fingertips stretched out touching the bricks on both sides. A sharp right corner, deep storage alcoves on both sides, deep beyond her reach, then a further lowered narrow doorway into the windowed room. A flickering bulb in the center of the bricked ceiling. It was a jail cell, the brig of the fort. *Desolate,* but her question was answered. She always had to know, to satisfy her endless curiosity. Kaarin bent down to enter. There was an odd shadow in the far corner. What was it? Then quick, back up to the parade ground, she would be late and she wanted as much time as possible to talk with Sugar and Serreta.

A small shelf-table built into the wall. To eat from, store in. Lord, so gloomy, depressing. She would go absolutely wild, caged underground in this murky dankness!

***

McGraw waited. He knew the mark would be coming. Tourists, dreamy honeymooners, people off the cruise ships, all over the fort. He shifted the camera with the long lens. He felt the heft, the solidity of the forty-one.

212

With it, when you hit, everything stopped, but it was humungous and uncomfortable to conceal. He kept walking, move with the marks, hit, then move on. Sweating in the heat, he carried a large cold ginger ale sipping it thirstily through two straws. He was early, no rush. This would wrap it up. The Jamaican would show, but he had given that black mother a later time to keep him out of the way. Smooth, professional, and on a plane to the world tomorrow. But that little blonde was damn spooky. Getting her would take a load off his mind.

A wide stairway with a sign warning of steepness leading to the underground portion of the fort looked clear of tourists. He stopped, looking for a trash barrel. Seeing one against a bench about twenty feet away, he lofted the can with two straws in a high floating arc. The amplified *ker-thong* of a perfect hit in the empty barrel was intensely satisfying and saved a minute of walking.

McGraw stopped a few steps from the bottom, removed his sunglasses to let his eyes become accustomed to the diminished light. Then he stepped down onto the gloomy central hall. He noted the galleries opening off the central area which curved gently around to his left. He turned right, wouldn't take so much time to check out, then back upstairs. Nailing the mark in a crowd, these small-town police would know a polished professional was in

213

action. He chuckled at his conceit, and stopped, hearing his muffled chuckling echoing around him. His soft shoes made no sound.

Black gaps in the wall were empty storage areas. Nothing. No wonder no tourists were down here, crazy. He stopped, faint echoes of light steps dissolving in the still dimness. Someone down that corridor. Why not? Might be something down there, then back upstairs. God, this was enough!

What the hell? The passageway was a dead-end! Then he made out a barred window. Silently, he walked quickly toward it, his curiosity fading rapidly. Nothing but endless boring bricks. There was only a struggling bare bulb against the ceiling. As he approached the wall, he understood immediately what it was; a brig! He turned, but caught a glimpse. Someone was inside the brig. He held still for a moment, then tossed both hands in the air. All right, numbnut, see who's there, then get the hell out and back to work.

The spook! The little blonde spook!

He was stunned. Christ, trapped in a damn jail cell, too good to be true! He instantly believed in prayer. McGraw turned to find the corridor entrance leading to the brig. A few seconds he would finish her, then the mark. A beautiful God-sent opportunity. He'd drop a little more in the poorbox next time in church.

***

Kaarin whirled to go, simultaneously a sudden icy chill poured down her spine, as she saw him! His broad face with its prominent jawline, smiling, leering at her through the bars, his eyes curiously gleaming in the struggling light. Kaarin's jaw dropped in shock. Trapped! Trapped underground with the white killer. He didn't move then started to grin, his teeth gritted together. He began to turn away from the barred window.

Kaarin's stunned mind finally grasped where she was, as she watched the killer start to come after her. Two, three lunging steps she was at the low narrow opening. No sounds. Where was he? Into the dark storage alcove across the passage.

"Shit."

She heard him softly curse. Reaching out with both hands, Kaarin sought the dark alcove, its curving edges against her fingers. She crouched low, her hands on the uneven floor, rapidly crab-stepped into the blackness until stopped by a cold brick wall. Can't stay. He knows I'm here somewhere. Kaarin removed her shoes, felt the cold moist brick against her feet. She'd use them as weapons. Couldn't make noise running.

Kaarin sensed him at the entrance to her alcove. A

215

bare three feet away. His breathing was dry, open mouthed. But he made no sound in moving. She pressed tightly to the bricks, away from him, holding her breath, fearful he could detect her racing heart. Kaarin carefully, slowly, pulled her legs up, ready to crab-walk to the entrance and run. One hand held her shoes. As his faintly limned form moved toward the other alcove, she started to edge forward. As Kaarin lunged for the small opening between his dark bulk and the curving entrance of the alcove, its hard edge scraped across her back, her hand smashed against the bricks, dropping her shoes. Her elbow brushed his trouser leg.

Kaarin ran!

***

He twisted, grabbed at her form with one hand only to feel soft hair float across the back of his hand. A second! Bending down to avoid the low ceiling, he waddled awkwardly after her, only four or five feet away now, clearly visible.

***

Her feet slipped silently on the bricks as Kaarin sprinted. The end of the corridor, right, into the lighted hall. She risked a quick glance back. He was coming out, his broad face grinning, his vulpine eyes glistened.

The broad steps. Her feet slipped as she tried to

turn, to leap up the stairs, to run to the sun and the tourists, to help. She stumbled, then staggered and regained her balance, he was too close. Run, run! Find something else, a door, stairway. Run!

He could run now in the high-ceilinged central hall. Her turning away from the stairway gave him a lift. Had her now, if no one interferes. Just grab her hair or sweater, pull her down. Three seconds to snap her neck and be gone.

Kaarin wanted to scream, but she realized no one could hear her down here. Skidding, she turned into the gently curved central gallery. A light ahead, bright, to the outside. She sucked air deeply, driving her legs against the hard crusty unevenness of the brick floor. *Agh!* Her right toe caught in a wide grout, she twisted, caromed off a wall. She pushed away, walking, trying to ignore the searing pain. Hopping, limping, she ran toward the arched doorway lighted with Bermuda sun.

He saw her stagger and pushed his bulk harder. Just a handful of yellow hair. God damnit! That's all I want.

Blinded by aching brilliance, Kaarin stumbled against a palm, the sharp edges of trimmed fronds tearing

217

at her sleeve. She ripped free, frantically blinked, squinted hard against the sun. A small dirt path lay ahead. Drawing deeply for air, she ran for the path, his hoarse breathing almost on her.

Christ! So bright can't see. There, easy to follow. Just keep her in view. Can't shoot, hand would tremble. Run. Sweat beading his face, he dragged his sunglasses from a shirtpocket and put them on as he ran. Now, get her, man, get her!

Kaarin dodged through endless flowers, the narrow path designed for strolling, not sprinting. Her bare feet dug into the dirt, accelerated her forward, they held at the twisting turns, her aching toe forgotten. An odd desperate thought: do a blindfold run?

Out of sight, damn. No, only a thick-leafed bush hid her for an instant. He sucked in the warm humid air. Ahead! By crashing straight through ferns and flowers and back onto the path, he'd gain a few seconds on her. He thought he could hear her gasping for air only a couple of yards ahead. Her long hair tossing back and forth on her back. Just a handful and it's all over. He crashed into the brush and ferns to gain another few yards but cats-claw vines held his heavy bulk for seconds before giving way. He ran on, deep red welts across his arms. His camera was somewhere back in the fort. Thrown out of the way. Probably didn't work anyway.

Kaarin saw a large floral-green bush with heavy hand-like leaves. Her wind was almost gone. Hearing loud snapping and slapping, she glanced quickly back over her shoulder. He was shortcutting through. But he wasn't in view. An instant, hesitation, then she dove under the bush, skidded head first, clawed frantically at the dirt with fingers and toes to pull her rapidly under the branches. Footprints? Would he see anything or was he as spent as she was?

Kaarin could hear her heart pounding, clogging in her throat. She breathed slow, shallow, open-mouthed, forcing her questing lungs, aching diaphragm to wait. She pressed as deeply into the soft earth as she could. When she pushed her pasted damp hair back from her eyes a tiny green anole lizard stared defiantly at her a few inches from her face. It suddenly dew-lapped. Pressed down, flat into the soil made breathing difficult. Kaarin raised her shoulders slightly to ease the passage of air. Sealed off from circulation, the air under the bush hung like hot wet wool around her. Where was he?

219

Where was she? Damn vines. He pushed harder. Can't let her get away. The mark? What time? Where is she? He brushed against a large floral-green bush with heavy hand-like leaves. The path curved out of sight. A minute, a goddamn miserable minute, for a breath. He staggered, tripped on an exposed root and fell to his knees. He pushed up and on. Get her! Maybe lose both of'em. Damnit! He ran, his lumbering legs shrieked for rest but he couldn't let the spook slip away. Not when she had been handed him on a silver platter.

Kaarin watched him disappear around the bend. He staggered, his clumsy steps erratic. He was as exhausted as she. What now? Her breathing was coming under control. She raised up higher, deeply inhaling the thick humid air, letting her slowing heart slip back into place. Wait? He'll be back, watching for her footprints probably. Run the other way, how far? She'd lost track. He could catch her from behind. He could suddenly reappear around that bend. Maybe he's just waiting out of sight for her to emerge, to give herself away. A sound! Behind her. Could grab her legs, while she lay. Kaarin curled them into a tight pre-natal position. She didn't know. Too worn for careful thought, her mind slipped away from her control. She didn't know what to do.

A cool chill flowed down her back, across and through her cramped legs. It was overpoweringly refreshing in the oppressive humidity under the bush. Kaarin seemed to know. He was still searching, running, no, more just fast walking now. Follow him. That was the closest escape. A stairway up the side of the moat to the parade ground. Yes, she had seen it from the drawbridge coming in. Follow, follow him. No! It's illogical, suicidal. She shook her head. Follow! No! Follow! Now! She shivered, her eyes went wide, she could actually glimpse him! Ohh, God. Like starting straight down a steep ski run.

The anole stiffened as she shuddered, her crystal eyes flickering a strange light, then it suddenly vanished into the upper terraces of the bush.

Kaarin dragged herself back onto the path, her legs at first not willing to support her, her aching feet bare. Focusing all her will on her stiff legs, Kaarin stumbled slowly forward, feeling led along the path, the enwrapping colors only an exhausted prismatic blur.

She picked up speed to a rapid walk, then to a slow trot, twisting, mechanically following the path, her arms hanging loosely, her lungs beginning to ache again with even that modest effort. Kaarin surrendered to whatever was leading her.

221

He could feel his panic rising. She wasn't on the stairway up the side of the moat. Must have gone on, afraid to risk getting caught in the open. He crossed the small clearing, a path leading off to the stairway, no footprints, he noted professionally; she must be lying low ahead. He slowed to a walk, staying on the pathway leading away into a clump of royal palms. Might lose the mark, have to get her. Twice, he cursed, he had her only to lose her by a hairsbreadth. He relished the thought of finally twisting her head back, watching the light fade from her strange eyes, the final snap of her neck. Stupidest job he'd ever been on. A deep breath, he moved ahead more rapidly.

Kaarin slowed, her lungs, her side corseted with pain. Crazy. Crazy. All she wanted in Bermuda was to do a good show and go on. Find her answers. Not dodge killers in a humid jungle. Sugar, Serreta. She looked at her watch, blinking back sweat droplets. 2:45. They'd be looking for her. There was a small clearing ahead.

2:44. That black mother with his stupid blade would be showing in ten minutes. What would he have to show him? Stinking, shoddy crap! He stopped, indifferent to the luxuriant walls of butter-yellow hibiscus with tiny orchids floating on the humid thick air. Screw it! She's gone. Get the mark. Get one of them, numbnut! He started back toward the clearing. Everything would be cool if he had never seen that spook.

Kaarin saw the stairway, the path leading to it. He wasn't in sight. She took another deep breath; run, hit the steps, get back with people, out of this insanity. Another breath, her legs trembled, her senses tensed for the effort. Now! Kaarin dug her bare toes into the soft earth, drove her heavy legs down and forward, toward the stairs, expecting any instant to see him appear from behind a bush or grabbing her from behind. Slapping, she pushed myriad greens away from her, Kaarin pivoted, dodged through hanging vines, avoided stepping into a clump of shiny green Spanish bayonets, their sharp falcate leaves menaced her legs. Breaking through into the cleared area at the moat wall, Kaarin fastened her eyes on the second step, and leaped heavily for it. Her bent toes crushed, grated against the cut stone, then the next step. Slipping, she sprawled on the steps. Kaarin sobbed. She pushed herself back up, one step at a time, just move, move. Pressed hard against the sun-warmed moat wall, she moved one step at a time, up toward the tourists. A couple looked down at her from the wooden bridge, their expressions masked by chrome

223

sunglasses. They turned away. She looked down through her yellow hair pasted across her face. He was in the clearing below looking up at her ! Oh, God. She had no more to give. A step, he seemed to move synchronized with her, a step, his step. Kaarin couldn't move any faster. She wanted to stop, just sit down. Cold water. All she wanted: cold water and rest. Cold anything!

How? She was on the stairway. He had just looked at it a minute ago. How had he missed her? He took a breath. Get her before she reached the top, still time. Do it. She slipped, wasn't moving. He moved quickly, his last reserves committed, along the path knocking leaves, branches out of his way, trampling purple flowers, crushing a bunch of stiff green plants, their sharp points gouged painfully into his ankle. She was moving again, a step slowly at a time. He could still get her, taking the stairs two at a time. He lumbered to the bottom of the stone stairway.

A step, another, another, Kaarin looked up over her shoulder. So many, too many to the top. He had burst out of the mass of green growth. How could he still run? She had nothing left. Another, a step, another. Her step, his, hers. He was at the foot, looking up at her through grayish sunglasses, grimacing, his heavy jaws clenched. Disgust appeared on his florid, sweat polished face.

She backed up, pressed against the moat wall. He wasn't moving. Why? She glanced out at the lush gardens below her, then back. He had moved up several steps! How? When? She felt growing paralysis in her legs and thighs. She thought of screaming, but couldn't get any sound past the constriction of her throat muscles. A short distance, only a few steps more. He looked up at her again. He seemed stopped, but she wasn't sure any more what was real.

The top! A fast look back down. He was still there, his mouth opened as though to speak. As she turned, a black hand grasped her shoulder! Her knees sagged.

"Hey, Kaarin, what's going down?" Sugar asked.

She looked up into Sugar's smiling, quizzical face. "Oh, God," she moaned and fell across his arms.

"You look like you just fought a war, lady. C'mon, Serreta's got the goods." Sugar looked past Kaarin down the steps. Kaarin saw his smile vanish. "Let's move, White Lady," he said, as he grasped her shoulders.

As he leaned against the sun warmed moat wall, he saw some people stop on the wooden bridge to look down. No chance. Quit it. Get the mark. He stopped, watching her stagger backwards, then, God damn it all! The mark

225

himself appeared at her side, supporting her, then drew the spook back. Their eyes met, as they had over DiMarco's still warm body in the church ruins. Everything blown! The whole damn thing! He turned, going jerkily down the stairway, suddenly stiff, awkward, and tired. That yellow-haired spook was bad, bad luck. Set it up professionally and she queers it just by being there. Something uncanny, weird about her. Sommers'll shit. He shambled back toward the path to retrieve the camera. No leavings, ever.

***

"Good God, Kaarin! What's happened?" Serreta stood, her smile of welcome faded as Sugar and Kaarin slowly approached. Tourists watched them passing, one young man with very close concern, others with mixed embarrassment. As Kaarin walked with difficulty, she stumbled against Sugar's body.

"Sugar?" Serreta asked. His somber face frightened her.

"A minute, Baby, a minute." He helped Kaarin to the bench at the picnic table. "Okay, White Lady, what do you need first?"

"Water, anything cold to drink, please." Her hoarse croaking voice shook her, her throat filled with wet wool. "And a bath," she managed, with a smile that barely bent her lips.

226

"Cold Chablis okay?" Serreta asked.

She nodded. Anything, anything. Her hand shook, spilling some of the wine across the picnic table. It was good, so good. She couldn't stop, draining the glass dry with long swallows. A deep breath, then she pushed the glass toward Serreta who filled it again. Kaarin drank half and stopped, her consuming thirst momentarily in check. She suddenly choked, sobbing deep gutted whimpers, then regained control. Curious tourists looked away when her eyes caught theirs. He wasn't in sight. She scanned desperately the other way.

"I was attacked again by one of the two men from last night," Kaarin started to explain, finding she had to finish the cold clear wine before continuing. She shook her head when Serreta offered to refill. Her head was starting to float dizzily.

Sugar sat silently at the end of the table, watching.

"My God, Kaarin! Are you really all right?" Serreta reached out to take her hands between her own.

Kaarin nodded, explaining between long breaths as she felt her body beginning to recover. "It was so, so close … but the warning sense didn't trigger until I was looking directly at him. Why? I don't understand. And under the bush, when I was hiding … I didn't know what to do. Something took over … took over my mind. I was too tired, scared, to fight it … I would still be shaking under that bush if it hadn't led me out. I … I actually … I think I actually *saw* that man" – she turned to Sugar. "I *saw* him, Sugar, *after* he was out of sight. Oh, Lord, what's happening to me?" She sobbed, caught herself, then couldn't hold back the tears, letting her head slump across her arms on the table. Serreta's gentle hands felt reassuring as she stroked her head and brushed her wet hair away from her face.

"Easy, Kaarin, nothing's going to happen now. Sugar, I think Kaarin should get back to her hotel. We can find another time to talk."

"Yeah, Babe, you're right. There was a couple of cabs in the parking lot. We can get one of them." Sugar frowned. As he stood he slowly looked around.

"Sugar?"

He nodded. "Yeah, the same."

"Oh, no, no." Her flawless face tightened. "What? "

"Talk about it later, Babe. Let's get Kaarin out of here. Can you handle the goods? I'll help Kaarin.

***

The wind in the open taxi window even at the Bermuda speed limit of twenty, was intoxicating, her tangled hair thrown back from her face. Serreta's arm was around her. Her tears had dried, but Kaarin felt empty,

228

exhausted and helpless. Sugar's sudden look of fear when she said the warning sense had failed haunted her.

Kaarin declined Sugar's offer to help her to her room. His smile appeared forced, something weighed on him. Serreta was silent, her face frozen in thought.

"Got some thoughts … maybe you've thought along those lines yourself … but I see some patterns in your visions. But we can talk later. Call when you're ready. Just get rest, White Lady, then call the police."

Mario raised his eyebrows when she passed the bell captain stand. "All right, Miss Larsson? Need help?" he asked.

Kaarin shook her head. "I'll make it. Accident at Fort Hamilton. My fault, fell down some stairs. A bath'll take care of everything. Thanks." She felt a piece of paper pressed into her hand. Her nod was brief.

Thankfully the elevator was empty. To be away from curious eyes. Dizziness swept again through her, emotional exhaustion pressed down. Kaarin braced herself against the elevator corner, her eyes closed, gripping the hand rails. When the elevator doors slid silently open at her floor, her step was erratic. The opening between the doors seemed unusually narrow. Her sore bare feet sank into the soft hall carpet. Light-headed, Kaarin walked unsteadily to her door. She saw a cleaning woman watch her closely.

Bath or police first? Kaarin called Keith Haggard. 247- 0…0… Her mind was wet sand.

Haggard listened without interruption, then asked: "Was the black with the broken nose there as well?"

"No, I didn't see him."

"We'll investigate the area immediately. Keep your door dead-bolted and chained. There will be guards in the hall. Rest. I will call you at six, after I get more input. Perhaps a quiet dinner?"

She agreed.

Haggard hung up and frowned. Fox had somehow missed the whole thing. Damnit to hell, she might be dead now! Somebody must have seen something. "Get Fox in here," he ordered.

16

Well, how could he have known? Sky clad and still moist from her bath, Kaarin stood with her hands on her bare hips and slowly rotated. Only two possible sources: the police and the Alberts knew she would be at Fort Hamilton at that time. And neither. *No!* Wait. *No one knew* the exact time she would be there because *she didn't*. And she didn't know herself that she would be in the brig. She didn't even know it existed until she was *inside it*. It had been a simple terrible coincidence. So the white killer was there for someone else and had been idling away time waiting, just as she had been. The fort's dark underground had drawn them both, drawn them together, both wanting to stay away from people until their time. Faced with the same circumstance, their thinking had coincided. The nexus sent a chilling wave through her body. Kaarin shuddered, clinching her fists. Who was he after then, if not her? But it confirmed that the first attack was no attempted mugging. She turned back from the balcony. Morgan, Sommers or Kane, or some combination, apparently wanted her dead, though she had not known any of them even a few days ago.

Kaarin went still. What did they think she really

was?

***

Keith Haggard had unusual trouble with the winding narrow coral-walled portions of South Shore Road. He had already slowed to just over ten miles-per-hour. He couldn't keep his eyes from Kaarin. Her face had become a delicate jade carving in the green instrument lighting. Her strangeness, so close yet beyond his understanding. What was she? He slowed a little more, joining Middle Road, turning right heading toward Somerset Village. Hannah Jack's little pub was just outside the village, almost on the beach, far away from Fort Hamilton.

He slowed further to cross Somerset Bridge. At twenty-two inches, he pointed out, it was the world's smallest drawbridge, used to allow the masts of sailboats to pass through to the sea beyond. Kaarin only nodded. Haggard started to describe it, but stopped. He didn't want to sound like a rote travelogue. Names, facts only get in the way. Bermuda was a unique feeling. He didn't want to interfere in Kaarin's quiet absorption of that feeling. Low darkened blunt hills paralleled them on both sides.

"What fort is that up there, Keith?" she asked, twisting to look back.

"Scaur. Nice place for a picnic, for reading a book.

232

Not a really heavy tourist place." Pressure built rapidly as her sheer blouse slipped down from her shoulder.

Kaarin suddenly turned back toward him. "Keith! Go right, quick! To the other side! Quick! Quick!" She shivered violently. "Quick, the other side!" she cried. She held up her hands as if to ward off an attack.

Haggard started, looked over at Kaarin, her instant transition from romantic languor to fierce intensity. Upright, her whole being focused on something. The other side of the road? A car coming around the rocky curve ahead couldn't pick up their lights in time, even at Bermuda speeds. He felt her hand, icy dry, grip his wrist tightly, her face transformed in the eerie stillness to -- he twisted the wheel sharply right, veering across the narrow lane until metal grated against coarse volcanic stone.

It was on them, through their headlights and gone, its dark shape smudged against the night. No headlights, the American side of the road, crazy, deadly. Haggard accelerated back to the left side. He caught a glimpse of red tail-lights flash on and swerve to the left. The driver, whoever the idiot was, had been shocked into what he was risking. As other headlights were now creeping up behind them, Haggard accelerated gently. Too tight to turn to pursue. No identification. He could only hope the fool had been scared enough to respond.

He looked over at Kaarin, slumped forward, her face in her hands, yellow hair highlighted with green glow. Her breathing was deep and slow. "Kaarin, are you all right?" She raised her head to look at him, her fingers still covering her mouth. "Okay?" he asked again.

Kaarin nodded slowly. "Close, so close." She said quietly.

"Yes, very close. You saved us both." He felt her fingers, warm and soft, touch his hand.

"Thanks … thanks for trusting me," she whispered.

Haggard nodded, but what had he trusted?

17

Braced by a tripod of rock and driftwood, Hannah Jack's pub sign was lighted by a single soft bulb. Neon lights are forbidden on Bermuda. A squared wooden arch stood oddly near the sign, its sharply uplifted curves and careful symmetric style mismatched with the small squat building behind it. Strangely positioned rectangular windows were outlined by wavering interior lights. A neatly bordered pulverized white coral path led under the arch to an open doorway faintly lighted by two gas-fired wooden sconces.

"Good evening, Mr. Haggard. Good evening, Ma'am," said a woman dimly outlined inside the doorway. Her voice was dense, rough.

"Hannah, this is Miss Kaarin Larsson. From the U.S."

"Miss Larsson, welcome to Hannah Jack's. Please follow me to your places. You are expected."

Their places were on a raised platform of broad crosscut planks round-pegged into heavy rough-hewn squared timbers, partially concealed by loose hangings of strung tiny seashells. Their chairs, also of thick planking but with smooth leather padding, were a few inches higher than normal, her toes barely touching the wide boards but which allowed easy viewing through a raised wide but very narrow window. Rich cedar permeated everything.

"Anything to start? Soft Rum, perhaps?" Hannah asked.

"Soft Rum?" Kaarin asked.

"A family recipe, Miss Larsson. Try it. If you don't care for it, I'll bring something else." Hannah's off-center smile displayed a row of blunt darkened teeth. Her smile broadened when Kaarin nodded. "Good. I'll leave the meal lists and return in a moment."

Haggard separated the two long pieces of heavy parchment, handing one to Kaarin. She couldn't recognize anything on the hand-written menu. "Keith, please order for me," she said.

Hannah suddenly, soundlessly, reappeared with a filled crystal ewer and two long-stemmed tulip glasses. She waited, smiling off-center, as Kaarin sipped the cool transparent liquid.

"Soft. That's a perfect description. I like it, Hannah." She sipped again, feeling the coolness turn warm in her throat.

"Now Mr. Haggard, don't take unfair advantage of this beautiful woman after she's enjoyed Hannah's Soft Rum."

'Yes, Ma'am," Haggard responded.

Hannah started to turn away, then turned back, ignoring her name being called from behind the seashell hangings. "Were you the woman on TV who drove blindfolded yesterday?" she asked.

Kaarin nodded.

"My cousin did something like that, but not in a car with all those cameras and crowds."

"What did she do?" Kaarin asked.

"She, Maedean … you could cover her eyes with anything and she could still see. When Maedean got older she had to wear glasses, except when she had her eyes wrapped. She said she could see better without her eyes. Maedean was a witch. Are you a witch?"

Haggard sat up. "Hannah!"

Kaarin quickly smiled. "No, Keith. It's not the first time I've been asked. No, Hannah, I'm not a witch. At least I don't think so." Kaarin looked up steadily into Hannah's glistening solemn eyes. "Is Maedean in Bermuda? I'd like very much to meet her."

Hannah shook her head. "She's dead. For three years. Just died one day. Like she said she would. Just dead." She spoke plainly without emotion. "Got to get to my other customers. Want more time to decide? Mermaid's Breath was prepared special for tonight."

"Tiger shrimp, Hoppin' John and glazed onions …
for both of us," Haggard said.

"Yes, sir. Now don't you let her get hot now."
Hannah moved away, scudding between tables,
occasionally placing a hand on the shoulder or arm of
favored customers.

"Hot?" asked Kaarin, sipping again.

"Drunk," replied Haggard.

Kaarin grinned. "No chance."

"Bermuda has a strong history of witchcraft and the
supernatural; other than that Bermuda Triangle nonsense.
And, of course, Shakespeare's *The Tempest*, in 1611."

"Yes, I know," said Kaarin. "I've had to do a
careful study of witchcraft because some of my clients,
audiences, expect me to know about such things. Actually
witchcraft is just an old pagan nature religion, not very
supernatural."

Haggard said quietly, "There are some people on
these islands who would be very reluctant to accept your
observation."

Kaarin smiled. "I wouldn't doubt that, Keith. Just as
long as they don't audition at the Duchess. I can't afford
more competition right now." She liked his quick smile, his
nearness. She sipped again. "I would, very much, love to
speak with them, sometime."

"Keith, how long has your family been on Bermuda?" Kaarin asked swallowing her last shrimp. They had eaten quietly, their plates now nearly empty.

"Three generations. My grandfather was a policeman, actually he served briefly as police commissioner. Then my father, who was an inspector, and finally me. We all came to the police from the British Royal Marines. Born in the UK, then over here."

"All stamp collectors too?" she asked. She held the tulip glass with the fingertips of both hands. Soft Rum was treacherously smooth. Her legs were beginning to feel disconnected from her body.

"Regrettably no. My grandfather could have gotten some superb deals in his day, but my father was the first in the family."

"What did you do in the Royal Marines?" She smiled. "My turn for questions. How long have you been trying to quit smoking?" She cocked her head to one side, the rim of the glass touching her lips.

"I'm that obvious? Seven days, almost to the hour." Haggard grinned. "Military counter-intelligence work in various places in the world. I can't really be more specific. No heroics. I wasn't a James Bond. And quitting tobacco is my toughest case." His eyes held hers for a moment . . .

"Smultronställe," Kaarin murmured contentedly.

"Smul … I didn't hear what you said."

She dropped her eyes. "Smultronställe … a wild strawberry place. A special, very special place to be shared only with those closest. An expression my mother brought from Sweden. I think Bermuda could become such a place for me."

"I'm glad."

Hannah suddenly reappeared through the seashell hangings. "More Soft Rum? I ask you, Ma'am … I don't trust good-looking men this time of night." She chuckled deep in her chest. Hannah raised an eyebrow when Kaarin shook her head. She picked up the ewer, raised the other eyebrow at Haggard and elbowed through the hangings, leaving them purling behind her.

Haggard's emotions were beginning to be a problem as his eyes returned again to her remarkable form barely concealed by sheer ruffles. Nicotine deprivation and Soft Rum were disconnecting his world. He turned back to Hannah's bananas and black rum sauce. But the question couldn't wait: "Kaarin, what did you see tonight, on the road, that saved us?"

Kaarin swallowed. "It's difficult for me to speak of such things. Even given what I do for a living, to demonstrate the curiosities of the mind, it's difficult, because people react with fear, with incredulity; and sometimes with biting ridicule. I saw the form of something coming on the wrong side of the road. It could only have been another car. I sensed the threat clearly, distinctly. I have learned to trust the feeling completely, and as a result it has grown stronger over the years ... though for some reason I don't understand, I had no warning of the killer this afternoon at the fort. I want you to know I don't understand what this extra sense is ... where it comes from ... and why me?" She hesitated, waiting for his reaction before saying anything further.

"I've read some Stephen King novels," Haggard said, "that have some strange senses, powers described in them. I thought such things were only the fevered inventions of fevered novelists. You're saying such events, happenings, can be real ... real in you?"

"I am afraid of that word reality," she said. "Escaping from that killer this afternoon and last night was real, certainly, and I was scared, panicked beyond words; but there have been other times, alone, in tranquil silence, when I begin to feel even greater terror, when I" – he placed his glasses beside his plate, his eyes held her, questioning – "when I let my mind go out from me. I sometimes feel I can't call it back, that I am forever gone, never to be me again. Then somehow, I'm not sure how, I

241

come back. And I become desperately afraid to let my mind wander free again, to let my imagination roam unbounded." She pursed her lips for a moment, tightly, as if holding in words. "But that was my job, back then, my profession, my love, my life. That is physics as I know it: To wrestle God for His secrets of the universe. As each year passed, I began to experience this more frequently, like a weird recurring fit."

She glanced out at the hooded moon, then continued: "Psychologists, and so-called parapsychologists, had no answers. Even 'experts' that a psychologist friend I had consulted had no answers. Only theories, experiments they wanted to run, Federal grants they thought they could drag from my tormented mind; they had all the time in the world, but I knew I didn't. I couldn't function … any longer. To do my job, theoretical astrophysics, to teach, I had to risk my mind *never* coming back. I couldn't. So I turned to someone named Mentavo, an old nightclub performer, and his mentalism, to follow a different path, to try to keep my mind while I searched . . . to stay … me. I have learned some …" Her voice softened and drifted away.

Haggard knew of her physics background from the FBI report. She had had a standard secret clearance because of a short involvement in an anti-missile project. "Kaarin, I need to be sure that I understand you. You have experienced, and can now experience, almost at will, something like clairvoyance? Actually sense beyond normal physical limits? Beyond what happened tonight on the road?"

Kaarin responded slowly. "Beyond the limen, the threshold, between real ... there's no word I know, except the empty jargon of floundering psychologists. Their jargon makes them sound like lawyers trying to justify a swollen bill, so I just call it what it seems, a warning sense, a seeing, a forepresence. And it changes, strengthens in me like some astral tumor. I don't know where it will end, how I will end, what I could be. So I fight it. I have, as I started to say, learned something about controlling it ... the warning sense, a little; but always, when I pause and look around, it's ... something's always there. So I try not to look. By ignoring it, I seem to keep it reasonably at bay. I say *it*," she smiled wanly, "as if I really know what *it* is."

Haggard lifted his hand as he looked through the hangings. Hannah caught his signal, walked swivel-hipped among the chairs and tables to reach their place, cleared the plates, then vanished again into the murmuring darkness.

"Have your contacts in mentalism helped? Have you found anyone who has experienced what you are experiencing, who could at least tell you what to expect?"

He spoke gently like holding a fragile porcelain doll in his hands.

Kaarin felt comfort in Keith's steady eyes. She shrugged. "Sugar told me he had thought of a direction at least to think. But we never had time to talk today. I was in no condition to talk. But now, it seems, I'm babbling." But it felt good to exorcise the demon again. Her head was feeling pleasantly light, some barriers lowering, a subtle warmth spread throughout her body.

Hannah returned, her off-center smile widened as she picked up the half-filled ewer of Soft Rum. "Neither of you can handle any more of this, if you're going to get home alive. Mr. Haggard, I hold you responsible for this beautiful woman's safety."

Haggard grinned, "She will be carefully watched over, Hannah."

"I know that. I was talking about her safety." Her deep chuckle lingered as she melted through the rippling hangings.

The night air, rich in cedar, was cooling. Kaarin drew her arms across her chest. "I need Sugar's insights. This afternoon, the killer, confused me further."

Haggard pushed his empty glass aside. "In what way? Didn't your warning sense work the same as tonight?"

"No. It didn't work at all. That's what I can't understand. When I feel that icy ichor flowing through me, I have learned that I can trust it but why, why didn't it trigger today at the fort?"

Haggard was silent, reviewing Kaarin's description of the afternoon, Bains' report of the search of the fort, the interviews of tourists and snack bar attendants, the finding of a discarded lens cap near the underground moat entrance, the prints on it too smeared to read. No one remembered seeing a bulky white man with a strong jaw line dressed as Kaarin had described. Nothing at all, like he had simply walked through the brick walls. But how had he known Kaarin would be there and in the brig?

"The warning sense didn't trigger, Kaarin, possibly, because you were not who the attacker was actually looking for. You were not the target. The killer at the fort, based on your description of his reaction, may not have even been looking for you. He may have been, probably was, there for some other reason. Therefore, until he actually saw you, you were not threatened."

So simple. Why couldn't she have seen it? When her eyes had met the killer's, then the warning sense gripped her in its icy paralyzing embrace. Kaarin was stunned. Keith saw so easily, so quickly.

"Keith, I think you're right. On the road tonight, I

245

was, we both were, the target … so it triggered. Yes, yes, of course." She held her breath for a moment, a burden slipping from her mind. She felt dizzily lightheaded. A single step of understanding, but the assurance that what she was experiencing had some underlying sense of reason, even logic to it, even if the whole thing was irrational. The sense of relief mixed with Soft Rum sent giddy waves through her.

***

Coruscating surf ran its fingers across the sand, almost to the low slabs of limestone outlining Hannah Jack's parking area. Kaarin stepped across the slabs to stand on the firm sand of the beach to look out at the rhythmic sea.

"Ely's Harbor," Haggard replied softly to her question.

She stood quietly. Errant shafts of moonlight that reached through a rift in the shifting clouds were almost tangible, touchable. A strange silhouette floated on the horizon. She turned toward Keith Haggard to ask and then return to his car. She didn't resist when he drew her close, gently kissing her upturned mouth, her question unasked and unanswered. When Kaarin could look back, the silhouette was gone but it didn't matter.

She pushed him gently back, moonlight across her,

her eyes half-shadowed. "We should get started," Kaarin said.

Haggard agreed.

***

The Duchess lobby was deserted as Kaarin crossed to the elevators. She had noticed that most of the room lights were dark as they approached the hotel's ornate entrance. She walked quickly, nodded in passing to a bored night bellman in an ill-fitting maroon jacket. Her rum and wind induced lightheadedness had subsided abruptly when Keith, as she left his car, gave her two ruined taupe shoes his men had found in a dark underground alcove at Fort Hamilton. The twenty-five minute drive from Hannah's back to the Duchess had taken over two hours. But seeing the shoes had squelched the evening in an instant. Was the man with the gun waiting for her even now? Where?

18

Kaarin stood motionless for a moment with the door closed behind her, the ruined shoes dangling from her fingers. Then she dropped them at the half-opened closet door.

Obviously the killer must know my name and hotel, the newspaper had that and the television. *My God! He had been at the blindfold drive!* The big guy in the red shirt with the cameras near the microphone. That's why his face was faintly familiar. She stepped out of her shoes, looking for her slippers. Without thinking, she cupped her breasts and rubbed her fingers across her nipples softly. His skin had been so rough, she could still feel his hands squeezing, touching. Ohh, she shook her head as though to clear it, dropped her hands, shaking her fingers as if flicking off water. Self-caressing was not her thing. But he was good, so good, but the whisker-burn still tingled around her mouth; his momentary hesitation when his fingers moved slowly through her hair and touching the ridges there . . .

***

A light rain was starting to fall, forcing Kaarin back into the room from the balcony, her gray silk robe drawn tightly about her. For some reason, it was the Alberts the killer was stalking. They were the only data point common to her two attacks, even if one attack was a coincidence. He certainly hadn't been at the fort as a tourist.

It had been Sugar who had stepped in front of Tony DiMarco in St. Louis, shoving him away after DiMarco had ripped her blouse open, and Serreta who had helped her into the elevator while shielding her from the curious people in the hotel lobby. DiMarco had been drunk and uncontrollable, gave Sugar a rough time, until Sugar had punched him, a hard uppercut to the side of DiMarco's jaw, risking his valuable fingers to help her. To break even one finger or knuckle would have seriously jeopardized Black Magic's income. But after St. Louis, there had been only postcards between them and sharing quick coffees in airport snackbars as she had drawn down her savings pursuing Mentavo's list. She did what shows could be arranged on short notice, usually late shows in comedy clubs where nothing was very funny. The Alberts had always been so busy rushing from one gig to the next, Sugar's wide cocky smile, while she had to claw for shows.

With her head slightly back, her eyes half-closed, her imagination carefully curbed, Kaarin stood with her hands on her hips, slowly rotating, as she sorted through each event since Machinegun Morgan's first phone call, looking first for obvious links, then secondary, to seek that constant key Jacob Mortmann had demanded in her research work. What are the real questions that need to be answered? She stopped. Untying her robe as she walked to the nightstand, she reached for the phone. Long distance information would have Dieter's fax number and Morgan's, throw on something to go down to the Duchess' communications center in the lobby; then to bed. If Dieter could give her answers, then dinner for sure, two dinners, since he just might be saving her life. And Morgan, well, maybe him too. Any answers she would share with Keith, but darn it, she would not be a damsel in distress clinging to anyone for protection.

***

Kaarin had pushed his hand away only after a lingering moment. When he returned, she didn't hinder his exploration, nor he hers. She buried her smile and warm cheeks into the pillow. Keith didn't need a second invitation. He had scarcely needed a first. Kaarin rolled back, kicked the sheets aside, her hands touching, moving over her body in poor imitation of his. She hadn't realized she'd gotten so incredibly horny. Her dream-generated yearning was deflated by a sharp metallic ringing. Her reverie evaporated. 10:34 am on the digital clock next to the insistent telephone. Her show was only eight and a half hours away. Kaarin forced her mind away from Keith as

250

she stretched for the phone well into its third ring.

"Good morning, Miss Larsson. This is John Nathaniel."

The name didn't immediately register amid the rapidly dissipating clouds of sleepy ecstasy. Pink Sands.

"Yes, Mr. Nathaniel," Kaarin said, as he started to speak again. "I'm a little slow this morning."

"I hope my call isn't inopportune," he said gravely.

"No, no, that's perfectly all right. What can I do for you?" Her mind was finally clear and functioning.

"Perhaps you can help me. The Alberts didn't appear last night for their midnight show. They left the Pink Sands sometime after the ten-thirty show without explanation. It produced some embarrassing moments at twelve, but I am more concerned about their welfare. Perhaps you could help explain their disappearance?" he asked.

Kaarin went rigid. "I'm sorry Mr. Nathaniel, I have no explanation. The last I saw Sugar and Serreta was early yesterday afternoon." A caress of fear touched her.

"I see," said Nathaniel softly. He hesitated for a moment. "Sugar seemed very nervous at the nine o'clock show. He and Serreta arrived very late, less than half-an-hour before show time. Normally they would be at least an hour preparing for the first show. To get their heads

251

warmed up, Serreta explained once to me. Sugar isn't at all nervous before a show customarily. Consequently, I knew something was certainly disturbing them both, but they chose not to confide in me. I had hoped they showed more confidence in you. They speak so highly of you as a performer and as a person." He paused. Before Kaarin could respond, Nathaniel continued. "The show at nine was very poor, their timing was off badly. Even Serreta's floating ball routine was clumsy. She dropped the ball, and, well, everything went badly. I had succeeded in convincing a prominent booking agent from the U.K. to break his vacation to come see their act. It was very unfortunate. Very." His quiet voice hardened for an instant.

Kaarin groaned, visualizing Serreta's loss of image, her anguish.

Nathaniel said, "Yes. Serreta was humiliated. But she seemed recovered for the ten-thirty. Sugar also seemed more in control. The show was more like what I know they can do, but sadly, Miss Larsson, the agent had already left."

"Oh, no." What damnable luck!

"Then they simply disappeared. Their birds were gone as well. Only their strange boxes and gear were in their dressing room. I am seriously concerned, Miss Larsson. I believe the police should be notified. Inspector Haggard has spoken to me recently."

"I agree. Keith should know as soon as possible. I wish I could help. I don't know where to start looking for them. I don't understand what is happening."

"Then I will call the inspector immediately. Thank you for your concern. I'm sure the inspector will be contacting you."

Kaarin sat for a moment after hanging up. Sugar and Serreta. They would never run out on a show. Something must be radically wrong. She started to get up, to dress, to get into the day as rapidly as possible but the phone rang again. She sat back.

"Kaarin. Marc Kane. Lunch? Remember?"

Kaarin responded cautiously. Lunch? When had she committed to lunch? "I'm sorry, Marc I just woke up. I'm slow this morning."

"That's okay. I'll give you time. Heard you came in pretty torn-up yesterday afternoon. Trouble? You okay for tonight?"

"No trouble. Just fell down some steps at Fort Hamilton. A few scrapes but they don't show. I'll be ready for tonight." Darn it! She hadn't committed to anything. She had only suggested "maybe later". He moved in like a bulldozer, assuming, forcing, but he was a key to the letter she needed, for a reference for her still developing booking brochure. A quick lunch, at the hotel only, then back to the

253

room for final prep; and a short walk on the beach later when the sun was lower. But the Alberts?

"Marc, lunch would be fine but it would have to be at the Duchess. I need preparation time." And to be available for any answers to her faxes.

He sounded disappointed. She was glad. "I heard of a unique place on the beach. Thought we might go there. Away from tourists. I'm getting a little cabin fever with these workshops at the hotel. How about it? Place is called Hannah Jack's, down in Somerset. Sounds typical Bermuda."

Kaarin smiled. She could agree. No. She couldn't face Hannah for lunch with another man. She wanted to keep Hannah's in the moonlight, not the sun. And the memory that Kane brought to mind still bothered her. Keep it short. "No, Marc, I've got to stay close to home. How about at the Rum n'Onions by the pool, at twelve?

Kane reluctantly agreed.

Kaarin began to stand when the phone rang yet again. 11:03 and she was still naked as Psyche on the rock.

"Kaarin, this is Keith. John Nathaniel just called about the Alberts. It looks like something is starting to break. I want you to stay at the Duchess all day … where my people can be around you." She could almost hear him smile. "Good morning."

"I will be at the hotel all day. I am having lunch with one of the conference organizers and . . ."

"Which one?" he interrupted. His voice was smooth, professional. Wouldn't he even hint at last night?

"Kane. Marc Kane."

"The American. All right. I've started a search for the Alberts. I'll call when we find something. I have an uneasy feeling about what's starting to happen." His voice was edged, hard.

"Yes. But it must be serious. Sugar and Serreta would never miss a show." Won't he say anything? Well, darn it, she wouldn't either.

"Keep your warning sense turned up. Sgt. Bain can get me if something comes up, or the Alberts call you."

"Good," she responded mechanically.

"Kaarin .... I can't get you out of my mind. The islands were the most beautiful I've ever seen them this morning. Be careful." He hung up.

She was elated but stared at the dead phone. Now she couldn't say anything anyway.

Kaarin stood, half-expecting the phone again as she started for the bathroom. In passing she touched the crumpled ruffled blouse. Next time. She smiled. Next time.

A sudden one-two-three knock at the door. Mario. Kaarin wrapped her robe over her nakedness, scuffling slippers on as she walked.

"Your brunch, Miss Larsson," Mario said pushing a cart through the opened door without waiting. Coffee, pastries, a fruit bowl, and orange juice. "Please sign here," he said, grinning. "You'll find some special bon-bons with the pastry. Good morning." He strode back across the room, closed the door, still grinning.

Kaarin's initial protest, that she hadn't ordered anything, died unspoken. Mario's and Will's notes were under the silver pastry plate. A glance -- oh – 11:22. Kane. She scanned the material rapidly. Dieter's comment about horny bankers in the sun was proving accurate, more like rabbits. Well, maybe suggest one liaison, to add spice if needed. Using any more could get her arrested. Sommers overheard on his cellphone with someone named McGraw. "Finish it tonight and get out" was all that Will had written. Sommers had been angry and nervous, tapping his fingers hard against the wall, Will had noted. Ellis Whitney, an investment banker from Colorado, was planning to challenge her. Bragged over drinks to his wife and another woman. Claimed he could stop any mindreader cold. He was an amateur magician and knew all the angles. Kaarin smiled -- good. Kane. *Need to remember the umbrella.* She etched that memory into her mind. The hotel had several big black ones stacked near the bell captain's desk.

256

Mario had listed other bits, but no time. Review her setup after lunch. She just might entertain and scare them, scare them good. But the Alberts, her heart went cold -- the police would certainly find them, keep them safe. They had to.

***

Marc Kane brightened, smiled boyishly as he pulled a chair back for her. Kaarin wore close fitting gray silk. Her wardrobe was running thin; in rags actually. The slightly humid air in the warm sunlit restaurant was reminiscent of the flowered moat at Fort Hamilton.

"Hello," he said. "You look really great."

Kaarin smiled. "Thank you. I'm sorry, insisting on lunch here when there's so much to see on Bermuda, but I must be ready for tonight. I hope you'll forgive me."

Kane tossed a hand in the air. "Forgiven," he grinned.

"Perrier with a slice of lime," she said to the waiter at her elbow.

"Don't drink on working days, huh," he said. "Gin and tonic." Then he added, "Make it with Plymouth, if you have it."

She edged back in her chair as he leaned forward, his massive shoulders almost surrounding her. The waiter disappeared behind a royal palm rising up through the glass roof. No one was in the pool, its water motionless.

"I've had enough rum here to last me until next Christmas," he said. "I'd go for a straight Jack Daniels now to wash out the taste ... but people'd probably think I'm an alcoholic."

"How's the conference going? Everyone getting educated and sunburned enough to satisfy the IRS?"

When he shrugged the whole room seemed to move. "Yeah, it's a good legitimate write-off. Some interesting deals have gone down." He paused, laughed. "Almost said something I shouldn't." Kaarin remembered Mario's notes. "Your bit yesterday and the way you handled Chet went over very well. He likes to f. . .screw things up. Some people have asked if you would autograph your memory book for them?"

"Glad to, any time. After the show tonight, perhaps."

"Good. You really know this stuff," he stated, his head cocked. "Memory and mindreading?"

She nodded as she leaned back to allow her Perrier to be poured. Several people were looking over at her from behind greenery, their eyes darting away when Kaarin made contact. Afraid she might poke around in their minds?

"Kaarin, that card stuff you did. Was that legit? I

258

mean," he said quickly, "you, someone, can memorize a pack that fast?"

She sipped the strong, bubbling flavor of the French water. She nodded. "Yes, anyone can do it. Card counters do it all the time in Las Vegas, Macau, and Monaco."

"You ever perform at those places?"

"No. Not yet. I'm not sure my material would go over. I work a little slow. I like to enjoy my audiences."

"Would you like to? I've worked some deals with the right clients in all those places. Can get you in, anywhere."

"My agent has me booked pretty well, Marc. But thank you. If my show and lecture are satisfactory, I would appreciate a letter from you and Roland Sommers saying so. It would help build my credibility."

"No sweat. Consider it done."

"One thing, Marc, if you could for tonight. Would you bring a big black umbrella?"

"A what? You going to do a rain dance?"

"No. But it could be a most interesting moment in your life."

"Hey, consider it done. I can't wait." He looked up. Their waiter had reappeared. "Yeah. What would you like?"

She heard herself say, "The seafood salad and

another Perrier." She watched herself look at red, tanned, and black and white humanity settling into white iron chairs, shifting tables, so absorbed in themselves. Yet, what was happening – to the Alberts – to her mind? How could she sit here talking meaningless nonsense?

"Tell me about your football experience. You planning to turn pro?" He grinned carelessly.

"Not yet. I'm still protecting my amateur status." Had she said that? What about – that waiter behind the trees – she blinked – what waiter? There were only thick clusters of tall bamboo stretching up toward the glass dome.

"No kidding … what kind of football did you play? Football's a passion with me."

"You look it. Just touch" – a waiter carrying a large pitcher of green drinks came out from behind the bamboo – "Just touch."

Kane frowned slightly. "Ever get hurt?" he asked, glancing over his shoulder, where she seemed to be looking. He poured more tonic into his gin.

"Just touch. Back in school… no time now." Her voice drifted. The waiter avoided a crowded table, with several shuffling and shifting white wrought-iron chairs. Like a gypsy dancer, he swung his hips clear of the customers, the tray held its position gyroscopically.

Something. Where was her mind?

"Ever get hurt?" he repeated.

She came back to their conversation. "Both arms and a collarbone were broken, and a shoulder dislocated." He sat up. "But the great thing," she said wryly, "was that it wasn't all in the same game." She was coming loose inside.

He laughed, a hard dieseling sound that squelched conversation for a radius of about three tables.

Kaarin edged back away from the table, tensed her legs and rose slightly from her chair. Kane stopped laughing, his mouth open. Others looked over at her. She didn't know what they saw.

"Are you okay?" he asked.

WHAT'S COMING? WHAT'S HAPPENING TO ME? I'M ME. ME. BUT WHAT AM I?

"Okay?" Kane asked, again.

His smile fixed mechanically, the waiter moved smoothly among the thickening lunch crowd, his loaded tray at his fingertips, poised high above, avoided the people like it had a life of its own. His eyes focused on his customers, table 36 between the potted birds-of-paradise. Stunning blonde with the big jock off to the side. Great pair of knockers under that gray silk. He looked back at 36. Oh, shit!

Kaarin suddenly stood and jerked back her chair.

261

She stepped two, three steps back when a woman, her vision blocked by a floppy sun hat, tripped the waiter as he moved to avoid a busing station. He reached, grabbed at the sliding pitcher of marqueritas, missed. The pitcher smashed across the wrought iron table in front of Marc Kane, cold green liquid sprayed up over him, and where Kaarin's chair had been.

A few drops reached her, lime spume staining her dress. She had been in no danger, but she had *known* something was coming. Her panic rose. What else would she see if she looked in their faces?

Kane, soaked from chest to knees, bellowed angrily at the waiter down on his back frantically scrambling to regain his feet. The floppy-hatted woman rapidly backed away, disappeared into the gathering, laughing crowd. Kane mopped himself hurriedly with a handful of napkins. He looked over at Kaarin's terrified eyes, strangely bright, like no human eyes he had ever seen.

Kaarin turned to push between two matronly women in shorts, shouldered past a short laughing man with a blue nametag, thrust away a chair with each hand – and ran! Away from faces she feared to look into – to see, to feel something coming, to run, to hide behind locked doors, her eyes shut, her hands over her ears, down in a corner, hard walls at her back! She ran, ran lunging between closing elevator doors. Kaarin swallowed, breathing hard, tightly gripped the brass railings, her shoulders pressed into the corner, her eyes closed, the empty elevator shut out the world, the faces; a momentary bump, then the elevator began to rise. Her eyes opened, her mind began to slow. Would Kane remember the black umbrella?

19

"Chief Inspector Nusam in?" Haggard asked. It was his first visit at the Hamilton Police Station in almost a month. He could readily recall the former four-floor Hamilton Station that had no elevator. With the detective offices on the fourth floor, no detective working then at Hamilton ever had a weight problem climbing those stairs every day. But the new station was in a seven level building with elevators.

"Yes, sir. Waiting for you in his office. Mr. Drummond from the states is with him. Drugs."

Two men looked up as Haggard entered. One, darkly tanned and balding, behind a metal desk in the white uniform shirt of a police inspector, the other, pudgy with sharp dark eyes and sunburned arms, slumped in a wooden chair, dressed casually in stone-washed jeans and a striped sport shirt, its buttoned-down collar unbuttoned at the tips and open. The spectacular sweep of busy Hamilton Harbor filled the windows.

"The Alberts' flat was empty, Keith. Beds were not slept in. Some strange stuff there," said Barry Nusam. "You know Brian Drummond, DEA, I believe."

Haggard nodded to Drummond. "Magicians. I

would expect that."

"Expect this?" Drummond put a small carved green box with black oriental markings on all sides on Nusam's desk.

"What's this? Looks like a conjurer's box for a rabbit." Haggard picked it up with both hands, rotating it, felt the satin smoothness of the finish. It was yellowed from years of nightclub cigarette smoke.

"Doves, actually," said Drummond. "An Okito vanishing dove box. A beautifully made piece of apparatus about 50-60 years old. Worth, I'm told, about a thousand dollars."

"So?" Haggard replaced it on the desk.

Nusam opened two small doors in the front of the box and slanted it back toward Haggard. The secret compartment in the top was open.

"It was used to transport cocaine as well as vanish doves," said Nusam. "There was white powder residue in the cracks of the secret compartment that has tested as coke."

Haggard grimaced. "Why wasn't I notified sooner?" he said coldly.

"Now is as soon as soon can be, Inspector," said Drummond. "We've been following some couriers to establish connections and ran across the Alberts more by accident. The magic apparatus was an obvious smuggling possibility. I was with some of your patrol car people when they were sent to the Alberts' apartment."

Haggard nodded slowly. "We need to check our '42nd Street' friends out on St. Monica's Road to follow-up on any possible local activity by the Alberts." St. Monica Road was a local drug bazaar – at times -- and generally peaceful, but that had been changing over the past several months with the increased aggressiveness of the four or five strongest gangs.

"Right," said Nusam. "We are on it. I will let you know immediately I get anything." He snapped the doors shut on the Okito box and slid it to one side. "How's that smashing blonde mindreader holding up? She's got plenty, what with killers and memory drives and whatnot on her mind. She looks much too young to be in the middle of all this."

Haggard was looking at the twisted black designs carved deeply into the green dove box. The care and touch of an extraordinary craftsman, yet, the real craftsmanship, the real workings were hidden, never intended to be seen. Hannah's. The night made more exotic by Kaarin's astonishing crystal beauty, the touch of her erect nipples against his hands . . .

"She's remarkable," Haggard said. "She has plenty

of nerve, but where she places in what's going on, I just don't know yet. This cocaine is another nasty element."

"Anyone who can travel widely, legitimately, must be suspected if they match distribution patterns. Professional entertainers, particularly." Drummond slowly got to his feet and stretched his arms toward the ceiling. "The DiMarco killing is your bailiwick. Thanks for your help over the past days, Haggard. Keep me on the list for any data from your '42nd Street' drug bazaar." He picked up a bulging Black Seal Rum plastic bag. "My tourist disguise. Not exactly Lon Chaney, but … cocaine, that damn stinking poison."

***

The police code-a-phone number is 295-1140. A recorded man's voice, recently changed from a very bored woman's voice, quietly encourages the caller to give confidential information that might be of interest to police or other government authorities, "to help make Bermuda a safe place for all". The phone was sometimes answered by a live constable, but often it was just the recording. It was Constable Ermaline Johnson's morning duty to listen to the recorded calls from the previous day then summarize the material in a daily report that went up to C.I.D., Special Branch, and Press Liaison Officer. They didn't have to hear the obscenities, which were usually brief attacks on the policies of whatever party controlled the Government, and sometimes were even humorous and inventive. The more crude, the briefer the call, apparently the caller quickly exhausting his limited imagination; though there were times she felt like responding in kind. She had come to recognize some voices who seemed to use 1140 as therapy. If it did something for them, why not? A means of yelling at the government, at the world, but only a lowly newly commissioned constable ever actually heard them. Obscenities never appeared in her reports, only descriptions as "severely distressed" or "agitated". But it was at least brief. It was the other, the rest of it that stretched her patience. She had scored the highest ever for a woman in shooting the police regulation .38 revolver, won a medal, and had drawn only fink duty.

There was no time limit on a code-a-phone caller. Every time Ermaline had recommended a one or two minute limit, it had been abruptly turned down. Better to err the other way, then to risk cutting off a vital message. But what in hell, she thought, was vital about finking on your neighbors, complaining about yelling at nights, running a car without a muffler, who's running into who's back door when the man is gone, why doesn't the government do this or that? They would carry on for several minutes, then hang up without giving a name or address. The pattern was so familiar that the husky feminine voice immediately stood out.

"Ah-h, whoever you are," it said, followed by a long pause. "Blue house on Tankfield Road, down from the Ice Queen. Something's funny. Man and a woman. Don't belong here. Don't belong *at all*. She was wearing some kind of silvery stuff on her face. Didn't look like she had any clothes on. Were sneaking in last night, like thieves. Wasn't sure if I should do anything." Silence.

Ermaline could hear her breathing close to the phone. Silence, then the connection was broken. Ermaline immediately picked up her phone to dial the C.I.D. Duty Officer. Her written report may be too late for whatever was going on.

***

Barry Nusam stood with Keith Haggard at the elevator. "Watching Kaarin Larsson's show tonight, Keith? Your duty naturally. Would be mine. Assuming she's an innocent victim."

Haggard looked over sharply at Nusam, then shook his head. "No. She is safest in front of an audience ... with some of my people watching undercover."

"Probably every maid, waiter and bell boy at the Duchess knows who the police are. Bermuda's a small place."

"Good. That will keep people at a distance. Her attackers weren't in CRO, so they may not be locals who could spot police."

"Inspector Nusam, Haggard!" A detective beckoned from his office. "Sgt. Bain is on the phone!"

Haggard was across the corridor in two strides. "Bain, Haggard."

"Found Sugar Alberts. In Tankfield Road, Paget. Code-a-phone report. Parrish constable checked it out. Socko is on the way."

Socko! Haggard stiffened. "What is it?"

"I talked to Constable Farrow. He is badly shaken. Reported a shooting. Said a man was shot in the head with an elephant gun. Nothing left. Never seen anything like it. Puked all over his uniform. First time since being on the force he couldn't hold it. Pieces of brain all over the room."

"Serreta Alberts?" Haggard demanded.

"No sign. No sounds last night, apparently. Operations starting house-to-house interviews. I'm leaving now."

"Have Penniston stay with the body to King Edward Hospital. Who owns the house?"

"Apparently unoccupied. Crowley's starting on real estate records." Oliver Bain coughed. "Pieces of brain on

270

the walls? God, Inspector, what is going on?"

20

Serreta had wiped the silver from her face and shaken her hair loose from the sorceress arrangement. A green sweater and long pants covered her costume. The toe and heel of her silver shoes, laced up her calves, were still visible. Five seconds, Sugar had said. Babe, only five lousy seconds between us and breathing free. But he hadn't heard the silenced shot. He had followed DiMarco, seen him standing there in the graveyard, turning slowly toward him. Sugar had fired. The little .32 sounded like a cannon, he had said. Then Sugar had seen him, the tourist with the red face and belly full of cameras and the big gun taped up in black tape, and a water bottle with the bottom blown out. Babe, I ran, but he saw me. I don't know who he was, but he's after me. Five lousy seconds! If I had just waited, I would have seen Tony had half his head blown away. But when I saw that asshole, I had to kill him, to get him off us, away from you. No more blackmail, no more threats about coke and jail.

Sugar had sobbed. The first time Serreta had ever seen him cry. The cool confident tall man had sobbed. I messed us up, he had cried, messed us up for good.

At the Tankfield house he had heard them coming.

272

But there was no gun, the .32 had gone into the ocean. Ten years is too long to play with, he had said. Run, Babe. I'll hold them up. Get to Kaarin. She can help. She's got something special in that head of hers. Run, Babe, run.

She had, out into the darkness, out the back of the Tankfield house, as sounds came from the front. Sugar said it was a safe house, guaranteed by the man on St. Monica's Road. Man who had gotten him the .32 for almost all the money they had.

No answer in Kaarin's room. The pay-phone near the bus-stop felt exposed, like tying her out as bait for a tiger. Serreta shifted, looked behind, then shifted again. "Miss Larsson has gone out for the evening, I believe," the desk clerk at the Duchess said helpfully. "Her key was left. No, I don't know where, but I couldn't release that information even if I knew. I'm sure you understand, Ma'am

She was still, in the darkness, in the shadows away from the light at the green and white pole marking the bus-stop. No cars passed. She had no watch. Sugar had said he would look for her at the Duchess with Kaarin. But the killer was after Kaarin, too. Sugar had said he was the one who was after Kaarin at Fort Hamilton. Why? Sugar didn't know. No – not the Duchess. They'd find each other, when Sugar got away, but not the Duchess, to bring the killers down on Kaarin.

A bus? Two headlights anyway. They were slowing. She edged toward the boundary between light and dark. Yes. A bus -- it was stopping. Serreta gulped some air and stepped away from the shadows.

"Where to?"

"I'm to St. George's," the driver answered her dryly. "It's on the front of the bus".

Serreta sat in the midst of a group of local women at the back, sitting as though a part of their animated conversation, if anyone looked into the windows. Once one of the women saw her silver shoes, Serreta instantly became the center of the group. St. George's was as far from the Pink Sands and Tankfield Road as she could go on the islands and not be under water.

After too many 2 AM shows in her life, she didn't need much sleep, only rest in a safe place, to wait to make contact with Sugar. She needed him, his warmth, his steady strength. In St. Louis, when DiMarco had changed his requirements to include her body with the cash to keep him from giving their cocaine smuggling to the police, they had run. Sugar had known John Nathaniel from somewhere. After so much work, their act had come solidly together, the spark! The real magic was there now. No more moving a few grams of cannabis, meth, or cocaine to keep money coming in. Risk money. Money that could put them into cages like animals for years and years. She didn't want it, but Sugar had said it was guaranteed. Until Tony DiMarco on a friendly visit after a show, had popped open the Okito dove box and the little plastic packets fell out.

She hesitated. The group of women had dispersed like a night mist at the St. George's bus-stop. As she walked up a dark narrow lane away from York Street, the shrill insistent whistling of thousands of tiny night frogs became louder. She easily touched both sides of the lane, coarse limestone walls, without straightening her arms.

"Zed B M," a soft woman's voice murmured. "Bermuda's music choice. Did you ever notice … maybe you have, but wondered what to do about it. Did you ever notice the secret messages some vinyl records have, if you play them backwards?" She laughed slowly. "I'm going to play this LP from Elton John … backwards. Catch his message."

Serreta edged past the open window. A fan was lazily rotating on the sill, purring in the night. She found the corner of a brick wall, a car backed near it. She wedged herself down between the car and the wall, to wait, to think. Sugar, Sugar, how're you doing? Run. Don't stop to fight, just run. All we need is each other and a little break. The Pink Sands was it. Our launching pad. Just five

275

seconds, the difference between making it in the spotlight and sitting here in the dark, an exhaust pipe digging in my back. She closed her eyes -- just for a minute.

***

Serreta stretched her arms up, standing on her tiptoes. She cast a long shadow in the sun hovering just above the horizon. A glimpse of calm rippling sea flashed between the pastel houses. Cool fresh salt leavened the air. Sugar would be out looking for her. She needed to call Kaarin to warn her and so she in turn could tell Sugar everything was all right. Then they could plan, get things fixed.

Like always.

That car was a blue Lancer, damn thing must have the sharpest tailpipe in the world! Maybe stay separate for a day or two. Maybe work something through John Nathaniel. Get out of this corner and make a run for it, somewhere. Somewhere, but not on a damned isolated island a million miles into the Atlantic.

Some people, locals, no tourists yet, were walking on York Street. She saw a group of young women on the other side strolling slowly, dressed for work. They passed the bus-stop across from the closed-up opera house. Must be working in the shops in St. George's. She was very hungry. She didn't think well when she was hungry, except before a show.

"Yeah," one of the women grinned. She wore a blue striped sweater wrapped fichu style over her shoulders. "Cunningham's, off Custom House Square around the corner. Serves breakfast this time of day. Only place open … except maybe the White Horse."

"No," another woman interjected. "White Horse is closed. Cunningham's. That's the place. It's simple and quick."

Cunningham's only customer, another local, sat at one of the two wooden tables. A large bearded man in musty blue overalls, he mopped up congealing egg yolk with a piece of toast while talking to the woman scraping the grill clean. Serreta carried her eggs and toast on a paper plate to a round metal table on the narrow outdoor decking.

A large white sailing yacht with glistening brightwork shifted restlessly in its moorings almost against her table. Stark empty yardarms of the Deliverance monument jutted above the palms and pine trees that were bending and bowing to the winds. A full low sun washed over the glowing green patina of a bronze statue of a man in a flowing great cape. Raising her head each time she heard scattered voices from the decks of the boats, Serreta kept looking for a big white man with a wide red face.

She swallowed down the last scrap of toast and

started to move away, but turned, picked up the paper plate, plastic fork and wadded paper napkin, and stuffed them down into a trash can. With food warm inside, her hopes rose.

Serreta leaned against the corner window of a perfume shop. Just around the corner was the White Horse Tavern, a man in a black White Horse t-shirt was sweeping the porch, another rearranging chairs and tables. Jessica at Cunningham's had said pay phones were at the police station -- no way -- and outside town hall, other side of King's Square. Serreta had lost her cell phone somewhere. She could see the phones across the deserted square, a row of three, next to the wide stairs leading up to ornate brass encrusted wooden doors of town hall.

Serreta hesitated, nobody in sight, then edged out of the shaded narrow street to start across the cobble-stoned square. A bank to the left with two punishment stocks and a whipping post out front for tourist photographs. To the right the harbor and The Deliverance replica set in concrete, its mahogany hull shining as it never did on the original that had brought the first settlers to Bermuda in 1610, or something. She didn't know. Any way she could have been followed? No. No sign. Get to the phones, get contact with Kaarin, then find a safe, quiet spot. Wait out Sugar's contact. Cunningham's clock had said about ten

278

after eight but it was slow. No one really knew how much.

Once out into the square, Serreta walked more rapidly, stumbling when her silver spikes caught between the stones. No one in sight, though she felt as though someone's hands were reaching for her. Like in a creepy horror movie. But then, then the hands were always Sugar's. She smiled, hopefully, the rascal, he wouldn't quit.

A witch-dunking stool was by the Deliverance. Highly polished wood, the ship glittered like bronze in the growing strength of the sun. Bermuda could be so beautiful, if someone wasn't after you.

The Duchess, Serreta couldn't remember. The D's were missing from the first phone book. She nervously grabbed the next one, ripping several pages, turning them as fast as she could. Oh, god! Finally. But the first phone was out of order. She seized the second.

A ring -- then the phone was torn from her hand as she heard: "A glorious good morning! The Duchess."

He slammed the handset back on the hook. It bounced off, he caught it with astonishing quickness and placed it gently back on its cradle.

"Could've saved you some money, if I was a little quicker, eh?" His thick lipped grin, full of blunt yellowed teeth, wrapped around his face. "What a waste." His broken nose cast a sundial-like shadow across his black face.

"Time to get moving, lady. Very quiet like. Day's getting old, eh?" He nudged her in the ribs with the hilt of a knife held flat against his forearm, his breath sweet. It made her think of pink velvet.

Oh, Sugar, only five seconds! King's Square was beautiful, so like a postcard

21

"You think it is going to rain, or is the roof leaking?"

Marc Kane jerked his head around. "Show up for dessert, Sommers, when the work's about done?" he said testily.

"Terribly sorry, Marc, just several critical things breaking at very inopportune times. Never intended for you to shoulder the whole operation." His smile changed, but didn't brighten his face. He slid his pipe from a jacket pocket. "Will strive to make it up to you. Two new venture partnerships coming together. I'll get you in, if you will allow me." He blew twice into the pipe stem, then began filling the bowl out of a white suede pouch. "However, it is odd to see one carrying an umbrella to dinner ... even in Bermuda. Perhaps customs in the States have changed since last I was there." He bent his face again in a smile, his eyes mocking.

"Kaarin Larsson asked me to bring it. For her show after dinner." That crazy lunch – that insane lunch with a lap full of ice cold margaritas. Her spooky eyes. What was she seeing when she ran away? She'd been full of apologies for running out when he had called, but he couldn't get her to leave her room, even for a Perrier in the lobby.

"How is our indescribable phenomenon? My business has prevented me from enjoying much of her attractive presence, and sadly, she will not be around much longer." His pipe was drawing smoothly.

The guy looks like he's floating, like he just sniffed a line of coke, but if business had been that tight, well maybe I'd be acting the same. "She's doing great. Her memory gig went down very well. Even Delano, manager of the Duchess, said some nice things about it. She is strange, however … like no woman I ever ran into. Kaarin has asked for a letter of recommendation from us. I told her she would have it."

"Certainly. Happy to sign one for her," he said. "But what is the umbrella to be used for?"

Kane shook his head. "Beats the shit out of me. She asked for it, so I borrowed one from the hotel. Kaarin said it would be an interesting moment in my life. I don't know what that might mean."

"But you can hope, I suppose. Can I be of any help in tonight's doings? I recognize I am very late in offering."

"Yeah, you are. No. I'll take care of things."

"Very well, then. We settle up tomorrow morning? Nine?"

'Yeah, nine."

"Good. I will have Rennie drop off particulars for you on the blossoming partnerships. Best."

Kane watched Sommers blend into the gathering dinner crowds. First, he isn't around, then he acts like my brother. I don't care if a guy likes little girls or little boys, but he's got to stay straight when the business is on the line; not disappear. Sommers' mind has been running a quart low, not at all like him. Weird. Kane felt stupid carrying the black umbrella to his table. It was going to be a night of pathetic jokes.

***

Sergeant Oliver Bain rubbed the back of his hand across his mouth. He had held his stomach in check, but just barely. Bits of brain, pinkish-gray jelly, on the walls, the chairs, hanging from the television screen. The bloody headless green parrot found in the kitchen! Sugar Alberts' body was being lifted into the ambulance for transfer to the basement of King Edward hospital when Bain had arrived. His stomach tightened. He forced his mind away. Wouldn't have to worry about staying on his grapefruit diet for a few days. Haggard looked up from the preliminary report on Sugar Alberts as Bain sat down.

"Serreta Alberts' photo in the papers, on-line, television?" Haggard's face was grave.

"Yes, sir. Don't know how effective television will

be, so many on the island using cable, streaming, and DVD's now. Put out circulars in the shops?"

Haggard nodded. "Superintendent approved it, even if our tourist visitors are a little disturbed. If we can't find her fast, we may not find her alive."

"Looks like we might be on the edge of a drug war?" Bain suggested. He hunched his chunky shoulders forward, then relaxed. Removing his glasses, he rubbed the bridge of his nose, then replaced them. His Bermuda was changing, ever since he arrived from St. Lucia with three years police experience. Just not the same.

Haggard pursed his lips. "Who owns the house?" Bain started to answer.

A policewoman knocked, then pushed the door open. "Sir, Chief Inspector Nusam on your direct line." Haggard punched the speakerphone.

Barry Nusam was grim. "Keith, no indications on the street of the Alberts actively involved in any Bermuda drug dealing. They may have done something elsewhere but apparently not here."

"FBI and DEA said they were clean … no arrests of any kind."

"Maybe just not caught yet," said Nusam. "Sugar Alberts was seen a few days ago near "42nd Street", St. Monica's Mission, by one of my observers … but for only a few minutes. Nothing passed. He made a special note because Alberts was new to the territory. We are now trying to find the man Alberts talked to but nothing yet. He was familiar, but my man couldn't make a clean ID. Alberts never reappeared that we can fix." Nusam spoke to someone away from the phone, then asked Haggard: "Narcotics or Special Branch have anything? They must be percolating about now. No one wants the islands a battleground for drug types."

"Narcotics had only small things, worth some bruises, cuts perhaps, but not an execution. Special Branch says no funny Jamaican passports have shown up." Jamaica was a principal source for hit-men on Bermuda, but there were others.

Haggard scanned the brief file from Constable Crowley and summarized it for Nusam and Bain: Tankfield house owned by the Deliverance Memorial Trust, a recently formed group of native Bermudian investors, together with two other trusts. Crowley's checkmark indicated he was identifying the other trusts. House recently put on the market. Unoccupied for seven weeks for renovation. Asking $870,000. Under the law, they can sell the house only to other Bermuda citizens. Non-citizens can sell houses only to other non-citizens with starting prices about $3 million.

"Barry, so far the ownership of the house looks clean. We're doing more work on identifying the owners. But why, of all places on the islands, did the Alberts go there, and why were they found so quickly, unless they were being watched? How did they know it would be empty?"

"Sounds like very fishy business. I'll have some street friends approached about the house. That place obviously is something special. Will get back to you quick as we can. Maybe drugs're not the point." Nusam hung up.

Haggard turned to Bain. "Anything from the bus drivers on Middle and South Roads last night? She had to take a bus somewhere, no taxi pickups in that area. They had no car when they arrived at the house, according to the code-a-phone report." He paused. "Unless she's trying to hide somewhere on the beach."

"Operations have reported on their search of the area. They found nothing. No identification on the Middle Road bus. Still trying to find the driver for South Road. Seems he's taken holiday today."

"Find him. He may be able to tell us exactly where she's at."

***

Moments after Oliver Bain left, Sergeant Vahe Babosian, Press Liaison Officer, waited at the door.

286

Haggard looked up at the Perot envelope. Kaarin. Kaarin. Keep that warning sense sharp, if you can. Something was circling her. What in bloody hell was it? He nodded to Babosian, dark, heavily mustached, who had been referring to himself as the Police Service's token Armenian for about fifteen years. But he wasn't smiling.

"Heat's growing on the Commissioner, sir. The government is edgy, and so is His Excellency, the Governor. Visions of drug wars on Elbow Beach and other politically unacceptable doings. I'm using up my IOU's to keep things quiet, but an American reporter here on holiday thinks he has gotten on to something. Local press will have my hide if he can publish first. I have to put a statement together for the Commissioner to have ready. Anything new?"

"Yes and no." Haggard closed the real estate file. "Let's go. I am briefing the Commissioner and Superintendent Montgomery-Beach. You can listen in. I doubt they will want to put out a statement just yet."

***

McGraw leaned against the wall. The dumb Jamaican didn't know the word professional. Probably couldn't spell it. Get the mark and move. Stinking mess at that house. Dumb place for them to run to – a dead end. He grinned at the unintentional pun. A mess, but you make do with what they give you. A howitzer for a .22 job. Jesus. But this Jamaican and his stupid blade. He only likes to cut, push and bully. Small time hood, thinks he's in the movies. Cut the head off a parrot? Jesus!

Grimacing, McGraw shook his head as he walked away from the closed door. The black could roust Alberts' old lady all he wanted. Wasn't his people, but the mark had to go. Now only the blonde spook. She wouldn't be easy. Sommers didn't know what he had hooked with her. She was something creepy, something dangerous. He sat down, the .41 bulging out of his coat. Damn thing. He pulled it out, his middle finger hooked in the trigger guard, letting the gun swing like a pendulum. Noise stopped in the bedroom. He'd like to pitch the cannon in the ocean, quick. Of all the guns to hide away. They think the marines were going to invade, for Christ's sake? He glanced up. The Jamaican was grinning like a death's head.

"Smooth as butter, man. A real piece. Worth the trouble."

"Get to it." McGraw didn't like knives. Had to get too close, run too big a chance, make too big a mess. "Finish her. One to go, then out of this mad house. We've got the tough one ahead. She can see us coming, I think. Jesus, what is she, that spook?"

***

Christian Montgomery-Beach, cold, relentless, was Superintendent of CID. A West Indian with extensive military experience, with a Bermudian wife, he was now a Bermuda citizen. Haggard had felt his talents were under-used on an island like Bermuda. Marseilles or Rome were more a match to Montgomery-Beach. He sat stiffly his back not touching the chair, his dark face impassive while Haggard reviewed his actions and the results.

Edward Swainson was a native Bermudian promoted up through the ranks and in his third year of appointment as Police Commissioner. He was hunched over his desk, a neat stack of reports topped by a letter from the Governor at his elbow. He listened intently without interrupting to Haggard's presentation. "You are convinced therefore, Inspector, the money found on DiMarco was a frameup?" he asked, when Haggard finished.

"Yes, Commissioner. Too many things do not come together. We have received immediate cooperation from the FBI and the New York police. The money was laundered through Bermuda and planted in DiMarco's rooms to suggest a motive for his killing. The setup falls apart under any investigative pressure. The money was here for some other purpose probably, then put to use with DiMarco. According to Kermit Morgan, DiMarco's agent in New York, DiMarco's income was about $450,000 annually ... and more if he chose to do the work. The income doesn't necessarily mean he never had money problems, but they would have had to have been big ones. He could meet any small ones by just working more shows." He had been astonished at learning DiMarco's income, just for memory stunts!

"If they didn't have time for a better frameup, the killing may have been hastily planned as well," said Montgomery-Beach, his voice a sharp whisper. "Summary punishment for a broken agreement, perhaps."

"Possibly," acknowledged Haggard. "We do not know yet who killed DiMarco or Sugar Alberts. Nor can we yet identify who has attacked Kaarin Larsson on two occasions, though the evidence of the .41 strongly suggests the same identity as the killer of DiMarco and Alberts. We do not have a motive for any of these incidents. The cocaine found in the Alberts' conjuring apparatus is the only hard evidence of a possible drug connection. FBI and DEA have nothing on DiMarco, the Alberts, or Miss Larsson."

"Finding Serreta Alberts is obviously of first priority," whispered Montgomery-Beach, "and that objective must be pursued with utmost vigor." He shifted toward Swainson. "Commissioner, I would recommend that Inspector Haggard and his men draw revolvers. When the Inspector's efforts locate these killers, I do not want those men going against God knows what kind of weapons with only billies and guts. A .41 magnum is an insane man's weapon."

Commissioner Swainson nodded slowly. "I must reluctantly agree. Inspector, you may draw regulation revolvers from the armory as you deem necessary for your men. You will inform this office if you do. I will, as well, Superintendent, alert Emergency Reaction Team. It appears time is starting to run against these people. They may lash out against others. We will need to quickly squelch whatever violence we encounter; though violence must be contained or avoided if at all possible."

Keith Haggard felt a cold chill down his spine. The ERT. Their M-16's, 9mm Uzi's and stun grenades didn't mix with happy tourists.

"No statement will be issued at this time, Sergeant Babosian, but prepare a draft based on our understanding at this time. Update as necessary, with a revision to me immediately. Keep the lid on tight, Sergeant," the Commissioner ordered. "I realize it is increasingly difficult – particularly with that American reporter rooting around."

"Yes, sir. Tight," snapped back Babosian.

***

The office door open, Haggard turned back toward Montgomery-Beach. "Sir?" he asked.

"I said: get those bastards, Mr. Haggard! I don't want any more blood spilled on this island," the Superintendent aspirated sharply.

22

Otis Parker was wasted, his swarthy face puckered like a cold Spanish omelet. His flesh served only to conceal his bones, giving no shape. His breathing was slow, hollow. "Possible, Mr. Haggard. Yes, possible," Parker said slowly, "but safe houses don' stay safe. So, one must be in the flow, so to speak, to know … or know someone who is in." His head was held as in a hammock slung between his arched thin shoulders. He sipped rum from a plastic cup, unaware of the beauty of the pink beach before him. Parker's body had been revved-up and betrayed by every substance he had touched. Too tough for the stuff, he had once bragged to Haggard; he could break an addiction any time he wanted. Any time now, if he wanted unbearable agony. "Don't know any safe houses. Don't use the heavy stuff. Can't take it any longer. It's like an itch you can't scratch. I still itch … but not so much," he finished slowly.

"What about houses temporarily empty for a few weeks?" asked Keith Haggard. He was wearing cutoff jeans, a blue-green Adidas shirt and running shoes, his other clothes were in his car. Parker detested uniforms and police, as a matter of principle, but Keith Haggard had kept him alive when no one else would lift a finger. Haggard didn't sip the rum in his plastic cup, only holding it at his fingertips briefly before placing the half-full cup carefully on the chopped slant of a palm stump. A bronze sun settled toward the horizon, closing a day of frustrating emptiness. Serreta Alberts was somewhere on the island, but where? Parker was a source not accessible to anyone else, but it had taken most of the day to find him, and supply him with a paper-wrapped bottle of Black Seal, Parker's favorite rum. He liked the label with the seal. A few gulls worked the tips of the monotonous rolling waves. Heeling over in the postcard beauty, a daysailer moved as an actor late for his scene.

"Yeah, yeah. Dealers'd have a tap into real estate action … can move big money easy there. Know when a house would be ready. But that kind of stuff was always on the street, at Court, at 42nd Street, Middletown. Only a total stranger, or a white cop, couldn't get that. This isn't a big place, not many secrets. When I was dealing, I always knew a plush place for a quiet snort or smoke. Trouble was, sometimes somebody else would make reservations, too. Make for a problem, Mr. Haggard."

Haggard leaned on his leg braced on the palm stump, his elbow on his knee. "That's what I've got, Mr. Parker. A problem … someone was set-up."

"Happens," Parker muttered.

Standing back, Haggard shoved his hands into his hip pockets. His shadow no longer fell across Parker's face.

Otis Parker rolled his eyes up at the waning sun, not moving his head, his face a mass of red and green peppers and chopped ham. "You asking me to suggest a name? Yeah, you would." He sipped. "Black magician blown away, I understand. His old lady's off running somewhere. Nowhere to hide here, except in a corner somewhere, down low. Probably was ... was, hell, why'd I set myself up? This isn't a violent place. It is a place with long memories, with hours to match. Minty, maybe, but ... Joe Socks ... Arturo Meglioni would setup anybody. But none of them would chance Her Majesty's hospitality at Westgate prison with a gun. They aren't stupid. They'd set up the wicket, then scat. Let somebody else use the muscle. But only a beating ... no guns. Hear a real cannon was used. No wonder you've got a problem, Mr. Haggard. A real problem."

A woman leaned over the stern of the daysailer, her long-barreled camera directed toward Haggard and Parker. Haggard glanced back at Parker sipping, sipping desperately, the bottle rested in the sand held upright firmly between his legs. Someone had sent the Alberts to the Tankfield house, then gave it away. Follow-up with Nusam.

Joe Socks. As ugly a human being as walked anywhere. Otis Parker would not give one name, he wouldn't be an informer, at least to himself, but Socks – Parker's sour grin at the name. Haggard looked back at the water briefly but didn't return the woman's wave.

"See you," muttered Parker, the rim of the plastic cup clenched between his teeth, his hands hung limply across his knees.

Haggard rounded the palm stump, slipping in the loose pink sand. He poured out the rum on the sand and crushed the cup into his pocket. Parker's slouched shoulders and bowed back didn't move. Haggard knew the outside world for Parker was as forgotten as a broken glass

23

Mario settled his maroon jacket on his shoulders and brushed back his hair with the palm of his hand. His bowtie was a little off, he straightened it, checked carefully again in the mirror opposite the elevator. Escorting the most beautiful woman he had ever seen, even in Italy, was not a casual affair; even if it was only down the service elevator and through the kitchen. "Can't afford to get lost in the pastry carts. Not very psychic," he had cautioned Kaarin, when she had asked him for the best way to get to the Royal Bermudiana Ballroom without being seen. Her laugh was music and she had agreed to his escorting her. Laughed! A beautiful woman with a sense of humor and humility. *Straordinario!* A beautiful woman, who was also a mindreader, sees with a blindfold on, and a memory like a computer. Also *incredibile*. A beautiful woman with icy eyes that see straight through you. "Now that's a little nervy," he had confided to J. Outerbridge.

He nodded to the policewoman dressed as a cleaning maid loitering near a linen closet, a new one. Policemen as waiters, bell men, desk clerks. He was probably the only one left working the Duchess without a warrant card. Whatever, there was something big on.

297

Kaarin Larsson? Why not?

Mario settled his jacket again and knocked: one, two, three. Her chief spy she had called him. Hell, if he had known how much fun it was going to be watching her react to his tidbits of dirt, he would have never taken her money.

God!

Kaarin was wearing a sleeveless silver-gray silk tunic which reached just above her knees. It fitted well, but not tightly, leaving her breasts outlined and subtle – as Raphael would have drawn her. Her yellow hair, a large curl swept over her forehead, fell to the middle of her back

Mario swallowed.

On her right shoulder a long gathering of silken black lace was fastened with a black stone set in silver, the lace reaching the floor in back and to her bust in front. It spread and fluttered as she walked, collapsing, clinging when she stopped.

Mario coughed. "Service elevator is this way." He straightened his tie again, knocking it askew.

Her tunic was cinched tightly at her waist by a wide black leather belt from which a black pouch hung by two short silver chains on the left, and a black handled dagger in a silver scabbard on the right.

"Tough looking knife you've got," he said. She seemed to float beside him; a mindstopping barbarian.

"It's an anlace, a two-edged ceremonial dagger from Northern Italy," she responded simply, without looking up at him.

"Ah, I know about knives in Northern Italy. I'm from Ivrea, just north of Milano. But nothing like that black thing."

"It's about three centuries old ... and still very sharp."

"You going to throw it at something?"

Now Kaarin looked up at him, a quick smile, as she stepped into the wide-doored service elevator. "Not likely. I'll use it to find a card someone is going to select."

"A card trick?" he grinned over at her. "Hold it against a guy's neck: 'That's the right card, man', huh?" He noticed her black high-heeled taleris sandals. She never stopped. "To your right as you get off. Watch you don't get tangled in the laundry carts. This is where we launder the money your IRS is always worried about." Well, at least she smiled a little, probably too nervous to talk much. More cops in the Duchess tonight than when the British Chancellor of the Exchequer was here two months ago. "Move it, man!" he barked as the doors opened. "We've got four hundred people waiting for this lady."

Kaarin waited as two men in sweat soaked maroon t-shirts wheeled an overflowing laundry cart into a steamy humid room filled with growling, grinding washing machines. She stepped away briskly, holding the black lace close, away from projecting corners, brooms and mops. She wore no jewelry, only a wide silver bracelet on her left wrist.

"By the way, Miss Larsson, Marc Kane has the umbrella."

Kaarin looked back, then stepped around a set of wooden storage racks. 'Kitchen Personnel Only' was over the twin doors ahead. "Good." That set up a key portion of the routine. No need to mentally rehearse the alternate stunt any longer.

After her flight from lunch, Kaarin had huddled down in the corner of her room, her back up against the walls, her eyes closed, her arms squeezed her knees tightly together. What would she have seen in their faces? Her eyes so tightly shut they could have been *seeled,* sewn shut like the lids of a trained falcon. Yet, even then huddled in the room she had seen – she had seen *the silhouette of Napoleon against a shaded moon* . . .

Kane's call had drawn her out of her *querencia* in the corner, erasing the image of Napoleon; but no, not the lobby, not now, not until she was Kaarin Larsson again inside, Kristen Larsson's daughter, not a strange creature who could see and feel what wouldn't be seen and felt by a normal human being.

Kaarin hadn't seen the faxes slipped under her door sometime in the afternoon until she opened the closet to start dressing for the show. She was still feeling a little dopey from a short nap. An attempt to calm and smooth her nerves before mentally rehearsing her routine and the backup stunt.

Morgan had written simply: "Black Magic was a marginal act, going nowhere according to Tony DiMarco. Have never seen them perform. Don't know any agent who has. What's going on? Bermuda cops asking a lot more questions about Tony, and a few about you."

Dieter's was more elaborate, including a copy of a negative *Wall Street Journal* article on Cognito Thought Systems and its fast neural computers. Apparently, as part of the deal to roll-over the principal note, Cognito's bank, Harris & Burke Trust International, Bahamas, had required the key investors, including Sommers, to personally guarantee the loan. This, according to Dieter, would put most of Roland Sommers' net worth at risk and cause serious uneasiness among his group. The guaranteed amount was $59.4 million. Marc Kane, on the other hand, appeared to be in decent shape.

It was obvious then, Kaarin reflected as she dressed, that both the Alberts and Roland Sommers were under

301

some pressure. She was disturbed that the Alberts had not been honest with her about the success of their act. But connecting a Zombie ball routine and a $59.4 million loan only raised more questions for which there was no time, but there had to be a connection; perhaps DiMarco. But finding the Alberts, to bring them to safety was the most important thing.

Through the crack of a quietly opened kitchen door, Kaarin could see the black umbrella lying like a dead condor next to Marc Kane's chair. In their first week together, Mentavo had led her to Lulu Abbott, an elderly exquisite doll-like woman, who with a pool cue had shattered Kaarin's confident understanding of the physical laws of nature. Standing on one foot, holding the cue in two hands before her, Lulu had challenged Kaarin to throw her over backwards by pushing on the wooden shaft. Not wanting to harm the older woman, Kaarin had reluctantly tried, then, goaded by Lulu, had pushed with all her strength – to no effect! The tiny woman had only smiled, remaining balanced on one foot. Kaarin tried again but Lulu was immovable, utterly immovable! It didn't make sense. It was mathematically impossible. Kaarin had all the leverage, the strength, Lulu was in her nineties, but still she held Kaarin at bay, even giggling in the process. Kaarin had been stunned. Then Lulu opened an umbrella, shyly saying they should forget it was bad luck to open an umbrella inside a house, then challenged Kaarin to hold the umbrella in place, to keep it from becoming a living creature! While Kaarin had held the handle and steel shaft of the umbrella as tightly as possible, Lulu had reached out her small white hand, gently touched the shaft and smiled brightly. Try as Kaarin could to resist, the umbrella began to move and with each of her efforts to bring it under control, the umbrella became more violent, transforming itself into a bird of vengeance, finally throwing Kaarin across a chair and onto the floor. Once Lulu had determined that Kaarin was unhurt, she smiled happily.

Then Lulu, smiling gently, had shown her the arcane subtlety of resistance magic, how to apparently overthrow the laws of physics at will. Later Mentavo had added more, until Kaarin had terrified a janitor at one of their motels by making his mop come alive and attack him! So subtle were the movements, that the line between the real, the physical, and the mind dust was blurred almost to invisibility.

Her adrenaline pumping hard, her nerves sharpened to the necessary performing edge, Kaarin looked over the tables for the people she would use, to manipulate one way or another. They wouldn't move far after the lights went down. She could find them easily or they may just seek *her*

– which would be – her dark expression was hidden from Mario standing behind her – satisfying.

She turned. "Tell Marc Kane I'm ready, Mario."

24

"Got off at St. George's, sir. Driver remembered Serreta Alberts was wearing all green, pants and sweater, and weird silver shoes. She was in a group of women. All got off at St. George's just up from the police station."

"Time?" Haggard asked into the car microphone, his eyes on the narrow road ahead. Police station. She had been only about two hundred feet from safety, unless she thought the police would also be after her because of the cocaine. Who knows? She probably believes Kaarin is her only safe contact. He looked at his watch. Kaarin's show was already on. Would she have concealed a call from Serreta? As he had concealed Sugar Alberts' death from her. He shook his head . . .

Oliver Bain said, "About 11:30 last night. Bus driver has been out fishing all day today. Operations found him only a few minutes ago at a pub in Somerset. We're almost a full day behind Mrs. Alberts now."

"We need everybody. Contact operations, have them saturate St. George's, find anyone who may have seen her. Check bus drivers and taxis for pickups. Damn. We're walking while she's running. She's getting away from us. We've got to get those hours back."

"Crowley, Reilly, and Fox are already on to the bus drivers. I have help from Narcotics on the taxis," said Bain. "We also have identification of the members of the other two trusts. All stalwart longtime Bermuda businessmen. Nothing bent about the Tankfield house so far."

"Except the Alberts knew it was empty and the killers knew they would be there." Haggard slowed his car, pulled into a driveway to turn around. "I'm heading directly the Duchess. Will call in. Should be there in about twenty minutes. Anything from the Hamilton office?"

"No, sir. Nothing yet. Otis Parker any help?"

"Joe Socks. Get on him. Minty and Meglioni are maybes, but Socks is probably it." He replaced the microphone in its dashboard slot. Serreta Alberts is running away, so far away we may never get her.

***

"Get her, Godamnit! You take all day for a simple cut job. Get finished!" McGraw snarled, his patience gone. The damn Jamaican was a mad man. Let me have her, the black had whined. Dumb shit. Sommers was insane to bring in this creep. He'd queer it for everyone. The woman's whimpering was shitty. Jesus, man, just put her away.

***

Their laughter was nervous, hesitant, like they

306

weren't sure if laughing was the right thing. Kaarin's smile was cold. Tonight she'd put fear into them, take them out to the edge without letup. It was black night when the unchallenged spirits of old Bermuda moaned across the islands and through the Royal Bermudiana Ballroom. Things were moving well. Ellis Whitney had not challenged her yet, but his time would come.

"Carla Carlson," the young woman stated, as though Kaarin obviously should recognize her. Dark haired, tall, in a flowered sweeping red gown, she shifted gently from foot to foot, keeping to a silent rhythm.

"Please hold this." A pack of Duchess playing cards was on the wooden tray.

"A card trick?" she said contemptuously as she took the tray.

Kaarin ignored her. "Please hold it firmly," she said. "In fact, could a man come to help Mrs. Carlson? Thank you." She waited as a thickening middle-aged man in red bowtie, wing collar, and double-breasted white tuxedo jacket rapidly moved between the tables. Faster, darn you. Carla's lover was Jeffrey Burnham, according to Mario's notes. Burnham was also married, his wife sitting next to him. He would come if called, Mario had assured her.

Breathing rapidly, he quickly nodded when Kaarin

asked if she could call him Jeff. He was the same height as Carla. "Carla, you can call him Jeffie, too," Kaarin said. Carla's eyes widened. She stepped back. "And to make things more relaxed up here, Carla, you must have a nick name too. Jeff, why don't you call her Carrie? Jeffie and Carrie. It sounds very together, don't you think?" Hot anger grew behind Carla's eyes.

Jeff shifted his feet nervously, sweat prickling across his back. He had first called her 'sweet Carrie' scarcely two hours ago. He looked out at the audience. Milo Carson was out there somewhere, watching; so was his own wife, neither of whom would tolerate any fooling around. Good God, what was going on? Was this blonde witch going to skewer his career for a laugh? How could she know, for God's sake?

Kaarin smiled again – a spider smile. "I have touched your minds," she said to the audience, "and you have responded. Now we will go deeper. Your minds will direct me … direct my arm, my hand. Jeffie, spread the cards face down on the tray. Then, Carrie, take the tray to someone in the audience … other than your husband, naturally … we do not want anyone to suspect you of arranging anything secretly" – Jeff started –"with your husband," she added after a second's pause. "When Carrie comes to you, whomever you may be, place a finger on one of the cards, lift it, look and remember it, show it to the others at your table, then replace the card and mix it back into the others. Naturally, do not let me see the card, or let Jeffie or Carrie see it either.

"Jeffie, let's you and I turn our backs while Carrie has a card touched." She took Jeff's arm, turned to lead him a few steps back from the tables. Following, Jeff plodded behind as in shock.

"For God's sake, lady," he whispered. "What are you doing? One wrong suggestion about Carla and me, and you could wipe me out."

Kaarin didn't answer.

"What are you doing?" he whispered tensely. "How do you know? What are you driving for?"

Kaarin looked up at him. His eyes went wide when they locked into hers. "I'm entertaining, *Jeffie*," she breathed softly. "Only entertaining ... but I know many things, many minds."

"Here," announced Carla in a loud voice. "Your damn card is buried somewhere in there."

Kaarin, still holding Jeff's arm, turned back toward the audience. "That's excellent. Do you know the card, Carrie?"

"No ... and neither do you," she retorted.

Kaarin relaxed Jeff's arm. "Please hold the tray

firmly between you about waist high. Good. Hold it tightly." Kaarin looked between the two nervous lovers holding the tray to the audience beyond. "Your thoughts now will guide me, whomever you are. Everyone, but those at the chosen table, please clear your minds so that no one … can be hurt." She smiled slowly, the audience visibly stiffened.

"Now," she said softly. "Now." Louder. "Now!" she screamed, the black handled anlace appeared in her hand, her hand raised high, then flashed down into the cards, the tray, knocked loose from their hands, clattered across the dance floor, the cards spinning and fluttering in the air. Kaarin raised the ancient dagger, her eyes glistening ice.

"The card! The card was?" she demanded.

"King of Diamonds!" was shouted in staggered chorus from a table to her right.

She lowered the dagger, a card impaled on its point – the King of Diamonds. A stunned silence, then nervous applause.

"A souvenir, Jeffie. Of old Bermuda … and its dangerous secrets." Kaarin extended the dagger toward him. "Be careful you don't cut yourself. That would be a messy affair."

Eyes wide, Jeff slid the card from the blade, a hole

slashed through the king's heart. He didn't wait and he didn't look back at Carla as he returned almost running to his table. Kaarin held the anlace at her fingertips for a moment to let it catch and splinter the tightly focused lights, then returned it to its scabbard. Kaarin smiled at Carla's suppressed fury as she moved back between the tables. A clean finish to an affair since Jeff would keep running and there would be gossip later, the best advertising.

***

"Clean, man, with a sharp blade. Clean." The Jamaican grinned across his face.

"Shitty mess," responded McGraw. "Let's move it. Now one to go … the tough one."

***

Marc Kane felt a fool as he stood rigidly, the black umbrella opened over his head, its shaft gripped tightly in his large hands. The audience was murmuring. Like a fool, yeah, but maybe no more stupid jokes about the roof leaking. He saw Kaarin wasn't smiling. She's been almost threatening, not what he had expected after the memory gig – some good laughs then. A strange woman.

"Tight! Tight! That the beast cannot be freed … free to attack!" Kaarin stretched her right arm out, almost touching the steel shaft, her fingers relaxed. "Life will flow

311

when I touch it. Hold firm … for your sake … *and for theirs*." Her crystal gray eyes drew Kane toward her, he couldn't look away, break away. He shifted nervously, watched her two extended fingers just touch the steel. Nothing.

The audience was silent, motionless.

A slight quiver that only Kane could detect. He swallowed and gripped until his knuckles were white.

Kaarin's smile was small, expectant.

It jerked! Kane's eyes went wide! He forced the shaft back, but it wouldn't rest, instantly ducking away. He quickly shifted his feet to brace against the umbrella. What the hell is this?

Kaarin dodged the swaying umbrella, her fingers still touching the shaft as life grew in the black shape.

Back again, then it darted away. Kane shuffled like a boxer, bobbing, gripping, gasping, his mouth open. Twisting, the umbrella lunged away. Kane lurched forward, lost his balance, recovered, staggered to the edge of the dance floor. Kaarin moved smoothly with him, her smile widened.

Cries, screams as Kane fell into a table, the people frantically dragged their chairs away.

"Hey! Hey! What's happening?" Kane shouted, the umbrella now fully alive, fiercely jabbed its sharp nibs at his eyes, dodged, gyrating, violently struggled to be free. Another table displaced, tilted up on two legs, balanced, then Kane knocked it over, scattering drinks, candles, and people.

Kaarin smiled grimly, dodged Kane's desperate lunges, still just touching the steel shaft.

Marc Kane was scared. He couldn't let go, but the stronger he held it, the more vicious the black beast became. Those eyes – what was she seeing? *Agh!* Over backwards, across another table, the audience was on their feet screaming.

Kaarin went still, pulled back her hand and stepped away.

Kane slipped across the tilted table with first the table, then drinks, flowers, candles and tablecloth avalanched down over him. He didn't move.

Kaarin stepped backwards slowly, back onto the dance floor. They would remember she was at a distance, not that she had ever touched the umbrella which was now wedged beneath a table, as the people backed cautiously away, not touching it. Lulu would have been pleased with the chaos, everyone on their feet pointing; then staring at Kaarin.

She waited for their anxiety to peak, then begin to subside. Kaarin smiled slowly. Time to finish, to slam the work home. "Please close the umbrella," she said. "It will rain tomorrow."

No one moved. She was pleased. Their fear went even deeper than she could have hoped. Kaarin walked coolly to the umbrella, stepped over Marc Kane's feet, furled it, snapped the strap closed around the lifeless black folds. She whirled, her black lace billowing out around her, and carried the lifeless umbrella at her fingertips. She shrugged then flipped it across the polished dance floor. She swept her eyes across the audience as they now hesitantly settled back at their tables. The displaced tables were upright, but the floor was covered with tablecloths, flowers, broken glasses and other detritus. The people darted nervous glances at her.

Marc Kane finally reached his feet with some help, his dinner jacket stained with drinks with hors d'oeuvres plastered to his chest like medals of valor. "Jesus, lady," he said hoarsely as he stepped away from the debris and moved clumsily back to his table. "You have a license for that black animal?"

Kaarin saw Roland Sommers at the edge of the tables, his expression one of strange recognition. He turned, nodded to someone behind him, then turned back toward her.

"Each mind a separate unique entity, but now

314

bound together by a common unique experience," Kaarin declared. "Now, a unique experience for each of you … your mind touched … but only if you so desire. I will not probe into your privacy. If I touch you and you want to withdraw, only raise your hand. I will stop, move to someone else." Several people raised their hands immediately, shaking their heads. Drive the fear in, let them laugh somewhere else, some other time. Etch her presence onto their memories, like hydrofluoric acid on glass.

"A new house, Harvel. The Harvels. You're concerned over a new house." A young couple waved their hands desperately. Kaarin smiled, nodded. "Very well, another thought." She turned abruptly back toward Sommers, a feeling.

"McGraw!" She said, pointing at him. Even at a distance she could see him blanche. "McGraw will fail!" Sommers face was tight, he backed away, raised a hand, backed further away, back into the darkness. Well, McGraw, whoever he was, hit a solidly resonant chord. Mario scored again.

"Wait a minute, Miss Larsson. Wait just a minute."

Kaarin turned. He was about sixty, gray hair thinning. He was pointing his folded glasses at her. It was Ellis Whitney.

"You've got these poor people scared to death of your so-called powers. If you were only entertaining, I wouldn't blow the whistle on you, but you've crossed the line, you have got all these people backed into a corner so they can't be sure what you are. So I've got to set things right. Your umbrella stunt was first done a long time ago by Lulu Abbott, as I recall. You do it well. Your card stabbing is a standard magic trick that I've used myself. That was also done quite well. And . . ."

"Test me, Mr. Whitney," she interrupted. "See if I am what you think."

He started at the sound of his name but quickly recovered. "Simple, Miss Larsson. Read my mind and tell me what is in this envelope." He withdrew a small blue envelope from his inside jacket pocket. "Right here." He tapped it. "Right here is the evidence of what you are."

Kaarin moved a few steps toward him, the black lace roiling behind her, then collapsing when she stopped in front of him. All sounds had ceased.

"I *am* an entertainer, Mr. Whitney. That has been my purpose tonight. But now *you* have changed the terms. And when I read your mind, Mr. Whitney, what then? Will you also deny that? Shall all these people trust your opinion, rather than the evidence of their own eyes?" Kaarin raised her right hand toward the audience.

"Don't try to weasel out now. Most of these people have known me for years. They don't know you at all."

"They do now, I believe."

"This envelope! What is in it?"

"Hold it up high, Mr. Whitney, so everyone can see it," she said. "Nothing, Mr. Whitney. It is empty, completely empty, which gives me little opportunity to read anything in your mind. Not a fair test, is it, ladies and gentlemen?"

Whitney slowly lowered the envelope. "Very clever, Miss Larsson." He looked around. "You must have seen that spotlight back there shine through it."

Well, true. You work with whatever is available. Kaarin moved back a step. "Put into your mind, Mr. Whitney, thoughts of your personal life that only you can know. I'll trust your integrity. Thoughts that, as well known as you are, no one here would likely know. Thoughts whose revelation will settle the issue you have raised. I will leave to the men and women here to draw their own conclusions about what I am, or am not. This, now, is only between you and I."

"Fine," he said. "I've got some thoughts you aren't going to touch. I didn't even know I would be here until a couple of days ago."

Kaarin laughed. "Colorado ... a place in Colorado,"

Kaarin said immediately. "The image is quite clear." If he responds push, if not then another go to another tack.

"What?" Whitney said softly.

"Greely, Colorado. Is that the place? I don't know Colorado, I've never been there."

Whitney was silent. His dark-haired wife, seated next to him, looked up at him suddenly.

"Geary Street. 3418 North Geary."

His jaw dropped as he sucked in his breath.

"Geary Street," she continued. "A white house with green shutters ... "

"My God! You're right." He paled.

"... and green doors. A woman, elderly, stooped, standing on the porch ... with hazel eyes, in tears ..."

"She is. Oh, my Jesus, she is!" he whispered. "Christ!" he said. "Get out of my mind! Get out!" He raised his hands to ward her off.

".... tears." Kaarin stepped toward him. Then another step. She raised her right hand toward him and suddenly flung her fingers wide. "A green and white checked apron ..."

"Stop! Somebody stop her." He fell back slumped into his chair. "No, she can't know, anymore." He muttered. "Stop," he sobbed. "I can't keep her out."

"... to match the house she always said." Kaarin

stepped toward him again, her face coldly rigid. "Didn't she?"

"Stop." A weak muffled plea. "Stop."

"Kaarin, stop! For God's sake, you've proven yourself." Marc Kane was on his feet.

"No!" Kaarin answered. "He challenged me!" She thrust out her right hand, her forefinger pointed at Whitney's face. "*He changed the terms.*" She turned back to the deflated banker. Only the people who think they have the answers, as Sugar had said, can know the real terror of the real thing – even if this time the 'real thing' came from a back page of the New York *Times*, Sunday edition, dug out of her garbage.

Whitney's wife rose unsteadily. "I know of what you're speaking. You are correct." She removed a large handful of bills from her purse and threw them at Kaarin's feet. "Please stop," she said simply, "or you'll destroy him. He has a loud mouth sometimes, I know, but he didn't mean to harm you. Take the money, it's all I've got with me. You've beaten him."

Cries began to come from other areas of the ballroom. "Stop! Stop you witch!"

Kaarin had raised her left hand high, her right hand pointed at him, the classic Isis position, but now dropped both hands and stepped back two steps. She breathed

319

slower.

"Keep your money. But, if there is a next time, I *will* take his mind." Her jaw was clenched tight, her eyes blazed in triumph; then she relaxed.

Whitney nodded heavily when his wife whispered to him. He rose as she gently led him by the elbow away from the dance floor. Shocked stillness spread throughout the ballroom.

Kaarin watched impassively, tens, twenties, and fifties formed a carpet about her feet. She bowed her head. She smiled. "Good night, ladies and gentlemen," she said softly and walked across the money toward the door to the lobby, the black lace fluttered cloudlike around her. There was no applause.

Only her satisfaction.

25

Keith Haggard had witnessed the mental battering of Ellis Whitney and now waited as Kaarin walked rapidly toward him with a cloud of black lace unfolding behind her like some dark flower. The rigid set of her face, her merciless handling of Whitney – she didn't even glance toward the hushed, cowed audience. Kaarin had been moonlight incarnate at Hannah Jack's, but now, a strange wraithlike creature. As she neared, a small emotionless smile of recognition appeared on her lips; a consummate actress, or what, he wasn't sure. Her face transformed as the ballroom lights began to come up. Must have been the blotchy darkness and the tenseness he felt in the air, in the shuffling manner of the people starting to move past him.

"Keith," Kaarin said, surprised. "Here long?" Her voice had lost its sharpness, its suppressed anger.

He took her arm. "Let's get away from these people. I need some questions answered urgently."

She frowned momentarily, then nodded. "They probably have seen enough of me here. Sugar and Serreta?" she asked anxiously. "You've found them? They're all right?" She hesitated for his response, wanting to share her faxes with him.

Haggard led her across the Duchess lobby. As scattered couples and groups began to leave the Royal Bermudiana Ballroom, they veered away to avoid crossing Kaarin's path, whispering, whispering. They didn't notice her stop, look up at Haggard's face, grasp his arm with both hands for support.

"Serreta? Where is she? Is she safe?" Sugar! Sugar dead! No, it couldn't be! She leaned against Keith, holding him close, squeezed his arm tightly.

"She's never called you, or made any contact?" He saw her eyes transforming into large glassy pools, but no tears fell.

"No," she said. "I've heard nothing from them." She wiped her eyes clear with her fingers, glassy pools immediately forming again. "Maybe they thought they would only bring me trouble." Tears began to drip slowly down her cheeks. "Oh, Lord. The world's tearing apart. We must find her. *I must find her.*"

Haggard gave her his handkerchief, looked down at her changing tear-streaked face. He rapidly explained the police efforts to locate the Alberts.

Kaarin shook her head violently, her hands taut fists. "No! We'll be too late, too late to help. Keith, you're too far behind. I … I must do something."

"What? Virtually everyone in the Service is mobilized in the search. What can *you* do?"

"I can try to see her, to project myself out, to tear down my barricades, to let go of my mind, to let in whatever is there. I don't understand what has been happening, but I must, *must* reach out for her."

They were standing outside the Duchess a few feet from the main entrance, near the open door to luggage storage. A zephyr shifted the black lace, wrapping it around her, brushing wisps of yellow hair across her face. The night sky was mottled with gray clouds, covering, then revealing a pale timid moon.

Kaarin looked up at Haggard again. "Something beyond a warning sense has taken root in me. I don't know that I will ever be free of it."

"But what happens to you … to you, if you surrender to it?"

She shook her head. "I don't know, but I must try to find Serreta … I must."

Kaarin moved away from Haggard. She stepped around a group of people disgorging from a taxi, their eyes on her as she walked slowly down the wide cobblestone driveway away from the hotel, toward Haggard's car in a no-parking zone. Cars, taxis, already slowing, swerved around her. Suddenly she stopped, stiffened, then raising

323

up, to her tiptoes, her arms out for balance, her head thrown back as an animal desperately seeking an elusive scent, her hair flying, tossing in the salt breezes.

Haggard ran toward her. At his step she whirled, wrapped in fluttering black lace, face rigid, her eyes had become vacant ice.

"East," she hissed. "East."

***

Haggard turned the ignition key, a quick glance over his left shoulder at Kaarin colored yellowish-green in the instrumentation lights. Damn. He twisted the ignition key again, the engine growled then caught. Kaarin had not moved, her hands clasped together in her lap, her shoulders hunched forward, her hair falling, her face concealed.

As he turned onto Harbor Road away from the Duchess, Kaarin abruptly sat up, her eyes wide. "No," she whimpered softly. "Oh, no, no."

Accelerating, Haggard swung sharp right up Stowe Hill. "What?" he asked, as he watched for traffic. He heard only a sigh, a short sob. A van blocked him as traffic came down the other side. Picking a spot, Haggard floored the accelerator, squeezed around the van on the narrow crushed lava road. "Did you say something, Kaarin?" he asked, simultaneously grabbing the microphone with his left hand.

Oliver Bain's radio voice was strained. "Found

Serreta Alberts, sir. Dead. Throat cut. Stavell Bay."

Haggard slowed the car after pulling onto South Road. Stavell Bay was the other side of the island, the opposite direction – not east. He pulled the car off the highway. "What have we got?" He saw Kaarin's shoulders sag, heard her gentle sobbing.

"Nothing to go on. It appears that she was killed somewhere else and the body left at Stavell. A honeymoon couple out for a walk found her. The bride has gone hysterical, taken to the clinic. Husband didn't see anyone, just the body behind some bushes. Starting to question people in the area. We're stretched real thin now."

Haggard slammed his fists against the steering wheel.

"Sir, Miss Larsson?"

"She's with me now. We're on South Road heading east." Heading east with Serreta Alberts being killed in the west. God take it! He cursed softly. "I'm on my way to Stavell Bay. Anything in St. George's?"

"No, sir. Nothing."

"Joe Socks?"

'He's disappeared. No one has seen him in two days."

As police radio procedure forbids cursing on the air, Haggard had to pause for a moment, take a breath, then

325

said, "Should be at the scene in twenty or so minutes. Notify the Superintendent. Socks now is our key." He jammed the mike back into its slot, then twisted the steering wheel and shifted down.

"No, Keith! East! We must go east. We must!" Her hand that gripped his wrist was cold, dry. Her eyes had widened, her face devoid of humanity. Like that moment on the way to Hannah's, when he had chanced it, trusted her and lived. But this time she had been wrong. Alberts was west, not east. Her hand fell away to her bare knees.

He hesitated, his hand still gripped the gear shift. "Kaarin," he whispered.

"East. We must go east! We're too far away. I can't see well from here. Get me closer."

"But Serreta Alberts was west, not east. How can you be sure?"

Her anger, when it came, was that of a beast prodded beyond endurance, spreading over her into her face, her hands, her taut body arched.

"East! East!" she spit out. "I sensed Serreta where she last lived. I felt she was gone. *I want her killers ... and mine!*" Her breathing slowed. Her eyes were shadowed in the sick light of the instrument panel as she faced toward Haggard. She shuddered. "Now ... east! I can't see from here. We must get closer ... to let me reach out, to see."

When Haggard still hesitated, Kaarin shook her clenched fists at him. "East!" she screamed. "I've given up my soul!"

Haggard pressed the accelerator down hard, throwing gravel and dirt, hauled the car around onto South Road – headed east. Once into fifth, he reached for the mike. East, to where? Why? Because a psychic storm shared the car with him? He held the microphone tightly, then finally pressed down the transmit switch with his thumb.

***

"Hit her leaving the hotel. Police won't find the black woman's body for days." McGraw felt some small satisfaction out of what was undoubtedly the messiest job of his professional career.

"How?" asked Roland Sommers. "She'd recognize you ... and him too, apparently. You can't get close." He stood behind his Louis XV desk.

"She's moving out to Shadowind tomorrow. I plan to hit her in transit. She's checking out early, so not many people on the road Saturday morning."

"Can you be sure?" Sommers sucked at his pipe.

"Bell captain's picking up her luggage at six-thirty in the morning. Going to do it personally. Says she's the hottest thing he's ever seen, even in northern Italy. Wants a long last look."

Sommers smiled slightly. "Miss Larsson predicted tonight that you would fail. That bother you any?"

McGraw put his beer down hard on the antique French desk. "Shit. When did you hear that?"

Sommers stepped over beside McGraw, picked up his glass and slid a plastic coaster under it. "That parquet does not like water rings." He was a few inches from McGraw's wide grim face. "Tonight, in her show. She waved toward me and yelled something like: 'McGraw will fail'."

"Pointed toward *you* and used *my name*?" He was incredulous and suddenly very scared.

Sommers nodded. "You may have been right. She may be more than just a trickster. But, regardless, she must go," he said, "or no final payments."

McGraw blew out his cheeks, making his head resemble a soccer ball. "Shit. I've hit a lot of people but nothing like this."

"What can she do to you? She has no gun, no weapons ... other than a knife she uses for card tricks. The police certainly are too professional to listen seriously to any of her psychic prattle. Get the job done properly ... then get out."

McGraw raised his arms, then let them fall. "I don't know what she can do. But, yeah, I'll get her. Just keep him

328

out of it."

The Jamaican didn't look up, only sipped his scotch and simpered at the big white man's growing stink of fear.

26

They were stopped on Mullet Bay Road, the former U.S. Naval Station behind them. Oliver Bain had been nonplused when Haggard had explained. Haggard was betting his career on Kaarin, on her ability to see further than diligent police work could achieve. After giving curt orders, he waited on Mullet Bay, sounds of laboring surf came through the open car windows. They had been waiting there almost five minutes when finally Kaarin whispered again: "East. East."

Haggard pushed the gear shift down with his left hand, pulled back onto the road. He called in, relaying his direction to headquarters and to the St. George's police station. A lot of uneasy people listening to that, maybe even the Commissioner himself.

Most likely.

Haggard kept the car at about ten miles an hour. Mullet became Wellington Street. There was no traffic, as though the whole island was stopped, even the spirits, watching, taking bets on his gamble on the small blonde presence beside him.

Wellington came to a fork: Duke of York Street to the left, Water Street down and to the right toward the docks. He stopped, looked over at Kaarin, who stared back, her face a blank.

"I don't know," she said, her voice quivering. "I don't know." She opened the car door, paused, then stepped out. She walked briskly to the heart of the intersection, black lace billowing up, wrapped around her body, then up around her face as she stood on tiptoes, her head thrown far back, her hair falling to her waist, roiling in the heightened cool breezes, she rotated slowly. A light came on in the second floor over a shop. A head was silhouetted, then two.

Haggard stepped out of the car, looked across the top at Kaarin revolving slowly, her hands outstretched. They probably think she's drunk. In that silk tunic, in this light, she looks completely naked.

Kaarin stopped, facing toward Duke of York Street. A police car creeping slowly toward her up York, transfixed her in its headlights.

Haggard quickly reached in, grabbed the mike. "Stop!" he ordered. "Lights out. Lights out!" The car halted immediately, its lights extinguished. Two officers got out and stood by the car, one in an inspector's white shirt.

"What gives, Haggard?" a voice said softly, but firmly, on the radio.

"Wait," he responded. "She's," he hesitated, "she's

trying to see the killers of the Alberts."

"Wha …?"

Kaarin rotated again, finally dropping her hands, arms, her shoulders slumped. Haggard wiped the sweat from his eyes. She started walking down York – bare-footed. He glanced inside. Her sandals were lying on the floor. He looked back as she walked past the police car, oblivious to it, and the men who silently watched her pass.

"What now, Haggard? She know where she's going?" the voice whispered again from the radio. "She looks like a mechanical doll … no life."

"I … I don't know. But right now, she's the best chance we have."

"Chance for what? This is insane."

"This is Bermuda."

Haggard drove carefully, following Kaarin down York, the door on the passenger side still swung open. The patrol car turned, fell in behind, only its parking lights on. One of the officers had remained, moving up the road to block any oncoming traffic.

Responding to orders whispered on the radio, another car left St. George's police station to seal off York from the opposite direction.

Kaarin stopped, then turned into a narrow, dark separation between two buildings, too narrow for a car to follow. She reached out, touching both concrete walls with her fingers.

"She's turned into Silk Alley. I'll follow on foot. Circle around on Queen Street. Wait there," Haggard ordered. He parked his car on the sidewalk and followed Kaarin into the darkness.

Kaarin glanced to the left. A compact car, blue or green, against the wall. She moved on between hard moon-encrusted shadows of other cars, coarse lava rock scraping her feet. What was in her, animating her? She brushed the black lace away, her hand hitting against the ancient anlace at her belt.

Keith Haggard followed, a featureless shape behind. A turn left, then right onto Printers Alley, up a gradual hill. He moved at her pace maintaining distance, two parallel forms surrounded by the shrill whistling of the night frogs. Only about an inch long, but there were thousands of them. Haggard's first nights on the island had sounded like a scene from Hitchcock's *The Birds*, but it had only been the frogs.

Kaarin stopped. A lane to the left, but she turned away, continuing on the road, curving right between tall walls. Another lane to the left. Ahead she saw a white police car parked partially into the intersection. Keith? She looked back. He was there a few steps away.

"I can see them now," she hissed. "*See them.* They're standing at an old table. But I can't hear them." Her brittle voice cracked. Then she turned back, her stride lengthening.

She sounds mad. She acts mad. I'm mad. Haggard saw Inspector Greenlaw's car on Queen Street. I'll come out of this either still a policeman, or in a strait jacket. But Kaarin, what's happened to her, to her soul? Needle and Thread Alley. Now where's she off to? He waved Greenlaw on with his flashlight and quickened his step.

Her eyes were closed, she slumped wearily against a wall, waiting until Haggard joined her. "Down there … in that big house at the corner." Her words were slow, slurred. "Second floor. They're there."

"Who's there? Do you recognize them?"

"The two men who attacked me at the Pink Sands, and at the fort. Roland Sommers! A black man I've never seen before. I think I'm hearing snatches of sound, but I can't understand. I . . . I think I am hearing . . ."

Rose Dale. Sommers' home. An elegant pastel blue and white two-story stucco with wide verandahs on both floors. A high wall encircled it, like many costly Bermuda houses. Haggard had driven and walked by it a hundred times. He had been in it only a few days before.

"What are they doing?" he asked, hardly believing he did.

Kaarin shook her head, opening her eyes. "Nothing. Only talking, arguing maybe, waving their arms." She walked slowly down the gently slopping lane, paused at intervals to put out a steadying hand against the wall, until she came abreast of the house. Someone abruptly drew back a curtain on the second floor, letting a sudden block of light illuminate the narrow walled street. Kaarin sprang back, crouching down on her knees. She looked up. *Napoleon!* Napoleon silhouetted against a shaded moon. She blinked and shuddered violently. The curtain was jerked closed almost immediately. She stood cautiously. Then she understood. Whale vertebrae mounted on the corners of the wall around the house. Back lighted from the right angle their shape became a silhouette of Napoleon in his distinctive campaign hat.

***

"She's down there, Godamnit! That spook is out there in the street looking up at us … like a ghost in a cheap movie." McGraw had turned a sallow white, his large mouth hung open. "Look out front," he demanded. "What's out there? Don't open that curtain wide." He reached for the black-taped .41 lying on the parquet table.

Sommers carefully drew back the edge of the

335

curtain on a corner window. A white police car was parked on Queen Street. "Police car on the street," he said blandly.

"Police? Jesus, what's go'ng on?" The Jamaican was instantly on his feet, slopping scotch over the floor. "How? No way they trace us. No way. They couldn't 'ave found her body yet." His hands were shaking.

Sommers turned back. "There's nothing unusual about a police car near this house. I often have valuable papers here. It's merely a courtesy extended by the police. The station is only down the hill in Custom House Square four minutes away. You're edgy, that's all. If the terms of your collective employment agreement had been executed correctly, you wouldn't even be here now. Believe me, I wish you all were a thousand miles away." He walked over to the other window, pulled back the curtain. "No one in sight. Only a quiet island night." He turned toward McGraw who still gripped the giant revolver. "You believe this Larsson woman is a witch," he said with disgust. "She'll haunt you in your dreams, even after she's dead. Serve you right for muffing it earlier."

"Hey, what's goin' on? I'm in for five thousand dollars for a setup and a quick yacht trip to the Bahamas. None of this hit this, hit that bullshit." Joe Socks was short, with powerful shoulders, copper colored skin, and a hairless head covered by a blue velvet beret. He didn't like a .41 magnum anywhere near him.

Roland Sommers nodded. "Quite right. The Hector will pick you up on Ordnance Island dock at six morning early. I want you out as far and as fast as those two. Then my slate is clean."

"Yeah," said Socks. "You dump me right next to the police station. We goin' to have breakfast at Cunningham's, too, just to stick a finger in Swainson's eye?" He scowled at McGraw. "Put the iron away. You could blow us all away."

"Shove it, man!" McGraw snapped angrily, then jerked his head toward Sommers. "What was that? That buzzing?" Christ, that damn spook had him coming apart at the seams, losing his moves.

Sommers slowly packed tobacco into his pipe. "The front gate has blown open probably. The buzzer triggers if the gate opens when no visitors are expected." He slid out a side drawer on the ornate desk, pressed a switch. The buzzing stopped.

"You goin' to check? Check the gate? Christ, this room is small!" Socks glared over at McGraw who still held the long barreled .41 loosely in his hand.

"Check the window yourself," said Sommers. "If necessary, I'll go down to close the gate."

Joe Socks brushed past the Jamaican pouring

himself another stiff shot of scotch. Socks pulled the curtain back – stared for a moment. "What the hell is that?"

McGraw was first to the window.

Kaarin stood holding the wooden gates open with both hands. She looked up. Strengthening sea winds spread the black lace behind her and tossed her yellow hair wildly about. Stark moonlight had erased warm humanity from her face. She raised her right hand, pointed up directly at McGraw.

He moved, grabbed a small leather cushion from a sofa and turned back to the window.

A sharp *thack!* The window exploded into hundreds of stiletto shards, the huge .41 slug ripping away a chunk of the wooden gate near one of Kaarin's hands; then silence.

"Shit!" McGraw shouted as Kaarin leaped forward on the ground, vanishing beneath the second story verandah sightline. He looked out across the wall. No police car in sight. The only real sound was the broken window. Get down there, get her. Get the spook!

***

Kaarin lay still. She looked up, pushed her hair back from her eyes. The second floor verandah railing cut off sight from the window. She crawled forward on her hands and knees. Keith was back there somewhere, but she crept deliberately on, toward the darkened lower verandah.

338

At the sound of a broken window, Haggard threw the mike on the car seat and then ran, bent down, toward the open gate. He carried only a hardwood truncheon. Reinforcements with weapons were on the way from Hamilton. Constables were running up from the St. George's station to positions on Turkey Hill Road, to cover the back entrance to Rose Dale. Greenlaw had already blocked Queen out of sight of the house. He edged around the pillar at the gate, a moon shadowed 'Rose Dale' at his shoulder. He saw Kaarin crawling toward the house, apparently unhurt, but now she was beyond reason.

For an instant the broken second floor window was dimly outlined behind the drawn curtain, then the light went out.

Rose Dale was dark.

Haggard lunged forward, around the pillar, went flat on the ground an arm's length from Kaarin. She stopped, looked back. "They're waiting for me, Keith," she hissed. "I'm going after them."

"No. Men and weapons are coming," he whispered, but he saw her raise up, then run crouched over to the verandah railing. Her mistlike figure floated over the railing and vanished into the deeper darkness, not even her hair reflecting any light. He pressed himself up, pulled his legs under him, then sprinted for the railing, cleared it silently, then hunkered down. He heard a soft, low laugh.

"Stay close, Keith. I can see them." She reached out, touched his arm. "I'll be your eyes." Her touch was cold, dry.

"Where are they?" he whispered.

"Huddled in the dark. In the room right over us. The man with the big gun and the bad aim, the big white man is scared of me." Her laugh was strained. "Sommers is holding his arm."

"They fired on you?"

"He missed me. It was the same gun as before," she said without emotion. "I must delay them. Hold them until more force arrives." She stood.

Delay, yes. Crash the front door. "Are they starting down?" he asked.

"No, no … they're only talking, arguing in the dark. I can't hear. They're … *ahgh!* … my head. It's splitting apart!" She whined in agony. "No much longer … I can last. Moving toward back." Falling forward, she squeezed her head between her hands to keep it from cracking open, gritted her teeth against the stabbing pain. She rolled, writhing, twisted into a tight knot, moaning. "Dear God, dear God." She was paralyzed, compressed by burning chains binding her. Wave after wave of trembling swept over her. A moment – then her body began to relax, her hands falling loosely. She breathed deeply, barely stirring, then started slowly to move.

"Stay still." Haggard's hand was on her shoulder. She was damp and feverishly hot. "We have men waiting for them in back. You can't do any more."

"Armed?" She pushed herself back to her knees, her hands clenched into tight fists, not feeling the fingernails tearing her flesh.

"No."

"Then they will be dead." Pain blurred her words as she rose unsteadily. Swaying, she moved as if walking barefoot on broken glass.

***

His body rigid, Superintendent Montgomery-Beach's face contorted with anger. Serreta Alberts' head was almost completely severed from her body, but it was the other marks, bruises, cuts.

"Miserable bastard!" he breathed sharply. "Tortured her before killing. Must be the same lunatic who beheaded that parrot. Must be loony as a man on salt water." He dropped the plastic sheet back.

"Sir, Inspector Haggard has ordered an armed squad and an ambulance to St. George's. Urgent."

"Then get them moving, sergeant! Tell him I am on the way to support. I want the creature that did this. Where

341

in George's?"

"Rose Dale, sir."

"Roland Sommers' home? Bloody hell!" he exploded. "Bloody hell, what is going on?" he repeated, his voice becoming a low snarl. "Move sergeant, move!"

***

Constable Clive Lashley breathed hard, his lungs heaving, his knees bloody from slipping and falling against a car in the darkness of Needle and Thread Alley. He had to run harder to catch up after searching under the car to find the polished black billy his collision had knocked from his hand.

"Welcome to the party, Lash," a voice whispered.

"Seal it!" he snapped. Limned by the moon, Rose Dale was a dark featureless hulk. Orders. Block Turkey Hill and watch rear of the house. Watch for guns. Follow, don't engage unless ordered. He quickly put his force of three in place. Only one constable left at the station on the radio. More coming. A real party. Not just getting drunks coming out of the White Horse, getting them hurriedly away from tourists' eyes. Tended to squelch their tropical romance watching police grappling with cursing drunks. He had repeated the gun warning to his men. Maybe a Kojak style shoot-out. Yeah, baby. All he needed was a lollipop.

***

Inspector Cy Greenlaw saw the mike on the car seat. Haggard was in a hurry somewhere. He looked up at the verandah visible over the top of the Rose Dale wall. No sounds after the crash of glass, no movement. But no Haggard and his strange blonde. Keeping near the wall he sprinted down to the wooden gates swinging in the wind. He could barely make out movement on the deeply shadowed verandah. Are they taking them on alone? No, Haggard had too much sense, but what that woman would do is anyone's guess. He could barely make out their still dark forms. He grimaced, torn between joining them and retreating to the radio as procedure required to maintain the com link. "Damn," he murmured, turned, and sprinted back to the car.

***

Kaarin pushed weakly against the Rose Dale front door. "Can't", she whispered, "… open it. I can hold them."

Haggard tried the door. Locked.

"We must make them know I'm coming … so we can delay them, hold them." Her voice was low, husky. She brushed yellow hair from her face.

"Stay there." Haggard stepped away, swung his billy and smashed in a large window. Jabbing with the truncheon, he cleared away the glass fragments left in the frame, then stepped through. "I'll get the door." She was right, hold them here, somehow, until the armed squad arrives.

***

McGraw froze. "Window. She's coming in. I've got to get her now. Where are the damn lights, Sommers? Light, damnit, I'm not a stinking cat."

"What's going on? Jesus, what are you people doing?" Joe Socks looked frantically around, blinking in the sudden light from a ceiling fixture, backing quickly away from McGraw's angry gesturing with the .41. "You crazies are throwing everything away because of a freaky woman. You're all crazy. Five grand isn't worth this hassle." He backed away from McGraw.

His hand still on the light switch, Roland Sommers felt certainty sinking inside. His face paled. A sure thing he had guaranteed to his investor group, and with the loan guarantee, a sure thing was what he desperately needed. And yes, it would have been without that confounded blonde mindreader. He heard the entrance hall door open, soft steps moving below. "Then get her! Get her and get out!" he snapped, immediately ashamed of revealing his sudden angry frustration, and his deep fear.

McGraw moved quickly to the head of the stairs, paused, listening. In the fringes of light, he could see the front door standing open. The spook was down there somewhere. He started down. Cool, easy, professional. Don't lose it at the last minute. Hit the mark and move, like always. His spirits rose. He was on the trail again, fix the problem and go. Downward, step by step, the cannon firmly cushioned and poised in his hand. Four chances in the cylinder, and a pocketful more. No sweat man, cool and easy. He could see the darkened entrance hall and living room, his eyes just below the ceiling. He was in the light from above, she hidden in the dark below. Another step down, another. His eyes moving, sweeping, any movement, blow it away. A wall switch. He grinned, reached out his left hand, gun ready. He snapped it on!

Haggard swung his billy, just missing McGraw's gun hand as the big man leaned slightly to reach the switch. The hardwood club bounced off McGraw's thick shoulder.

McGraw pivoted around, fired, the room exploded, something glass shattered.

"You want me?"

McGraw looked back toward the door. Jesus! The spook right there pointing at him! He whirled around, fired. She was gone. There! Huddled low against the banister. He lunged down the last two steps, his heavy bulk carrying him over solidly against the door. She was back on her feet – facing him – could almost touch her!

345

Haggard threw his billy at McGraw's head, then dove at his gun hand, knocking Kaarin away.

The big man staggered back, the club glancing off his shoulder across his jaw, then rattled off the door behind him. Too close to fire -- he slashed the revolver hard across Haggard's head, crumbling him at his feet. Now the spook. He started to straighten up, froze as Kaarin screamed.

The ancient black anlace, raised high, gripped in both her hands, she thrust the dagger down into the side of McGraw's wide neck. Her teeth were bared, whites showing around her eyes. McGraw shouted in rage, going to his knees, trying to turn to his right to bring his gun up, his left hand clawing at the knife.

Her body pressed hard against his shoulder, Kaarin twisted the blade, wrenching it free, raised it and plunged it down again, cleanly severing a jugular, slicing through his windpipe, blood gouted out over her face, across her chest. She struggled to pull the knife free, to stab again. She shrieked! It wouldn't come out! Screaming, snarling, she pulled with both hands, twisting. Saliva dripped down the sides of her jaw. The anlace was out! She stepped back, McGraw's heavy body slipped down between her legs, wrapped in black lace, his gun fell heavily on the floor. Raising the blade again with both hands, she screamed and plunged the dagger deep into his back. Twisting, shaking –

346

she finally wrenched it out, but suddenly Kaarin couldn't move, her arms pinned to her sides. Screaming, she struggled, clawing, biting at the arms holding her.

Greenlaw desperately gripped one of Kaarin's wrists slippery with blood to keep the dagger away from his face, his other arm across her chest, pulled her over backwards, the black lace, anchored under McGraw, tearing, ripped away the shoulder of her silk tunic. She was an animal gone mad! Everywhere was the thick coppery odor of fresh blood. He dragged her backwards through the door, her legs flailing the air, writhing, spitting, biting at his arm. Greenlaw squeezed, twisted her wrist sharply, the dagger fell away. Another set of hands on her arm. Greenlaw glimpsed Oliver Bain, a pistol in his hand, rush past him into the house. One of his own men had Kaarin's arm. They pulled, dragged her backward down onto the verandah. In the light from the door he saw blood smeared across her distorted face, her mouth, her bare shoulder, her bared white teeth in a maw of red.

"Get her legs, Mitchell. I've got her hands."

The constable shifted quickly, grabbing both her ankles and sat on them.

"Good God, Cy, what are you doing to her!" cried Haggard, blood streaming down the side of his face. He staggered, then fell to one knee on the verandah. Kaarin's struggling gradually subsided, her breathing fell into a rhythmic gurgling as saliva bubbled over and dribbled down the side of her mouth, becoming crimson foam in the drying blood.

"Easy, man. She's gone totally bonkers. Trying to keep her from killing anyone else … including herself." Greenlaw jerked his head toward Mitchell, who promptly lifted himself off Kaarin's legs. Her breathing slowed, she lay still. Greenlaw cautiously released her wrists, waited a moment, then laid her limp arms across her stomach, and stood up. Her eyes were closed, McGraw's thickening blood drying over her face and chest.

"Keith . . .," Greenlaw started.

Haggard shook his head. "I'm all right. Get Kaarin to hospital. She saved my hide. But what's happening to her, inside?"

Greenlaw nodded, Mitchell ran for the ambulance, its lights flashing, but no siren, coming up Queen Street. "She just went crazy in there," he said. He looked past Haggard.

Roland Sommers was standing in the doorway, a pipe in his mouth, a pained look of disgust as he surveyed his damaged house. He shrugged. Oliver Bain appeared beside him with Joe Socks in cuffs.

***

Lashley knew his men, and had placed them accordingly. Guthrie, only two weeks since taking his oath, inexperienced; Outerbridge, macho, but slow in movement; Lister, ex-marine, a fucking tiger, spoiling for action. Lister was placed at the bend in Turkey Hill Road, the last resort if they had to stop anyone, however many there may be. He didn't know. Lashley rolled his billy over and over in his fingers intently watching the dark lifeless house.

Lights! Second floor. He tensed. Scraping. The sound of a door opening. A soft shuffling of feet. One man coming! He snapped a whispered warning. The sound of a gun shot!

A gate opened slowly, creaking, a shadow slipped through, directly toward him. Light from the shifting moon reflected from a knife blade. Lashley moved his feet, spread slightly, his weight balanced.

A uniformed figure moved, down at the intersection. "Stop him!" Montgomery-Beach bellowed up the street.

Two strides, Lashley moved instantly to the middle of the narrow road, the cool moonlight overshadowing the face of the man coming at him.

"Move, cop! I can slice you up, and any friends you got, before you can breathe." The Jamaican held his blade forward, away from his body, moving smoothly across the

349

crushed lava rock of the lane. He laughed. "Just sliced meat. That's all you'll be, cop. Your whole career … just the guts of a sandwich."

Lashley was motionless, his truncheon gripped tightly, about three inches up from the butt, his left hand out for balance. In the cooling evening warm sweat trickled down his back.

"Stay in place, men," he ordered. "This bastard is *mine*."

He was on Lashley, the knife slashing eagerly at his throat. Lashley leaned back, not moving his feet, then leaned forward and stepped inside the arc of the blade.

The Jamaican stepped back, surprised. "Lucky smartass fool!" he grunted, slashed backhanded again, grazing the constable's arm, then thrust straight at his throat.

Rotating swiftly, Lashley stepped into the thrust, deflecting it up, away with his left forearm, then lunged forward his full weight behind his arm, speared the Jamaican low in the groin with the billy, pivoted, swung the butt of the club down hard against the back of the Jamaican's head. He instantly collapsed, sprawling across the stones, a sharp agonized groan squelched by unconsciousness. His knife clattered away. Breathing hard, Lashley pressed one foot onto the neck of the fallen man, and shifted his weight down. There was no movement under his foot. The constable stepped back, adrenaline pumping, making him giddy, ready to fight the world.

Someone was running up behind him. Lashley instantly pivoted, legs spread, his billy braced for another attack. He started to give an order.

Montgomery-Beach slowed to walk a few feet away. He nodded, looking down at the prostrate body on the street. He nodded again. "Done with commendable dispatch, constable," he aspirated sharply.

***

Roland Sommers sat comfortably in the interrogation room in the Hamilton police station. His Savinelli was drawing smoothly.

"I must warn you that Joe Socks has talked freely of your arrangements with him," said Montgomery-Beach, "which clearly makes you and he accessories to murder."

"I am not surprised with Socks. He, of necessity, was the most extemporaneous element of my planning and ultimately the most unreliable," responded Sommers. He waved his attorney to silence. "From ample experience, I know when a situation is lost. I should have recognized that when I had to seek out that flyblown creature. He was one more factor that increased the chance of failure with my time running very short." He pursed his lips, his gaze

351

focused for a moment on the fragrant wisps of smoke rising from the warm pipe bowl.

"It had to be a sure thing, you understand, Commissioner. I promised my investors no risks, only smart returns with Cognito. Very impractical, but I sorely needed the additional capital to cover other, unrelated, problems, so that not all their investment went into Cognito Thought Systems. Unfortunately, Cognito soon became faced with possible bankruptcy unless serious developmental problems were expeditiously overcome. Their principal bank, located in the Bahamas, had refused to roll over a maturing note, unless definitive technical progress could be demonstrated. The most efficient way was … to steal what we needed from Cognito's most advanced competitor, Digital Intellesis, who appeared on the verge of sweeping the market, the investment in Cognito Thought, and me, completely away." The whole business had seemed so tractable, a straightforward certainty only a few weeks ago. A very awkward loan guarantee, yes, but . . .

"Digital's security system ensured no one could physically or electronically remove any documents or devices from their plant. However, no system can stop what is in the human memory. I hired Mr. Tony DiMarco, upon strong recommendations as to his discretion, to memorize the necessary data, the necessary lines of code, in order that Cognito engineers could duplicate Digital's software technology with minimum cost and time, and satisfy the banks. A bribe or two, some connections, placed Mr. DiMarco inside Digital's laboratories, where he performed as required."

"Why then was he killed?" asked Montgomery-Beach.

"Ah, well. Discretion. Mr. DiMarco was a pig. He was paid quite handsomely ... far more than his fee for reciting drivel a hundred different ways ... but he wanted much more. So he held back a portion of the data and demanded more payments. Blackmail no less! Cognito engineers, unexpectedly, were able to rebuild the balance of the data from the portion he had delivered ,,, making Mr. DiMarco, obviously an unstable element and thus dangerous, immediately expendable. Mr. Roger McGraw was suggested by a source in New York as an accomplished and discreet professional. Regrettably, there were complications ... some of which I do not yet understand. Why the black magician wanted to kill Mr. DiMarco, I haven't a clue, but that event appeared to develop the initial crack in my plan. Alberts saw McGraw shoot DiMarco and therefore had to go. When Miss Larsson arrived I knew, through Mr. Kermit Morgan, that she had known DiMarco in some way, but I was most disturbed to learn that she knew the Alberts as well. There could be no open points, as I am sure you understand, so reluctantly, she had to be dealt with as well. An increasingly awkward business, slipping beyond my control as many new factors had to be accommodated."

Sommers stopped. Gripping the pipe stem between his teeth, he reached into his jacket pocket for the white suede pouch, withdrew a few strands of rich black tobacco and replaced the pouch. He rolled the strands between his fingers, held them to his nose to enjoy their special nutty fragrance. He leaned back in the metal chair.

"Factors! Four people are dead on this island, Mr. Sommers," Commissioner Swainson said coldly, spitting out his words, "because you had to have a sure thing." He slammed his hand hard on the metal table, stood up, his hands thrust deep into his pockets. He loomed over the emotionless banker. "Four people! They weren't saints, paragons of virtue. One was even your own hired killer. But an innocent young woman was driven to kill, to take a life … an act that will surely mark her the rest of her being, the rest of her years. But four souls!" Realizing his anger was getting the better of him, Swainson turned away.

"Yet, Commissioner," Sommers said calmly to his back. "Without whatever lies inside Miss Larsson's odd mind, it would have been only Tony DiMarco … a swine who richly deserved his fate."

Swainson turned back, shaking his head emphatically. "Fate is not for you to decide. We will talk more in the morning … with your fellow investors. Charge him, Sergeant Bain."

Montgomery-Beach followed Swainson through the door. They walked silently down the hallway together, the sparkling lights of Hamilton Harbor visible through some of the windows.

"Miss Larsson is recovering?" asked Swainson.

"Yes, sir. According to Inspector Haggard who is at the hospital with her. She will be the night in hospital."

"A very strange, and very courageous young woman."

"God help us, Commissioner," said Montgomery-Beach. Edward Swainson looked over at the tight-faced policeman walking beside him. "God help us all," the Superintendent repeated, aspirating sharply, "if there are any more like her.

27

There had been a large thick envelope from the New York Public Library in the pile of junk mail stuffed into her mailbox. Kaarin laid it on the table next to the telephone with its blinking message light. She pressed the button as she swung the white attaché case from her shoulder onto a chair. The suitcase and garment bag were by the door. A large postcard from the Archdiocese of New York slipped out onto the floor. She picked it up as the messages began to play.

How many saints? The postcard read. It is impossible to know with any certainty because the standards for canonization have changed widely over the centuries, but are now very strict, and please recall that it wasn't until the 11th century that canonization was reserved exclusively for the Pope. But if you need a number: *Butler's Lives of the Saints* lists 2,565 saints, and *Delaney's Dictionary of Saints* gives 5,000. The mix between male and female appears to be about equal in both references. Hope this is of help. Call or write if you need more. It will take some little time to get more specific, and then we may have to contact the Congregation for the Causes of the Saints in Rome. Sincerely.

Edsel Bingeton was wrong! Nobody knows! More female saints because women *are prone to it!* Bull ... shit Bingeton!

"Kaarin ...call-me-asap. Cruise-ship-opportunity-coming-up-next-month-New-Zealand-and-Australia. Dinner-next-week? What-happened-in-Bermuda?"

Machinegun Morgan could wait; for a while. She cleared her throat and slipped the postcard into her pocket. And Sarah Randolph, too, could wait for a day. There was a second package from the NYPL. Then fine tune the Randolph challenge routine; about an hour should do it.

Kaarin started to turn the messaging off, then changed her mind. Leave it. Her computer was off. Just didn't need any e-mails. A sagging fence to hold off the outside world for a time. Kaarin carried the library package with her to her bedroom. For a moment she looked out the window at the hazy New York afternoon. A bleary Sunday, streets almost empty. What had she become now? Like on a mud slide through life without control and no stopping.

As she undressed she chuckled, remembering Keith's telling her how the police press officer had kept an American reporter at bay. By getting and keeping him drunk on Soft Rum at Hannah's, with Hannah's help. The press officer was still in tough shape when Kaarin had gotten on the plane, while the American was unconscious in his hotel. Keith had given her a bottle of Duty-Free Bermuda Gold to bring back with her as the unique liqueur could not be exported from Bermuda. She could now make her own Rum-Somethin's, her throat caught as the happy memory of being with Sugar and Serreta at the Pink Sands surrounded her. She wiped at her moist eyes and turned away.

Rose Dale. The seeing. Seeing. Kaarin winced at the memory of scalding pain. Screaming. Her screaming was still in her ears. An incomprehensible montage of faces. Her right wrist still ached. It had hurt just to pick up and hold the full orange juice glass she held. Keith, his head bandaged, had explained patiently to her when she had regained consciousness in King Edward hospital, her head throbbing. Killed! She had killed a man with the anlace. Sitting down slowly, Kaarin sat hunched on the side of her bed, the packages on her knees. Killed a man. Killed in self-defense Keith had said. Saved his life. No legal charges, but there may be some questions as the interrogations of Sommers and his associates continue. Then seeing her bewildered, he had explained patiently to her once again. Yes, she had seen at a distance, when she had to, *after* surrendering her mind.

But it wasn't that that so disturbed her. It was that

first feeling, that feeling *without her being threatened* that the waiter would spill drinks over Marc Kane. The realization then that she was changing, apparently couldn't stop it, couldn't hold it back. Had she actually surrendered her mind, or had, whatever it was, finally just taken over? Pushing the packages aside, she wrapped her gray silken robe tightly about her.

Kaarin shook her head, put the empty glass on the nightstand and lay back on the bed, cradling the library packages absently in her arms. "I'm Kristen Larsson's daughter. I'm me, damnit, the me I've always been." She recited softly, wistfully, her familiar prayer of confirmation that she had repeated so many nights in the darkness of the orphanage after her parents and sister had been buried, and the driver of the semi who had killed them walked away free, who, with his local political connections, couldn't be touched. She closed her eyes and dozed, drifting, dreaming troubled dreams of running the halls of the brutal children's institution, the lesbian keepers screaming after her, her head beginning again to throb.

***

Kaarin carried the soiled plate back to the kitchen, ran hot water over the yolk stains, then refilled her cup with fresh coffee and went back to the living room. She had laid out the stapled library photocopies chronologically in a crude mosaic on her dining table, the tesserae of suggestion. Someone at the NYPL had noted that the two recent papers by John Notvik on her list would be sent in a few days. Returning from a government committee meeting, Jacob Mortmann had been impressed with Notvik's intellect enough to mention it to Kaarin. "For a soft scientist, Notvik's got heavy guns in his brain," Mortmann had said in a rare compliment.

"Wish you had some psychic power over nicotine," Keith had laughed at the airport. "I'm going to need help. Eleven days with no let-up in needing a quick cigarette. Come back to the islands, very soon." Oh, yes, she thought, as soon as possible, return to Hannah's, and so much else

***

Dated earliest, 1919, from the *South African Archaeological Bulletin*, it was a simple, though reasonably detailed description of the findings of calvaria, mandibles and limb fragments on the river Mooi near the village called Boskop, without elaboration or speculation.

A suggestion of speculation emerged in a 1954 article in *Man*. Though known since 1919, the findings described had been held back for unexplained reasons. Scratched or carved marks, indentations visible on an odd stone implement seemed to be aesthetic, not functional, though no aesthetic indications were evident in any

360

artifacts found in contemporaneous sites near the Boskop find. A separate race, or species, of small, fine boned, lightly muscled people surrounded by ample evidence of hardier, more sturdy man-like primates. Clearly the Boskop settlements could not compete successfully for food, or territory, against their much more robust neighbors. Darwin's right again, Kaarin mused. But the brain case capacity, calculated from the skull fragments, suggested a brain size almost double the volume of the average modern man. What was in those massive brains? How was their capacity used in getting through each day surrounded by brutal, lethal hostility?

Several anthropologists had immediately dismissed the possibility of a parallel unsuccessful species of man, insisting the Boskops were only the Ice Age forerunners of the modern Kalahari Bushmen.

"But Bushmen, even now, do not have brains twice the size of modern man," Kaarin murmured. Who does? She lightly touched her temple with the fingers of one hand.

Antropologiska Studie, 1931, a Swedish journal. A brief letter, remarking on a find of human remains near Kalixfors, a village on the Kalix River well above the Arctic Circle. Light boned, small, undifferentiated teeth, well developed cranial cavity. A longer article followed in

1932. It contained a sketch of how the inhabitants of the vanished settlement might have appeared. Kaarin laughed. Ridiculous! It was like a creature from a sci-fi story on human evolution. Small childlike face, great bulging skull, small body. The brain evolving, leaving the body behind. How many fevered short stories, Star Trek episodes, films, and novels, Wells' *Time Machine* came to mind, how many had depicted those characteristics as the final form of man, of life itself, a growing consciousness with less and less physical presence, but tens, even hundreds of centuries into the future, *not back* -- back at the fringe of the Ice Age in South Africa, and two thousand years ago in Sweden.

Utterly ridiculous! At least her physics was a reasonable science with demonstrable logic.

She paused. Would she ever be able to go back to her physics, ever? Ever be free of the raw ache in her mind when she tried to bear down intellectually? She set aside her half empty cup and slid over the last article. The doctor at the King Edward hospital had told her to take it easy, she had suffered a severe trauma, give herself a chance to pull things back together. Don't push it.

She frowned, people, people had frequently remarked how young her mother had looked. However, her father, a carpenter who loved the outdoors, had a tightly curled reddish beard that concealed much of his face.

362

Kaarin pressed her fingers again against her temples, letting them slide through her thick hair along the sides of her skull, feeling the familiar ridges. She had heard one of her mother's friends once remarking about her mother's very delicate features. Oh, hell, I'll get to be as crazy as that old porno-psychical researcher Bingeton. Her grin was quick. Maybe I already am with what is running around inside . . .

Kaarin slammed her hands down on the table. She so missed her equations and the thrill of the hunt, that chance to see something for the first time, to make it to the top of the hill before anyone else. She sobbed, feeling suddenly, desperately empty.

Kaarin wiped her eyes. A Norwegian journal, *Nordske Fortidsminder,* a paper on a finding of human remains at Hellemobatn in northern Norway, that referenced both the South African and Swedish material, but that had drawn down severe criticism on its author in a subsequent note for a technical blunder in his brain cavity calculations and his dating of the bone fragments to the late eighteenth century. Clearly, his critics insisted, the author was incompetent or was attempting to manufacture a hoax. There was, evidently, no reply from the author that the NYPL reference librarian could find. The Norwegian paper was dated 1947. The author had been tried and convicted of Nazi collaboration, according to a footnote photocopied from a 1948 editorial in the same journal.

But was the author right, Nazi or not? Politics instead of science. Eighteenth century. Why the recurrence of these evolutionary misfits? Atavism or not, nature wouldn't keep bringing a species back after it had been eliminated, like the Boskops in Africa. Are dinosaurs and passenger pigeons going to make a comeback? Bingeton's comment had been so damnably off-handed that maybe he hadn't been serious, or so convinced of the completeness his own experience that his own mind was utterly closed. He wouldn't be the first scientist she'd encountered with that condition. And he had been wrong about female saints. There couldn't be a connection between the findings – it would be utterly illogical – *unless,* unless the Boskops had not been completely wiped out on the banks of the Mooi, or of the Kalix.

"Confound him!" Kaarin snapped aloud in frustration. "It probably doesn't mean anything. A bunch of darned *freaks* that lived maybe two hundred years ago at the most recent … and that's if you can believe a *Nazi* scientist." She threw the article back on the table. There had to be more, perhaps in Notvik's papers.

Financially she could handle things all right for a while. No need to rush back to the road, for a couple of weeks anyway. And the Randolph threat had to be dealt

364

with, but finance is not the problem, lady. Your head is the problem. What is loose in there now? *Because there is something.* She hit the table with her fist. Confound it, there is!

***

Kaarin couldn't stay cooped up in her apartment any longer thinking and dreaming about little people with bulging heads. There was a cheap Italian restaurant a few blocks away, but oh, to be with Keith back at Hannah's on the pink beach. The pasta restaurant's windows were painted black and there was no sign, but the menu, other than the sometimes stale day-old bread, was decent.

There were few people on the streets, a Sunday evening in New York with the weather turning messy. Kaarin had thrown on her black psychic sweatshirt and white jeans with still dirty knees, and a raincoat to walk to the restaurant. Stuffed meatballs and a little red vino eaten alone certainly didn't need anything more formal. She brightened; she would write Keith when she returned. They had agreed to. His eyes had lighted so when she had asked him to write about Bermuda stamps. She wanted to learn. No e-mails. That was too mechanical. Letters. He had agreed.

A well-dressed young couple walked rapidly past her, the woman wrapped in a fur-trimmed white suede coat with her beautiful long red hair in a single braid, lost in their conversation and each other. Kaarin smiled weakly as they drew away from her, so intent on reaching somewhere as swiftly as possible. His place or hers, Kaarin mused sadly.

She suddenly found herself running after them, her mouth open to cry out. They had already turned the corner and were out of sight. Someone was there, the unmistakable chill in her spine that wasn't the weather. Not a flash or vision, *something*, her head throbbed dizzily. As she ran, she put out a hand to catch the corner of the building, to swing herself around quickly, to warn them, to . . .

The couple was standing at a glossy blue Porsche 911, his car. The woman slipped sensually down into the low seat, he closed her door, went around, got in, and they pulled away from the curb into the empty street. As they drove by her, their faces indistinct in the instrument lights, Kaarin could only stand silently, feeling the sprinkling rain on her face, the pain in her head gradually subsiding, like eating ice cream too fast. Her hands on her hips, she rotated slowly, looking carefully into the shadowed doors and windows. Nothing, no one, there was no threat to anyone. She blushed. What a silly fool she would have been, rushing up to them with her precious 'psychic' warning.

366

Oh, Lord, she'd look like a real New York nut case. Puzzled, she rotated once more, to see something. An empty parked car half a block away, but there was nothing, nothing at all. She stamped her foot angrily and turned back toward the restaurant. The sense had been the same, the feeling so familiar, but wrong? But in Bermuda she *had* seen -- there was no doubt of that, but could that seeing, sensing, always be trusted now, or had so many screws come loose in her head that? Her hands thrust deep into the pockets of her coat, its collar pulled up around her face against the blowing cold rain, Kaarin walked rapidly across the street toward the restaurant. Maybe, she thought, dodging a pothole, she should call a psychologist, not an agent.

***

An indistinct form moved up into view in the parked car which quietly began moving slowly toward the small blonde, then, after pausing to watch as she entered the restaurant without looking back, turned at the corner in the direction of the blue Porsche and accelerated away.

***

Stunned, Kaarin dropped the newspaper, her hands covering her face. She moaned, twisting around, kicked the paper away. "I knew, I knew," she sobbed. It had to have been that parked car up the street, somehow. The pictures of the charred bullet-riddled hulk of the blue Porsche, two body bags being lifted into an ambulance. Her mind throbbed, aching, she tore at her memory, but no clear image of the parked car emerged from the pain. She had been too tightly enwrapped with her angry frustration to take careful note of anything else. She had thought her senses had failed her.

That couple had been a threat *to her*, that was what she had felt. If her timing had been off, if she had come around the corner a few seconds later perhaps she would have been a part of the attack right there. According to the paper, the woman was running away from her husband who was under federal investigation for running a cocaine network with ties to Mexican cartels. They had looked so romantic and she had so envied them being together.

Kaarin fell into the rocking chair, squeezed her head tightly between her hands. Forget Mentavo, forget mentalism, forget, forget. Edsel Bingeton, he had been wrong about the saints and so much about him was absurd, but could he be right, anyway? Who could tell her?

I long

To hear the story of your life, which must

Take the ear strangely.

The Tempest V.i

28

"Thank you for seeing me, Professor Notvik," said Kaarin, settling onto the leather sofa he had designated.

John Notvik's warm smile reached across his face and up into his eyes. He wore a plain red sweatshirt over black jeans, and running shoes. His hairless head glistened in the sun filling his family room. Pictures of children were everywhere, on the walls, on bookcase shelves, on his work table.

"Not at all, Dr. Larsson. You said the magic names: Mortmann and Bingeton. Two extraordinary men who couldn't be more different, and whose works I greatly admire in different ways. Bingeton's stroke last week was sad. He died so alone, yet he did so much original work, even in pornography, I understand. Sometime, I would like to hear more about your encounter with him. I met him only once. And I am vaguely familiar with your work, though as a mere anthropologist and naturalist your cosmology is beyond me. I need bones and dirt between my fingers." He grinned as he leaned back, his hands locked behind his head.

"But now you are in show business?" he asked. "That's a remarkable path for an accomplished scientist as yourself. Though if you will allow me, for a moment, to be a normal male homo-sapien, your beauty is extraordinary itself, and should not be hidden in the back of even Mortmann's laboratory. Though you appear much younger than the maturity of your work would suggest." Kaarin smiled, quietly pleased anyone would remember her work. "And someone trained by Jacob Mortmann is always worth listening to."

She had been very nervous calling him. The author of a dozen books on anthropology and evolution, two even becoming popular best sellers, John Notvik's work on defining human evolution had been quoted to her by Jacob Mortmann as the quintessence of scientific discipline in an emotion laden field. She had explained her circumstances to Notvik on the phone as succinctly and bluntly as possible when she had finally connected with him after several attempts. His long silence when she finished had frightened her – oh, Lord, he thinks I'm just a nut case – then he had gently invited her to his home in West Chatham on the elbow of Cape Cod. She had put off Kermit Morgan, but

370

Sarah Randolph was waiting. Sarah had caught some kind of flu that put things off, but even that didn't matter. Randolph she could handle. She had to understand, to talk to someone who just might understand as well. It was apparent now that her answers had never been in Mentavo's lists, in mentalism, in the paranormal, that was clear, but was it, was it here?

Notvik suddenly swung forward on his swivel chair to stand, a large lump of a man, dark bags under large brown eyes, heavy horn-rimmed glasses hanging from a thong around his neck.

"May I call you Kaarin?" he asked shyly, smiling when she nodded. "I'm John to my grad students, and certainly to a fellow professional snoop. And to all these kids I am Bompa, Gramps, Uncle, Grandad, and whatever else their young vocabularies can manage."

Notvik beckoned to her to follow him to a small table near the window. She had dressed too formally in a blue silk suit; a fact he had gently pointed out. Cape Cod was informal, *always.*

Kaarin stood beside him as he opened a wooden box on the table. He carefully lifted out two large dome-shaped pieces of thin bone from the packing.

"Boskop," he said. "I found these six years ago up the coast about a hundred miles or so from the original

Mooi river find. There were a few other remains along with some odd as yet unexplained artifacts, but nothing so complete as this skull-cap. A female I think, but can't be absolutely certain since the Boskop skeletal structure seems to be relatively undifferentiated between sexes. Cranial capacity of this skull is about 2,200 cubic centimeters." The bones meshed exactly when he gently held them together, to form an almost complete skull-cap down to the top of the eye sockets. Kaarin reached out, her fingers hovered. Notvik nodded. Touching the bones sent an electric thrill through her. He carefully replaced them into the box. "A scientist back in 1918, Broom by name, proposed designating the Boskop as the new species, *Homo Capensis,* but it didn't catch on, as some felt the Boskops were simply the progenitors of the Kalahari Bushmen." He grinned. "As a scientist, Kaarin, you know the drill." He walked back toward the center of the room and Kaarin resumed her place on the sofa. "I haven't published anything on this find yet. I want more data than just the skull-cap, but I did ask an illustrator I had used for an earlier book to render this skull-cap and other artifacts into a rational representation of flesh and bone. She's very good, knows muscle structure as well as anyone I have ever worked with." Notvik pulled a large red three-ringed binder from the top shelf of the bookcase. Children's books filled the lower shelves. "Take this while I get us a refill on the teapot."

Kaarin settled back on the sofa, the book on her lap. She took a breath, and opened it. *Oh, God!* It wasn't like that weird caricature in the Swedish journal, it was so like her sister, Kristianna! The hair was rendered short and kinked like the modern Bushman, but the whimsical facial expression was uncannily Kristi's. She placed both hands tightly at the sides of her temples and slid them back feeling the familiar ridges. She closed her eyes, her hands still holding her head. It was there, the expanded braincase. No one had ever said anything about it when she was young, but then why, *since for us it is normal*. When Kaarin opened her eyes and lowered her hands, Notvik was standing there watching her carefully, the steaming teapot balanced in his hands. She slowly turned more of the pages, noting other renderings by the artist, J. A. Danton, of large-skulled diminutive humans in primitive exotic settings. Then a comparative portrayal of a Boskop beside the figure of a much larger, heavier shouldered human, much like an early Marc Kane. She put her finger on it.

"What is this?" she asked.

"The local competition, at the time," Notvik said. "Whatever the Boskop had in those amazing brains wasn't enough to succeed surrounded by superior brute power.

Some remains suggest, but not prove, that the Boskops may have actually formed part of their competitors' regular diet. Only about one-third of the Boskop remains we have found over the years had the large cranial cavity. The others seemed to have brains about 10-15% larger than that of modern man. If your experiences can be taken as an valid example, and you may be all the data we may ever have, unique mental capabilities apparently did not develop until late adolescence, possibly too late for consistent survival of the species in that early environment."

"But some survival, of some type," she said quietly. Without her parents' guidance, and her sister dead in the same automobile accident, on her own since she was twelve, she had fought against what was happening in her mind as hard as she could, for as long as she could until, apparently, she was overwhelmed by her own DNA.

He nodded, then hesitated. "May I, ah … may I touch your head, Kaarin?" He placed the teapot on his work table.

"Yes."

She closed her eyes as he let his stubby fingers flow slowly through her thick yellow hair following the ridges to the base of her skull. He swallowed and stepped back.

Kaarin smiled awkwardly. "I suddenly feel like a coelacanth out of water." She explained about the drawing and Kristi.

Notvik walked to the window, looked out between the scrub pines at the dark windblown waters beyond, his hands held loosely behind his back. He was quiet for several minutes, then turned back to her, grinning sheepishly.

"Turning my back on a guest ... my very Polish mother would have skinned me alive. Please forgive my rudeness, but you have unsettled many years of study and complacency."

He walked back and sat next to her on the sofa. He spoke very deliberately. "An enlarged braincase, Kaarin, is not by itself proof of being a Boskop descendant since such things happen randomly in the normal course of humanity, but not often. Those individuals involved, according to the very limited data collected, exhibited no unusual intellectual or psychic capabilities. And even the Neanderthal had brains generally ten percent larger than modern man. But the extraordinary pedomorphism of your features, the odd happenings you've experienced in your mind, and your reaction about Kristi, could firmly suggest that you may have the Boskop lineage somewhere in your DNA."

"Pedomorphism?" she asked.

"Part of our jargon, forgive me. It is one of several terms we use that relate to the retention of infantile features into maturity. Not just physical, but psychological as well ... the ability to laugh, act foolish, and so on. An adult gorilla exhibits little pedomorphism, while an adult human demonstrates relatively much more. It's not an exact quantitative measure like your physics. We can measure jaw compression ..." He stopped. "I don't want to start throwing jargon around and giving half-starved ideas the appearance of sound scientific data. I don't want to mislead you as to the level of our understanding of the Boskop."

She nodded, said nothing, and waited.

"There certainly had to have been some interbreeding for the Boskop DNA to survive through the centuries. Contemporaneous remains have been found up the eastern African coast at Singa on the Blue Nile, in the Sudan, so they moved major distances even then in their search for survival.

"The original Boskop were certainly Negroid in some ways, but during their interbreeding and drift northward, the unique Boskop physical features apparently reappeared in a more Caucasian form ... as suggested by those materials found near Kalixfors in Sweden back in the early thirties. I could not even guess how all that may have happened. Did you ever meet other members of your family, aunts, uncles?"

Kaarin shook her head. "No. Never. But they all lived in Norway and Sweden, north, far away from the cities." John Notvik's friendly acceptance of her and willingness to consider even what appeared to be mad nonsense caused a unique peacefulness to begin spreading though her. She wasn't going crazy – *but she was a freak.* But freaks can still do physics – can't they? She really was Kristen Larsson's daughter, the me she had always been.

***

John Notvik turned to his wife as he watched Kaarin's car disappear down the low hill and around the corner of Oakridge Circle toward Sulphur Springs Road. He and Kaarin would meet at his office at M.I.T. in a few days to begin detailed interviews regarding her childhood, her family, some X-rays, physical examinations, blood tests, DNA sampling, while he would give her everything known on the Boskops. Her identity would be kept secret throughout. Even faced with possibly being the last fragment of a distant forgotten race, she seemed so encouraged and talked eagerly about returning to Bermuda.

"An extraordinary young woman, John," Martha Notvik said, closing the door behind them.

He smiled quietly. "Oh, yes. If she is what she appears, then a very new life started for her today," he said, "and, Martha, for the rest of us."

Oh, wonder!
How many goodly creatures are there here!
How beauteous mankind is! O brave new world,
That has such people in't.
The Tempest V.i

The End

Acknowledgements

First, the Bermuda Police Service for their professional patience in past years in answering my many questions about the paradise of Bermuda from the police perspective. I have, however, taken some liberties with police procedures. To Heather Wood, Lifestyle Editor of the *Royal Gazette,* for her generous interest in *Beyond The Tempest* which led to a full-page interview, And to several collectors of Bermuda stamps, who asked to remain anonymous, who were delighted to find a dedicated compatriot in the novel.

You can follow Bermuda daily on the *Royal Gazette* website www.royalgazette.com. After the closure of the *Bermuda Sun* after 50 years in June, 2014, the *Royal Gazette* became the only newspaper published in Bermuda.

The charm of Bermuda is unforgettable, in its remarkable people, the pink sands, its amazing history, and those unfinished church ruins with red warning signs about

379

falling bricks,. signs that remained in my mind, but which I had to move physically for plot reasons.

Unforgettable.

***

For information on the Boskops, I would recommend the book where I first learned of their existence: *The Immense Journey*, by Loren Eiseley, (Vintage Books, New York, 1959). The chapter is called: "Man of the Future", page 127. Anything by Professor Eiseley is worth reading and re-reading. A highly respected naturalist, the man was an astonishing writer and poet.

In addition, the following papers on the Boskops are original sources:

Singer, R., "The Boskop 'Race' Problem", *Man*, p.23, 1958.

Van Riet Lowe, C., "An Artifact Recovered with the Boskop Calvaria", *South African Archaeological Bulletin*, 9:135-137, 1954.

Broom, S., "The Evidence Afforded by the Boskop Skull of a New Species of Primitive Man (Homo Capensis)", *Anthropological Papers of the American Museum of Natural History,* Vol. 23, Part 2 (1918), pp.63-79.

***

And about the astonishing memory feats of the Shass Pollak:

Stratton, George M., "Mnemonic Feat of the 'Shass Pollak', *Psychology Review,* Vol. 24, (1917), pp. 244-47.

***

The techniques of resistance magic, generally called the Magnetic Girl act, is described completely in the definitive book on the subject, *The Georgia Wonder*, Barry H. Wiley, Hermetic Press, 2004. Bringing an umbrella alive is only one of several amazing stunts developed by various performers over the decades since its first performance in 1884.

The world of mentalism extends far beyond the magic shop door to include people in the U.S. and Europe whom I would like to thank, but whom I have agreed not to name. Some of those who have given valuable help and understanding whom I can thank publicly are: Ray Goulet of the Magic Art Book Co., Watertown, MA; Max Maven, "The Thief of Thoughts" and our exchange of letters about female mentalists; the late Fr. Cyprian Murray, for perceptive insights into showmanship and the nature of the magician; Rev. William V. Rauscher, who led me to the strange world of the occultist and palmist, Cheiro, and has

381

been supportive of many of my projects; the late Mostyn Gilbert, patient searcher in the karstic reaches of the human mind; the late Walter B. Gibson, creator of **The Shadow** and confidant of Houdini and Dunninger; and the late Dr. Eric J. Dingwall, psychical researcher, anthropologist, and authority on pornography, for an amazing afternoon on a dismal rainy day on the south coast of England, for many answers, and not a few new questions.

For those interested in digging further into mentalism, its practice and performance, I leave them to their own devices. There are literally hundreds of books on the subject, with more every year, but, be cautious, as some publications are only expensive trash. It is up to the individual to sort it out, as mentalism is a highly personal, if invisible, art.

And for the curious:

Rum Somethin'

1 oz. Gosling Black Seal rum
½ oz. Plymouth Gin
½oz. 12 year Highland Scotch
A splash or two of Bermuda Gold liquor

Stir vigorously and pour into crushed ice in a highball glass.

(Based on an early Barbary Coast recipe)

Kaarin Larsson will return in

The Tempest Incident

Kaarin Larsson is working with Dr. John Notvik at MIT in his examination of her DNA and other aspects of her apparent Boskop heritage while, in New York she is preparing for her pending encounter with Sarah Randolph, meeting with 'knowledgeable' friends, in the course of which she discovers something in Sarah's background that could threaten both of them.

Machinegun Morgan has notified her of an opportunity at the Duchess. Roger Delano, general manager of the Duchess, wants her to perform for two weeks, during a special government promoted tourist program.

While Inspector Keith R. Haggard of the Bermuda Police Service must explain the finding of the dead body of Robert Malcolm Fitzgerald adjacent to a road near Little Sound. There are no marks of violence on the body, and the autopsy shows no internal damage to vital organs, nor the presence of any poisons in his system. How did he die? Sergeant Oliver Bain jokes that RMF is the first murder by magic spell the police have ever encountered. Haggard doesn't laugh.

Kaarin returns to Bermuda to the Duchess and to Keith Haggard, as they both seek out the answer to the RMF killing, and to what may lie behind his death. Kaarin's strange capabilities, along with her growing knowledge of the occult becomes the key to Haggard's investigation.

They also seek answers to their own growing relationship.

Look for updates on the author's website:

www.barrywiley.com

Other Books by Barry H. Wiley

Tales of a Thought Reader, 2016.

Stuart C. Cumberland (1855-1922) was the premiere thought reader of Victoria's vast realm, whose career is described in the non-fiction book, *The Thought Reader Craze,* noted below. Cumberland became the first millionaire mind reader. *Tales* is a collection of short stories with Cumberland as protagonist and narrator in which he encounters death spells (a genuine death spell from 1724 is key to one of the stories), an impossible crime in Vienna, a remarkable *magush*, an Afghan mystic, in India, and even, for the first time, meets Sherlock Holmes.

Available on Amazon in print and ebook formats.

The Thought Reader Craze, McFarland & Co., 2012.

A non-fiction study of the intense search by scientists, academics and others to establish telepathy as a fact of human nature, and perhaps the first scientific proof of life-after-death. The book also tells the story of the men, woman and, occasionally, children who so successfully hoaxed the scientists; as well as the parallel story of the creation of the one-man minding act one Monday morning in 1873 in a Chicago saloon. The stage performers used the scientists to gain public credibility, while the scientists used the performers to maintain public interest in their work. In the end, the performers gained and lost fortunes, while the scientists gained and lost reputations. Available in print and ebook editions on Amazon and on the McFarland website.

A Spirit of Fraud, 2014.

Set in 1876. A British occult Brotherhood under the apparent direction of the Archangel Uriel plans to seize defenseless America in the waning months of the Grant administration. Only the celebrated spirit medium, Annie Eva Fay, detects the threatening presence of Uriel's minions. Gaining the help of the Pinkertons, Annie moves to stop the Brotherhood. But Annie's spirits are all fake. Is the Archangel a fake as well? And will there be time enough for Annie to learn the truth?

The novel was reviewed October, 2014, on *Kings River Life Magazine* which favorably compared *A Spirit of Fraud* to *The DaVinci Code.* (www.kingsriverlife.com)

Available on Amazon in print and ebook formats.

The Indescribable Phenomenon, 2005, Hermetic Press.

Harry Houdini called Anna Eva Fay "the greatest female mystifier". Annie (1857-1927) was raised in a form of slavery in northeastern Ohio called "fostering". She never attended school, learning as could while working seven days a week. Finally, throwing off the fostering, she went on the road at eleven, bare-footed where she discovered that if should could convince people that when she talked to the dead, the dead answered, she would never have to chop wood again. And she could even sleep in a bed.

Annie became one of most famous spirit mediums in the US and UK. In England in 1875, after close investigation, the British scientist William Crookes declared publicly that Anna Eva Fay was genuine, that she could exercise a "non-human force at a distance" a force that Crookes called "a psychic force".

In 1894, when profits from the spirits declined, Annie went on the vaudeville stage to become acclaimed as a greater showman that Houdini himself.

The biography was considered for a film by Walden Media.

Available only in print format from Amazon, and the Hermetic Press website.

The *Adventures in Second Sight* series The series follows the extraordinary life of young Kyame Piddington.

The first book, *Revelations of the Impossible Piddington,* is set in 1890-1895. The story follows Kyame Piddington as she tries desperately at the age of eleven to take her dead mother's place in the family's second sight mindreading act as she and her father travel the American West. Kyame struggles to learn the secret codes and techniques of the act, while she learns to deal with hostile audiences, killers, bank robbers,

Jadoo-wallahs, swindlers, and the constant rejection of society as only a "theatre girl".

At sixteen she is disturbed when a Chinese astrologer in New York City tells her she has the soul of an implacable assassin. Kyame encounters the Bing On tong in San Francisco where she must kill the tong master, Wong Woon, who has murdered her father. Only seconds from her own death, yet Kyame leaves the body of Wong Woon in his windowless office with a silver knife in his heart and then vanishes, leaving the only door to Wong's office still barred from the inside. The tong members are astonished as the white woman had to be dead. They believe she is a *tulku*, a Tibetan occult wraith that passes through walls and locked doors, kills and then vanishes. The tong is almost right. The reader learns how Kyame's wonders are performed.

The second novel is ***Shadow of the Tiger.*** It is 1896. All British agents in southern France have been murdered except one in Monaco, code named Muffin. America is asked by the British Prime Minister to send agents to temporarily aid them until other agents can be transferred. The PM must immediately discover what may be threatening the Empire. President Grover Cleveland has no agents to send, and turns to the informal group that reports to his Secretary of State, the Anglo-Oriental Marine Insurance Co., of which Kyame is a member. She is the only one with the necessary range of talents. Cleveland is concerned that the only aid America can offer is a seventeen year old girl. Traveling to Monaco, Kyame soon begins to encounter the presence of Imperial Germany with its apparent plan to threaten the Suez Canal. Kyame must use all of her strange talents, even to using the yellow *ruhmal* of the Thugees, to defeat the Imperial plans.

Both books are available on Amazon in print and ebook formats.

The third book, *Pi Ying Xi, The Shadow Play* *is* set in 1897 in San Francisco, Honolulu and Tahiti. Its release is planned for early 2017.

For more information on the stories and books of Barry H. Wiley visit his website at www.barrywiley.com, and follow his blog "Plotting the Impossible" on Goodreads.

www.ingramcontent.com/pod-product-compliance
Lightning Source LLC
Chambersburg PA
CBHW070356260626
47161CB00001B/157